For Blood nor Money

For Blood nor Money

Timothy Lawson

To order additional copies of this book, contact:
Xlibris Corporation
1-888-7-XLIBRIS
www.Xlibris.com
Orders@Xlibris.com

To one of my favorite songbirds!
Thanks for letting me be a part of your life.

[signature] 1-15-04

I thank God for those who helped make this book a reality:
To Dempsey, Ethan, and Rob for their undying support;
my brothers-in-arms (if not in blood), Derek and Dale;
my folks for opening up the world of reading for me;
and the two women in my life, my daughter Mariah, who is a
constant source of inspiration, and my wife Sandy without who's
love my life would be an empty shell.

Chapter 1

Martin Daniels strolled through the doorway leading into the lab and waved to coworkers as he went. Julie glanced at her wristwatch, and nodded to herself. Right on schedule, thirty minutes after sunset. She crossed the lab, intent on bringing Martin up to speed since she had decided to come in early, then pulled up short when she reached him.

"Damn it, Martin," Julie said on closer inspection of him. "You told me you were going to get some rest today. And, don't try to lie to me." She raised a hand to cut off his intended excuse, "I can see that you haven't slept. Got any good reasons?"

"Yes, Mother. I practiced my violin when I got home this morning, lost track of the time and the next thing I knew, Geraldo was on and I wasn't sleepy anymore."

"Bullshit, Martin. Nice story, but it's bullshit. You went home and worked some more, didn't you. Couldn't leave it alone."

"That's what I like about you, Jules, you have such a way with the English language," he said as he patted her cheek. "It's nice to see you too. And, thanks for your concern."

"Who's concerned?" Julie said brushing back a strand of her auburn, shoulder length hair that had escaped the pony-tail holder she was wearing. "I just don't want to have to redo one of your screwups because you're too tired to think straight. I can see the obits now," she said to his retreating back, "Martin Daniels, mid-thirties, dedicated-very dedicated-chemist found dead after working himself to death. There was no one to mourn him, because he was such a stubborn butthead!"

Martin laughed to himself as he set about his work.

Martin barely looked up from the bonding agents he was working with when Julie informed him the others had left and she was calling it a night. He did lean back with a long sigh of appreciation when she came up behind him and started to massage his shoulders.

"Listen, Doc. Martin. Seriously," Julie gave his shoulders one last squeeze, "give it a rest. I know you're after something, but it won't do you any good if you're dead, or if you have to rework something you missed due to fatigue. Besides, you won't be able to take me out this weekend if you exhaust yourself."

"We're going out this weekend?"

"Of course. You just haven't asked me yet."

"Oh." Martin leaned his head back and looked up into chestnut eyes shining down at him. "I have a couple of things to button down here and then I'm through. I promise."

"You promise, huh?"

Martin crossed his heart and held up two fingers.

Julie knew he would keep his word. It was just that a "couple of things" could run a couple of hours.

As Julie made her way out of the building towards the parking lot where her faithful Geo Prizm waited, she mused upon the man she had just left in the lab. Dr. Martin Daniels. Chemist extraordinaire. Friend. And, something more.

He drifted in front of her mind's eye. Average height with a lean, muscular build and chiseled features. Black hair that was just starting to show hints of gray. Beyond the physical attributes, which were definitely appealing in themselves, was his mind. The man was brilliant. He had come up with some breakthroughs in neural regeneration and gene splicing, but had taken none of the credit himself. He had said, "Let someone else have the glory. My work is it's own reward."

That was one of the other endearing qualities about him that she found so attractive, sometimes he was just plain corny. Then there was the question she always asked herself: Why he had picked her as an assistant? No slouch herself, being a graduate student at UCLA with a GPA of 4.0, she was still intimidated by him sometimes, and felt she was nowhere in his league. During a break once, she had asked him why he had chosen her and not someone else.

"Aside from having excellent credentials," he said, waving a Twinky for emphasis, "you have moxy. That, and you like to work nights."

"Oh." At the time, she hadn't known if he had complimented her or simply made an observation.

"Face it girl," she said to herself as she reached her car and placed the keys in the lock, "you're just plain lucky."

Or, so she thought, until she saw the reflection in the driver's side window.

She tried to turn and run, but it was too late. A

gloved hand clamped viselike across her mouth as another snaked around her body, pinning her arms to her sides. Her assailant lifted her effortlessly and melted into the darkness.

Martin switched off the desk lamp and leaned back in his chair. He had decided that the couple of things could wait until tomorrow night. He rubbed his eyes feeling the ton and a half of sand grating behind his lids and decided he definitely could use some sleep.

He smiled thinking of Julie reprimanding him. She was a true diamond in the rough. For all of her lack of tact, he cared for her. No, his feelings were deeper than that. As he logged off the computer, he knew that was one of the things he admired about her. She spoke her mind. She took chances. She was one human he knew that truly lived.

"Why can't life be simple sometimes?" he thought as he flipped off the lab lights.

Pete, the fatherly fellow that worked the grave-yard shift at the front desk, waved as Martin passed on his way out. He walked down the steps to the parking lot and shook his head when he saw Julie's car still there.

"I'm going to have to talk to her about being overly protective," he thought, and started across the lot to where she was parked.

Ice formed in the pit of his stomach when he reached her car. Julie was nowhere around. There was no sign of any struggle. But, she was definitely gone. The only thing that gave evidence of her having been there at all were her keys hanging from the door lock of the burgundy colored Prizm. Martin's mind raced. He looked up and down the lot, saw nothing and started back to summon Pete when he caught a familiar scent. Martin tested the air again and found that the scent led through the low bushes that lined this side of the parking lot.

He glanced at his watch.

"Damn," he muttered and started off through the shrubs.

Julie found it hard to keep her thoughts straight. Whoever had grabbed her had not forced her into a waiting vehicle as she had presumed they would. Instead, he had tucked her underneath an arm like a child's toy and started down the street at a dead run, his hand still across her mouth. Bounced around the way she was, it was hard to focus on anything, but she was sure that her assailant had just hurdled a six-foot chain link fence without breaking stride. They made several twists and turns so that Julie was totally confused as to their whereabouts. From the sounds and the stench, she guessed she was in the low rent district not far from the lab. Her captor slowed, ducked down an alley, then stopped in front of a dilapidated dumpster. He checked both directions and then used his foot to move aside the large metal bin. Behind the dumpster was a hole in the brick wall. She was carried through the opening and then set upon her feet as her abductor pulled the dumpster back into place. When he had removed his hand to move the dumpster, Julie started screaming. The other arm released her and she backpedaled into the far wall and continued screaming. The person who had released her started to laugh as he turned to face her. Mid-twenties, he was an attractive man with shoulder length, brown hair, perfect teeth set in a square jaw covered by a close cropped beard and wide, muscular looking shoulders beneath the black, full length coat he was wearing. If it was the air of evil about him that caused Julie to pause in her call for help, it was his eyes that froze her. They were the eyes of a shark. Jet black and lifeless, they bore a hole right through her.

She pressed her back against the dank concrete wall and stood there like a cornered fox facing the hounds.

"Please. Don't stop on my account," said the man in a rich, baritone voice that should belong to a late night DJ. "You may keep screaming if you like, though it will do you little good. Even if someone were to hear you, no one in this neighborhood would help. Better to not get involved, you know. Oh, do forgive me." He inclined his head in her direction and put forth his right hand. "Nelson Straun here. Pleasure to make your acquaintance, Ms. Baxter."

At last her rage and fear found voice, "Y-you goddamned-son-of-a-bitch! Where do you get off grabbing someone off the street like that—and how do you know my name?"

Straun stood with a feigned look of shock as Julie delivered her tirade. "If you're quite through, let us go elsewhere and get better acquainted."

The way he said "acquainted" set her hair on end. Julie didn't know where she was going, but she knew she wasn't staying there. She feinted right and turned left to run. She had not even taken a step when Straun's hand snaked out and snagged her by the hair. She yelped as he pulled her up short and put his mouth next to her ear.

"Don't try something like that again or I'll tear your scalp clean off your head. But, look at the bright side, you were headed in the right direction."

Straun hustled her down the corridor at a brisk pace whistling as they went as if they were going to a business luncheon. Julie could barely see her hand in front of her face, but Straun negotiated the turns and steps with ease. She could only guess that they were in a deserted building or some type of access corridor that had been forgotten about. Straun told her to stop and not to entertain any silly ideas. Although she couldn't see it, she knew he would be wearing that same smug expression and she found herself wishing for a method to erase it. There was a grating noise and then light flared into the corridor momentarily blinding her.

"In we go." Straun grabbed her by the arm and propelled her through the open doorway. He slid the door back in place and slammed the bolt home, securing the heavy, reinforced wooden door, then turned those shark eyes toward her. "Nothing like a quiet evening alone, eh?"

When her eyes had adjusted, she saw that she was in a large room, not necessarily dirty, but Spartan to say the least. The only furnishing in the room was a well used couch and a low coffee table. On the far wall Julie saw a pair of manacles secured in the wall. Straun shoved her towards the wall.

"Now wait a Goddamn minute." Julie spun around to face Straun. "You're not going to use those on me!"

"Oh, I believe I will," he said smiling down at her, "you see, I find them to be extremely helpful tools of the trade."

Julie looked over her shoulder at the restraints hanging there, then kicked her right leg out catching Straun off guard and between the legs. She started to sprint past him when lights flared inside her head.

She woke to the sensation of cold metal digging into her wrists and pain in her shoulders as the ammonia fumes worked their way into her consciousness. Straun held the capsule under her nose again and the whole room snapped into focus.

"Nothing like the sweet aroma of ammonia to clear the head, eh, Julie?"

She wondered how he had known her name, then saw the contents of her purse dumped on the table.

Straun stared into her face. "It's amazing how you can find out so much about a person by what they carry in one of those things, you know," Straun said turning away as he pulled a photo out of his pocket, "Your sister, or your friend? No matter, she's important to you seeing as how you have more than one picture of her. She's very pretty. I suspect that you would like for her to stay that way."

"You're too late there. She's dead already. Has been for years, so piss off."

Straun was undaunted. "No matter. We'll find out if that's true. And if it is, then I'm sure we can find someone you're close too. It's just a matter of time and I've got all the time in the world. That is, of course, if it comes to that, and I don't think it will. I can be very convincing."

"You son-of-a-bitch."

"Julie, Julie, Julie. Flattery will get you nowhere," Straun said with an oily smile.

"All right, Straun, or whatever the hell your name is, let's get on with it. What is it you want?" Julie tried to force more bravado into her voice than she felt.

"Not a whole lot, actually. But, it's the little things

in life that can tell you so much. You see, I'm a thief. An exceptionally good one if I say so myself." Straun paced about as if he were on stage playing to a captivated audience. It was obvious to Julie that he was thoroughly taken with himself. "I work for whoever pays the most."

"Fine," Julie said trying to think of any way to extricate herself from her present position, "whatever it is, I'll double it and you let me go free."

Straun looked at her in genuine amusement and laughed out loud. "I've read your dossier, Ms. Baxter, and you don't have that type of capital. Besides, even if you did, I have a reputation to uphold. How would I ever find future employment if I sold out my contract. No, that wouldn't do. You see, one of your competitors thinks your people are on to something and they want to know what it is."

Her mouth dropped open. "You mean all this is over industrial espionage? Kidnapping is a little much out of line for this sort of thing, isn't it? I mean, why didn't you just try to hack into our system?"

Straun crossed his feet as he leaned against a support post facing Julie and looked at her with a studious expression. "Yes, I could have tried to access your computer, but there is the chance, however small, that I might not be able to get in. Besides, it would take too long. You see," he said waving his hand looking for the right phrasing, "my employer is in somewhat of a rush, and there would be reams of information to sift through. Not only that, what if what I was looking for wasn't in your system? That would be a shame, wouldn't it?"

"A real heartbreaker," Julie muttered under her breath.

"That's where you come in," he said stepping

AWS

towards her. "Extracting information this way is much faster," Julie flinched but didn't look away as he slowly traced a finger down her jaw line, "and much more enjoyable."

Julie tried to calm her breathing as Straun leaned down to eye level with his nose almost touching hers. Julie was again reminded of a shark as he stared coldly at her out of emotionless black pools. She was determined to not let this asshole intimidate her.

Straun spoke to her slowly and with much emphasis, "I want to know what you and Dr. Martin have been working on and where are the research notes?"

"I didn't know our work would interest you," Julie smiled sweetly. "I don't know, and even if I did, I wouldn't say. So, in short, Straun, fuck you."

"In due time," Straun said cupping a breast in each hand. "But, business before pleasure."

Julie felt the bile rise in the back of her throat and fought to control her fear and anger.

Straun continued to massage her breasts through the fabric of her blouse. Suddenly his hands closed violently, his fingers digging into the fleshy mounds. Julie cried out in pain.

"What are you working on and where are the notes?"

A part of her mind asked why. Why her? Why was he was doing this? Why fight it. It wasn't as if she were guarding national secrets. It would be simple just to tell him what he wanted. Another part of her mind told her the longer she held out the better her chances of being found alive. And, if for no other reason, she was stubborn.

Then, just as quickly, the pressure was gone.

"You were about to say?"

"Up yours," she spat out.

The pressure came again, only worse than before, ripping the screams from her throat. She felt as if he were pulling part of her body away.

Straun's voice cut through the haze in her brain, "Once more. What are you working on and where are the notes?"

"S-Sunscreen," Julie cried out.

Straun released his grip and gently massaged Julie's breasts again. "There, that wasn't so hard, now was it? What's so special about this stuff?"

Julie was almost grateful for Straun's manipulations of her breasts as it helped to ease the pain. She glared at him as tears of frustration and pain ran down her cheeks and the fact that she was crying in front of him frustrated her even more. "How the hell should I know? I work for a frigging suntan company. The stuff keeps you from getting sunburned. O.K.?"

"Well, I have a suspicion," said Straun, "but, they don't pay me to wonder why. They pay me to get the stuff and that's what I do. Where are the notes and all his backup disks? Would he have any at home?"

Julie thought of not answering but a shift in Straun's grip persuaded her otherwise.

"The notes are in Martin's office, you asshole. I don't know if he has anything at home; he works there, but I don't know on what. It's not my week to watch him. Everything else is in the top file cabinet. And, I hope you choke on them."

"Thank you, my dear. As I said earlier, business before pleasure." Straun slowly traced a path between the buttons of her blouse. "Well, business is finished."

Straun jerked at the front of her blouse, ripping out the front of the garment in one motion, shearing the bra as he went.

"Nooo!" Julie flailed at him with her feet.

Straun laughed, placing his face between her breasts and reached for the front of her pants.

With a scream of tortured metal and wood, the door at the other end of the room exploded in a shower of splinters and tangled steel. Dust bellowed into the room as a figure emerged out of the maelstrom.

Straun whirled to see what was happening, spied Martin crouched there in the middle of the storm, and stood wide eyed for a moment.

Straun's pause was all Martin needed. Julie stood fascinated as Martin closed the distance between the two in an instant and hit Straun in the middle of the chest. The blow knocked Straun off his feet and deposited him in a crumpled heap. Martin didn't relinquish the attack. He kicked Straun viciously as the other man tried to get to his feet. Straun crashed into the back wall forcing Julie to pull her feet out of the way. She couldn't believe this was the same man she had left in the lab a short while ago.

When Straun hit the wall he immediately rolled to one knee as Martin's foot lashed out again. Somehow Straun managed to dodge the blow and Martin's foot exploded one of the concrete blocks in the wall and was momentarily trapped there. Straun smashed Martin in the ribs, driving the air from his lungs. Martin grunted in pain but gave no pause as he backfisted Straun in the face, snapping the larger man's head around. It was like some bad dream to Julie as she watched with a feeling of detachment. Martin wrenched his foot from the wall and turned to face Straun who had recovered his footing as well.

Julie's heart sank as she looked at the two combatants. Straun was a head taller than Martin, wider in the shoulders, heavier, and probably ten years younger. Martin's chest pumped rapidly as he tried to catch his breath and she knew he had lost the element of surprise.

"What's the problem, old man," Straun said smiling like the Cheshire cat, "are the years catching up to you?"

Martin's reply was like the low growl of a dog that is certain to bite if pressed further. "You, above most others, should know that appearances are deceiving." And, like a good guard dog, Martin had placed himself between Julie and Straun.

Then Straun attacked. If the situation had not been so grave, Julie would have been entertained and amazed. The two men were a blur in the flat light of the room. Finally Martin spun, driving his foot deep into Straun's stomach sending him sprawling once more to the floor.

"Not bad, old man," Straun coughed, blood frothing on his lips. "She doesn't know, does she?"

The question caught Martin off guard.

"You actually care? Your weakness, not mine." Straun produced a switchblade, thumbed the release and rolled up to throw the knife. Not at Martin, but at Julie. She didn't even have time to scream as Straun released the knife.

The next instant, Martin was there. He caught the blade through the palm of his hand and then rolled as he slammed into the floor next to Julie. He pulled the knife free and turned to face Straun who had fled the room. Martin could hear his laughter as he disappeared in the corridor. For a moment Julie thought Martin was going to give chase as he looked first to her and then to where Straun's foot falls were echoing in the distance. With a savage cry, Martin hurled the knife, burying it in the opposite wall. He turned and grasped the chains holding Julie and pulled them from their moorings in the wall and then popped the manacles binding her wrists. Julie stood, mouth agape, staring at Martin as if she had never seen him before.

Martin gently draped his jacket around her shoulders. "Come on, let's get out of here."

Chapter 2

Julie winced as Martin administered the antiseptic from the lab first aid kit to the split in her lip and the abrasions on the side of her face.

"Didn't anyone ever teach you to duck?"

"Cute, Martin, real cute." Julie rubbed absently at her wrists where he had removed the manacles and ran a trembling hand through her hair. "God, I can't get over the whole thing. That monster appears out of nowhere. Oh, wow." She clasped her hands together in front of her, trying to still their shaking. "If you hadn't come along when you did," she let her words trail off to a horse whisper.

"I've never been so scared in my life."

"You're safe now," he said stroking the side of her face.

"Oh, God, Martin, your hand. I've been so wrapped up in myself that I forgot about it. You need to see a doctor."

"I'll be fine," Martin said making a big deal out of repacking the kit.

Regaining some of her bravado, Julie grabbed his hand, "All right. No more of this macho-hero bullshit. Understand? Let me see."

She twisted the palm of his right hand up then gasped in amazement. She grasped his other hand to make sure she had the correct one. Where there should have been a bloody puncture wound, there was nothing to indicate anything had happened at all.

Martin gently pulled his hands away. "I told you I would be fine."

"Wait a minute. Wait-a-minute," Julie pressed the sides of her head trying to push the thoughts there into some semblance of order. "Something's not right here, Martin." Julie's voice turned empathetic. "After all the time we've spent together, you've got to know that I'm crazy about you. I know it sounds cliché, but I've never met anyone like you. And, if anything is going to happen between us, I've got to know what the hell is going on around here." She stood and started to pace, her arms making wild gestures as she talked, her voice rising. "First, some guy grabs me and runs down the street with me like a football, then knocks my lights out. When I come to, he wants to torture me and then play feely-grabby. Then, you show up out of nowhere after Straun says that no one can find us. I didn't hear an explosion, but the door blew up anyway. And, what about that Kung Fu crap—not that I'm griping mind you—but the way you guys were moving was simply incredible! I couldn't keep up with your movements. Not to mention your hand!" She stopped pacing and looked at Martin, "What was that other stuff about, 'She doesn't know . . .' Doesn't know what? Martin, I've got to have some answers when I go to the police."

His head snapped up. "You're going to go to the police?"

"You bet your life I am!"

"That's exactly what I would be doing."

"What do you mean that's what you'd be doing. What are you talking about?"

Martin leaned back against the workbench. The lack of rest and proper nourishment had strained him, and the fight with Straun had pushed him beyond his limits. His head throbbed and he wished that he was anywhere besides where he was at the moment.

"You're not going to let this go, are you?"

Julie's exasperated face said it all.

"No, I suppose you're not," he said quietly turning to grip the edge of the bench. He stood with his head bowed and shoulders slumped for several moments.

Julie moved to him and asked, "Damn, Martin, you think I should let this kook get another shot at me and not call the cops?" She could see emotions play back and forth across his face and then a look of resignation settle there. "Martin, what is it? What's wrong?"

"Do you believe in monsters?"

Julie stood in silence staring at him.

"You mentioned monsters earlier," Martin pressed. "Do you believe in them?"

She shook her head that she didn't understand and pulled out a stool to seat herself.

"That's what I am by some human standards," Martin continued. "And, that is why I work so hard. I won't be able to stay here that much longer. I've been with the company for over ten years. I've even started tinting my hair with gray, but all this won't work much longer. The fact is, I haven't aged in over a hundred years. A hundred and fifty-seven to be exact. That is the reason for my odd behavior."

"Wait a minute." Julie put her hand to her forehead. "Doc, I think maybe you really have been working too hard lately."

"I understand your reaction." Martin looked away. "Anything that contradicts our established beliefs, goes against the status quo, or is distinctly different, we disregard it or destroy it. I've only told two other people about myself. One tried to have me committed, the other tried to kill me."

Martin slid his hands into his coat pockets and stood with his head bowed seeing a time long past. "I admit that even I had trouble believing it at first. Oh, it would have been easy to go insane, to give into the—urges." Martin stood silent, the steady thrum of the air conditioner the only noise in the room.

"Julie," Martin's eyes caught hers, "I, am a vampire."

Julie slowly pushed back the stool and got to her feet. She didn't know if she should hold Martin, laugh, or turn and run. Julie was a person who prided herself on being able to deal with anything, but Martin's last statement, piled on top of the rest of the evening, was too much. She forced herself to think logically. For all his brilliance, Martin was in need of professional help.

"Martin, I believe that *you may think you're a vampire,* but I find it pretty damn hard to accept."

"Would it be easier if I grew fangs or turned into a bat?"

"Well, honestly, yes."

"I can't turn into a bat, Julie."

"See, I told you, Martin, it's all in your head."

"I said I couldn't turn into a bat." Martin parted his lips in a toothy smile to reveal two, one inch fangs where his canine teeth had been. "Pretty impressive, huh?"

The color drained out of Julie's face. "It's a trick, right?"

"Oh, no. They're quite real, I can assure you. You can touch them if you'd like." Julie shook her head no and clutched her hands in front of her. "It's all right," Martin said in that same calm voice Julie had become so accustomed to, "I won't bite you."

Julie stood rooted to the spot and watched in amazement as the two fangs slowly retracted until once more, Martin was just Martin.

Julie's ordered mind reeled from the impossibility she had just witnessed and Martin caught her before she hit the floor. Her eyes strained to focus. When they did, there was Martin's face, very close to her own.

"NO! Stay away!" She crabbed backwards until she hit the bench.

Martin's head dropped in despair. As he stood, he felt the full weight of his hundred plus years of existence. He turned to face her and she could see the tears welled up in his eyes.

"I am not a monster, Julie," he said softly, "I'm just a little more than human the way you know it. And, your actions make me feel far less."

Julie sat mesmerized. Conflicting emotions raged inside her. She had been taught all her life that things like this didn't happen. That was why she embraced chemistry and science in general, for the structured logic they provided. But, here in front of her was something she couldn't explain. Julie got to her feet and stared at Martin. What she saw was not some evil creature in a cape lurking in the dark somewhere, but rather the man she had come to love, and he was hurting. She started to step forward, then withdrew, still unsure.

"The truth is, I love you, Julie. I have for some time now, but I could never tell you." Martin clasped his hands together, "And, I could never hurt you. Even if it meant destroying everything I've worked so hard for. I could have kept up with the story about my having a rare skin disease and then pass off the cut to just being a nick and that I was just hyped on natural adrenaline; but, instead I told you the truth. You deserve that much." Martin took a deep sigh, exhaling slowly, then looked at Julie with a half-hearted smile. "Well, at least now you know why I didn't go for any afternoon strolls with you."

As he spoke, a gleam appeared in his eyes, "But, all that could change." Before she could respond, he continued, "What you and I have been working on is not just some new tanning agent. Oh, we've been doing the company's mundane work, but some of that stuff you were unsure about, that was what I've been working on personally. What I've developed is the ultimate sunscreen. I know. It sounds corny like a cheap commercial, but what this stuff does is amazing."

In spite of herself, Julie found herself caught up in Martin's enthusiasm.

He was starting to pace now as he spoke, "You see, I'm not impervious to pain and I can die. Under normal circumstances though, it would be a real bitch to kill me." He stopped in front of her. "However, if I decided to try to catch a few rays at the beach, it's adios." Martin brushed the side of her face with his finger. "See, I can still make you smile."

Julie dropped her chin when he reached to touch her, but didn't pull away.

Martin awkwardly cleared his throat and stepped back.

Julie looked at him, "How-I mean, I don't understand . . . I mean, how did . . ."

"Oh, right. How does one become a vampire?" Martin said forcing a nonchalant note in his voice that he didn't feel. In fact, he was so tired, it was all he could do to stay on his feet. "Well, the person is infected by the bite. The disease, a virus actually, is carried in the saliva. That's the only way it's transmitted. It enters the blood stream, attacks the body's cells and invades them. And, I mean the whole body—non selective. Once inside the cell, it supersedes the DNA's code and alters the chain, causing some drastic mutations. Cellular activity is increased, the regeneration system is boosted off the scale. Even loss of major nerve tissue can repair itself. Muscle tissue becomes unbelievably dense and there is an immense increase in fast twitch muscle. Consequently, the increase in strength and speed is unbelievable. Trust me, I would be great at the Olympics. And, there's the teeth. Nifty little trick. The canine teeth are loosened in their sockets and tissue similar to erectile tissue is formed. The tissue fills with blood forcing the tooth downward. When the tissue empties, the tooth retracts. You learn to control that after awhile." A rueful smile played on his lips, "So, as you can tell, there are some advantages to being a vampire." The smile died as he turned away not looking at anything in particular. "But, they're not worth the tradeoffs. Besides the lack of sunlight, the body can no longer digest regular food. Only blood."

"Why?"

"I don't know why. There's so damn much we don't know." Martin pushed off from the table he had been leaning against and jammed his hands in his pockets as he shuffled along talking so low that she had to strain to hear him. "It's bad enough never seeing the sun, outliving your friends-the one or two that you have-but, then, there's the urges. It's like being addicted, only worse. The madness is over-whelming. Even with help, most are not strong enough to master the urges that well up inside them. Although I hate to admit it, even I have trouble re-pressing it now and then."

"Wait a minute, Martin," Julie said as she moved to come up behind him. "You keep talking about an 'urge'. Just what the heck are you talking about?"

Martin whirled on her so fast that his spin was instantaneous. "Haven't you been listening to any-thing I've told you?"

For the first time since she had met him, Martin had lost his temper with her. The sheer force of his voice was like something physical striking at her.

"What have we been talking about for the last ten minutes. Vampires, Julie. Real, honest to God, vampires. And, what do vampires do? They attack people for their blood and turn them into things like me. Things that never get to see the light. Things that wait in the dark with hyper senses and strength to boggle your mind." Martin's voice was taking on a note of hysteria. "We don't rise from the grave on the third day or the first full moon or whatever that bullshit is on the TV. If the vampire is a glutton, or if they attack in a group, they will drain all of the person's blood, and it kills them. They're the lucky ones. Others will kill just for the thrill of it. The fact of the matter is, THEY-KILL-PEOPLE, JULIE!"

She looked on as the tears streamed down his face. Martin slumped to his knees, his head leaned backwards, eyes shut tight trying to block out the images before him and his lips moved, but she couldn't hear what he was saying. Then his voice rose in pitch and volume until it knifed her ears. But, she knew the pain she was feeling was nothing compared to the agony that was carried in Martin's soul.

Then he looked at her through eyes that begged for understanding. In a hoarse whisper he told her, "I have killed people."

Chapter 3

Julie lay beside Martin in the darkness of his bedroom. He had been physically and emotionally drained and had been in no position to argue when she insisted on taking him home. Julie propped him up in the elevator and tried to give as casual appearance as possible as they made their way out the front door together, arms around each other. Julie called to Pete, telling him she promised this was the last time they would bother him tonight. Pete called after them saying that they were no trouble and that it was nice to see them together, that he had told the Mrs. that they made a fine looking couple. Martin managed a wave and then let Julie lead him out the door to her car. He had protested when she started to help him into his house. She ignored his complaints and weak attempts to walk on his own. Once inside, she half carried him into the bedroom. There, she undressed him and spread the covers over his body, watching until his breathing became deep and regular.

She then decided to make an inspection of the house not really knowing what she was looking for.

The only thing she found was a neat, well kept,

typical three bedroom home; with the exception that everyone of the windows had been sealed up. Not a ray of light came through any of them although she knew that the sun was well up by this time.

"No sunshine," she thought as she looked around, "this is crazy. Stuff like this just doesn't happen. This isn't the middle ages. We don't hide under our beds because of superstitions."

She began to wonder if Martin was indeed in need of psychiatric help and then just as quick dismissed the thought because this wasn't something someone had told her about. She had lived the experience, had been right there when it all happened, and there was no other explanation for it.

In the back of her mind she half expected to find a casket or something lying around in one of the bedrooms. At least that would help explain some of the craziness that had been going on.

One of the bedrooms had been converted into a library with books lining the walls. Some of the volumes where very old and still in excellent shape. She wondered to herself if he had bought them new or picked them up later at an antique sale.

She discovered the house had a full basement and Martin had set up a lab there. Although not as large as the one they shared at the company, it was impressive none the less. Over in one corner of the room, past the rows of beakers and sample trays, Martin had hung a punching bag to work out with, as well as free weights, jump rope and other exercise equipment. In the living room she found an impressive amount of electronic equipment: An entertainment rack complete with CD player, surround sound, VCR and large screen TV. He even had a Sega System. She wondered if he had bought it recently because she didn't remember him saying anything about owning a video system, or if he was embarrassed to tell her he liked to play video games. The thought of a video playing vampire definitely amused her. The kitchen was well stocked and contained an array of culinary utensils, though the refrigerator, typical of a single person, was sparse. There was the usual staples, as well as a can of peaches, a carton of eggs, and a half empty bottle of prune juice. With a sigh, Julie closed the refrigerator and walked into the room were Martin lay.

She could just make out his form in the light reflecting from the kitchen. Her heart went out to him and she longed to lie beside him, to take him in her arms and hold him there until all his hurts went away. But, she knew what he needed most was undisturbed sleep, so she quietly shut the door and waited.

He lay in the complete darkness of his room for a few moments gathering his wits about him. Finally he sat up in bed. "Hi, Jules. And, since I didn't say it earlier, thanks."

"How did you know I was here? It's pitch black in here."

Martin stifled a yawn. "I could smell you, hear your breathing; I could feel you in the darkness sitting by the door."

Julie's mouth dropped open in surprise. She had been sitting in the overstuffed armchair by the door. She reached out with her hand and flipped the switch filling the room with light. "Gees, Martin, you look like shit."

Martin squinted against the glare, "Thank you, and a good morning to you."

"Morning nothing," she said uncurling from the chair. "It's after three o'clock in the afternoon you lazy butt." Although, she admitted to herself, that if it had been her she would still be asleep.

"That long, eh?" Martin rubbed at his eyes and leaned his head back into the pillow.

She swaggered over to the end of the bed, "Even vampires have their limits, huh?"

Martin looked at her with mock contempt. "Yes, even vampires have their limits and I had reached mine. Would you please be kind to a poor soul and fetch me the bottle of prune juice out of the 'fridge."

"Oh, I'm here a few hours and already I'm your slave?" Julie's voice was droll.

Martin threw one of the bed pillows at her and propped himself up with the other one. "Be gone and bring a man his breakfast before I crawl out of this bed and gnaw on your leg instead!"

No sooner were the words out of his mouth when he realized what he had said. If they made Julie feel ill at ease her laughter gave no sign of it.

She opened the refrigerator and reached inside for the bottle. As she closed the door, a thought struck her. She unscrewed the lid and peered inside. It didn't look like prune juice and it smelled like. . . .

"Holy shit!" she muttered to herself, hastily putting the lid back. She hurried to the bedroom and handed the bottle to Martin eager to be rid of it.

As he raised the jar to his lips, she asked him, "That isn't really prune juice, is it?"

Martin lowered the jar and slowly shook his head no.

"I didn't think it was." She played with a spot on the carpet with her foot. "I just want to know one thing. Is . . . "

"No. It's not human blood."

"You read minds also?" she asked visibly relaxing.

"No, just an obvious question. Does it disturb or surprise you?"

"It's getting to where not much surprises me where you're concerned. I would be lying to you if I said it didn't disturb me a little. Still, I had best get used to such things if I'm going to 'hang' around with you." She jabbed him in the bottom of the foot, "that's a little vampire humor there. Hang around. Oh, never mind."

Martin managed a smile as he hefted the jar once more. He was acutely aware of Julie's intent gaze and closed his eyes as he took a deep draw from the container. When he finished the last of the liquid, he replaced the cap and set the container by the bed. "Well, I feel much better now, thank you. I've got to get cleaned up and back to the lab."

"Oh, no you don't. Not after having pushed yourself into exhaustion. It's Friday and you're spending the rest of the weekend with me right here."

"Believe me," Martin said, "I recuperate much faster then you think."

She put her finger to his lips to silence him. "I've already called in sick for you and," she pushed him back into the bed, "I'm going to stay here and play nurse maid to make sure you give yourself a chance to recover. Besides, you'd hate to make a liar out of me, wouldn't you?"

"You are sly, aren't you?"

"You know we wanton women."

The weekend passed too quickly. In the fleeting hours he was able to totally let himself open up. And, in doing so, Martin realized what he had missed the most in those long years of self imposed isolation. More than being able to rise with the sun and feel the warm rays on his face or thrill to the sight of wild geese flying overhead, it was the feeling of true companionship. He had been able to talk of things that he had mentioned to no one in over a hundred years. And, he had been able to share in another's dreams. Martin thought about this as he sat on the couch, and looked down at the sleeping figure leaned up against him. As he ran his hand lightly through her hair, he felt his heart break. Their time together was growing short.

This time it was Julie who slept past midday. It was just past two when Martin entered the room carrying a tray loaded with fresh fruit, coffee and danish. He had snuck out to the local food mart before day break which wasn't difficult since he had insisted on sleeping on the couch.

He sat the tray down on the bed and kissed her gently on the nape of her neck. "Hey, sleeping beauty. You going to sleep your life away and make me do all the work or what?"

She rolled to her back, stretched like an over grown tabby and groggily replied, "I think this fits into the 'or what' category."

Martin laughed and brushed a stray hair from her face. Then he took on a more solemn air. "Unfortunately it appears there is work to be done and not much time to do it. The lab called and the worst has happened."

Julie sat upright and put the tray aside. "What do you mean, 'the worst.?"

"It appears that the company was broken into last night. They're calling it simple industrial espionage. The police have no leads as to who broke in, but I know it was Straun," Martin said sipping a cup of Swiss mocha. "I made the mistake of thinking he was just another one of those bloodsucking bastards." Martin sighed heavily, cupping the drink in his hands, "I'm afraid this is all my fault."

"Yours?" Julie moved the tray further and motioned for Martin to sit with her. "How do you figure that it was your fault? And, for that matter, how do you know that it was even Straun?"

"It's too much of a coincidence. I should have seen it coming," Martin said as he sat beside Julie, "because Straun, if that is his real name, is not one of the ordinary leeches. Not if he was able to pump you for information and was inclined to assault you sexually before killing you." Martin gave her a lopsided grin as steam curled around his face. "But, I will admit that I was somewhat preoccupied this weekend."

Julie shuddered involuntarily as her mind recalled the fiery pain in her breasts, Straun's touch and the look in his eyes; a look that bored it's way through your consciousness with a sheer force of will. She wrapped her arms around Martin trying to block out the mental picture of Straun's face.

"You see, Jules," Martin said putting an arm across her shoulders, "chances are he was a thief to start with. Then somehow he managed to control the madness. Or, perhaps he is mad. You know what they say, . . . there exists a fine line between madness and genius. At any rate," Martin waved away his rambling, "ours was the only division broken into. And, let's face it, what we were working on is not Earth shattering. It could be that this was a simple case of industrial espionage and the buyer found a thief extraordinaire, not realizing what Straun is. If he takes the information to his employer, then they have all the data you and I have been working on together. If someone is able to find and crack my hidden files, then they get one hell of a sunscreen, which in itself, is no big deal. But," Martin crossed the room to stare at the scene pictured on the large TV screen and watched as tree limbs danced lightly in the breeze and the flowers turned their leaves to the sun, "if Straun is as intelligent and resourceful as he appears and decides to check out what he's stolen, then he'll be the one able to brave the daylight."

Martin turned and fixed Julie with a look that made Straun's intensity pale in comparison, "We've got to get that formula back."

Chapter 4

Later that evening, well after dark, the pair pulled into the parking lot of SUNCO, Inc. and came to a halt. Water from the automatic sprinkler system showed like gems on the leaves of the shrubs that lined the parking lot, glinting in the light from the overhead lamps. Martin sat staring at the tiny diamonds sparkling there and switched off the engine.

"You O.K. Doc," Julie asked tentatively.

"I was so close," Martin said not looking at her. "And, then to have a walking cesspool like Straun turn the whole thing on it's head. . . . "

"Come on, Doc," Julie said laying a hand on his shoulder, "this isn't like you. I mean, you don't know how bad the damage is yet."

Martin looked at her across the seat. Although the interior of the car was dark, he could make out the details of her face easily. He traced her jaw line with his finger and spoke with the voice of a man who's options have all but run out. "It isn't just that, Jules, I'm stuck between a rock and a hard place. Never in a million years did I anticipate something like this." Martin gave a sigh and leaned his head against the seat rest. "When I called the lab earlier today, they wanted me to come down and verify what was taken during the theft. I told them that I was out of town on an emergency errand, that I had checked my messages, and was calling long distance. I told them that I could have my assistant fill out the report. Nothing doing." Martin pulled the keys from the ignition with disgust and pushed the release on his seat belt. "The powers that be said I would have to fill out the paperwork myself and to report to the department head tomorrow during regular business hours. I told them that was impossible due to the malady I suffer from. They didn't want to listen."

"What malady? I knew you had an aversion to the sun, and now I know the truth, but what malady are you talking about?"

Half chuckling to himself, Martin said, "You mean for once, the front office actually kept a secret like they said they would? I told them I have a form of CEP and that that was the reason for my strong desire to work for their company. I asked that they keep it under their hat, because I didn't want to be subjected to a lot of questions."

"CEP?" Julie looked at him expectantly, waiting for him to answer her unspoken query.

"Congenital erythropoietic porphyia."

"OK." She motioned for him to continue.

"It's from a handful of genetic disorders known as porphyrias. The thing that is common to all these disorders is a defect in the assembly of hemoglobin. CEP is also one of the rarest. One of the complications of the disorder is the inability of the body to break down toxic protein precursors of heme, called porphyrins. These proteins build up to extremely high levels in the bloodstream and urine, and when the patients are exposed to any kind of light, the proteins react in ways that blister the skin. I told them that my form of CEP didn't react to all light, rather just the sun and that was the reason for my staying out of the daylight."

"Wow. Nice cover story. Any of that true?"

"No. But, it is ironic that the disorder that helps to protect me today, is probably a reason for vampire legend. Anyone afflicted would discover that they would need to stay out of the sun and only come out at night and some of the porphyrin deposits on the person's teeth would produce a reddish color making it appear that the person had been drinking blood. The superstitious lot of the middle ages probably mistook these symptoms for actual vampirism."

"And they gave you the job anyway?"

"I told them it was because of my affliction and the excellence of their company that I wanted to work for them. That line of BS, coupled with my credentials, landed me the job. Working in this environment, with their resources and not having to do all of it myself, has definitely speeded up my results. Not to mention that if I had secluded myself in my dusty, dungeon laboratory at the castle, I would never have met that lovely lab assistant of mine."

Martin's eyes caressed Julie's face as he looked at her. Then the storm clouds passed back over his features.

"I don't know how I'm going to handle this one. If I try to show up tomorrow, I go up in flames. If I don't show, I implicate myself. I can maybe stall them for a couple of days. I don't know." Martin ran a hand through his hair, "Let's go get this over with and see what kind of damage they've done," he said swinging the car door open.

The cool night air struck him and he stood for a

FOR BLOOD NOR MONEY

moment looking at the stars overhead, taking in the night, then turned to look at Julie across the top of the car.

"I arise from dreams of thee
in the first sweet sleep of night
When the winds are breathing low,
And the stars are shining bright. "

"My God, the man recites poetry as well." Julie closed her door and rested her forearms on the top of the car and gazed at Martin.

". . . I arise from dreams of thee,
And a spirit in my feet
Has led me—who knows how?—
To thy chamber window, sweet!"

Martin raised his eyebrows in appreciation, "Nicely spoken, M'Lady."

Pushing away from the car she said, "Well, Doc, science manuals aren't the only thing I read, you know."

Martin vaulted across the top of the car and landed lightly beside her. "Jules, you're one in a million." He bent forward and kissed her gently on the mouth.

When their lips separated, she leaned back a little and asked, "Is this the same man that a minute ago was ready to throw in the towel?"

"I figured what the hell. I've been down before." Martin shrugged and then put his arm around her shoulders, "The way my luck is running, I'll get audited by the IRS. Wouldn't that be a hoot," he said starting them towards the building, "I can see it now:

AWS

Yes, Mr. Daniels, we'd like to review your tax records for the years 1874 to the present."

"They didn't have income tax back then."

"All right smart ass, it's my joke."

They were both laughing as they entered the building and were almost to the guard's station when Martin's head snapped up in alarm.

The guard stood slowly and said, "Hi ya, Doc. Been expecting you."

Martin snarled and shoved Julie behind him as he took a step backwards.

"Whoa, chill out, Doc. Like, put your fangs away. We're supposed to be one big happy family here at SUNCO, remember?" The young man behind the desk sat back down and motioned to the video cameras trained on the desk. "Don't worry about them; we're not being taped. I've set up a loop to run while I answer any questions you might have. After all, that's what we do here at the information desk." The guard let out a dry laugh having amused himself. "Damn, Doc, you have no sense of humor."

Martin ignored the guard's comment. When he spoke, it was the low, warning growl of a wolf. "What have you done with Pete?"

"You mean he's one of them," Julie asked peeking around Martin. "Holy shit, I'm not ready for this."

The guard talked to Martin but kept his eyes on Julie. "You mean the old fart that usually works here? Well, his shift got changed and just for your information, he's alive and well—for now."

Martin started for the guard.

"Uh-uh, Doc." The guard didn't move from his seat and looked at Martin with a look produced by someone who knows they are in total control of a situation. "Straun said you were fast for an old man, but think about it. Too many people around. And, you never know when I'll turn off the loop."

Martin realized he was right. The custodial crew was out in force and it was early enough yet that a few of the daytime staff were still working.

"You filthy son-of-a-bitch," Martin snarled under his breath, "if anything happens to that old man, there won't be one place on this earth where you'll be safe from me. I'll track you down and rip out your spine."

"Believe me, man," the guard said as he pushed his chair back and placed his hands on the desk top, "there's nothing I'd like better than to jump over this desk and kick your ass. But," the guard spread his hands in acceptance, "for the time being, I was told that you were off limits and that you and I were to be real buddies. So, buddy, you might want to check out your lab. Seems someone broke into it."

The guard was still laughing as they rounded the first corner.

Martin expected the worst as he gripped the knob to the drab, gray door that opened into his lab.

Julie, tagging close behind, said, "Ease up, Martin. You almost ripped it off the hinges."

They both stood in the open doorway for a moment and took in the scene before them.

"I've been watching too much television," Julie said, "I really expected to see all the equipment smashed, papers thrown around; you know, have the whole place trashed."

"I'll admit I wasn't really expecting this. But, it makes sense."

"What do you mean," Julie asked as she followed him into his office.

Martin talked as he shuffled through papers and

other materials piled on his desk. "Straun asked you specifically what you were working on and with whom. He's not after equipment. If he were, he could go to a lot less trouble and just knock off a warehouse. No," Martin grabbed his chair and rolled it in front of his keyboard, "He knew what he was after and where to find it, so there was no need to trash the place. All he wanted was information. He said as much." Martin logged on to the main frame and booted up the PC sitting nearby at the same time. There was a moment's pause and then the words SURPRISE filled the screen of his PC. As Martin continued to stair at the screen, a message started to scroll.

> Greetings, Doctor. I have been expecting
> you. I have to admit that what you have here
> is not that interesting . . . on the surface.
> But, I can see why my employer is intent on
> obtaining it. Of course, you'll notice that I
> took the liberty of borrowing all your backup
> disks.

Martin hadn't noticed. A quick glance confirmed the message in that the locked file cabinet had been forced open and was standing empty. Martin turned back to the screen as it continued to scroll.

> Also, just in case that you're thinking of
> some way to try and retrieve your data,
> I wiped anything remotely connected to
> you from the main frame, and as for
> your hard drive, well, your system
> is going to crash. Right about now. Ta-ta.

Martin scrambled to shut down the machine, but for all his speed, was not quick enough. He stared in numb disbelief at the blank, lifeless screen before him.

Julie, who had been reading along with him, laid a hand gently on his shoulder.

"Martin, I'm so sorry. I feel like I'm responsible for all this. If I had been paying more attention in the parking lot then maybe he wouldn't have been able to get me and the information he wanted. I'm sorry. What are we going to do?"

Martin pivoted in the chair and looked up at her. "For starters, you're going to stop blaming yourself for something that was beyond your control. If he hadn't grabbed you before you made it into the car, he would have ripped the door off the car and got you anyway. No offense, Jules, but playing with this guy is way out of your league. Hell," Martin slumped back in the chair and drew a long breath, "he might be out of my league for that matter." He reclined back in the chair putting his hands behind his head turning the whole situation over in his head. "I mean, who is this guy? He makes it in past all the security measures, accesses my PC and personal files on the main frame, and dumps my system." Martin stood up and started to pace across the office. "Ours is the only department broken into. With not much damage done and ours the only office affected, there won't be a lot of major publicity. Thank goodness for that, but you can bet they're going to be looking up my ass with a microscope. They'll be wanting to know what I could possibly be working on that someone would think would be worth stealing. And, that if I was on to something, why wasn't I a team player and share the wealth. Or, worse yet, they'll think that I was the one that came in, made it look like a break-in and sold information myself."

Martin stopped for a moment and looked sideways at Julie who was giving him a lopsided grin. "I was rambling again, huh?"

Julie slowly shook her head yes.

"I do that when I think out loud, don't I?"

"But, you're so cute when your angry. The thing is, what *do* we do now?"

"Let's get out of here before they decide to arrest me and hold me for questioning. Let's go back to my place. We can plot on the way there."

The vampire guard was still there when they passed the front desk. Martin cast a menacing glance in his direction as they walked toward the front doors.

As they passed outside, Martin heard the guard call after them, "Ta-ta!"

Chapter 5

Shortly after midnight, Martin and Julie came to a stop in front of his house. The breeze stirred the shrubs below the windows and sighed through the trellises on the front porch. Martin cast a glance around the sleeping neighborhood as he fished the house key out of his pocket and inhaled deeply. He stood with his eyes closed as he identified the different scents on the night air.

As he turned the key he spoke to Julie, "The night can be so like a beautiful woman; lovely, yet concealing so many secrets."

Julie looked at him for a long moment with raised eyebrows, "Doc, I'm hungry and you're full of shit. You don't have much here, or at least anything I would be interested in, so I'm going to get something to eat. I personally don't know of any blood banks with drive through windows, so is there anything else I can get you?"

"You can get the hell out of here," then in a really bad Bella Lagosie imitation he added, "before I put a permanent hickey on your neck." He tossed her the keys to the Honda. "Whatever you get, I'll take the same."

He watched Julie pull out of the drive and start down the street then pushed the door open and stepped inside.

As soon as he entered the house, Martin knew something was wrong. The hairs at the base of his neck raised as he realized the all too familiar scent was everywhere in the house. He looked out the door, but the Honda was already out of sight. He felt fairly certain that Julie was not their intended victim this time. Of course not, he admonished himself. They would be after whatever information he had here at the house.

Martin felt behind the door and found his walking stick. A quick twist of his wrist caused the locking mechanism to unlatch and a thirty inch blade slid with a hiss from it's resting place in the shaft of the cane. Martin didn't own a gun. Above all, he wanted to avoid attracting the attention of the police, so the sword was the perfect weapon for him. Martin padded silently across the room probing the darkness with his senses as he went. He flowed from room to room and found nothing except the smell of where they had been. Martin cursed to himself as he moved toward the opening to the lab. As he got closer, their spoor became stronger. Either the parasites had been there the longest or they were still in the lab. Martin edged forward, rounded the corner at the top of the stairs and ran face to face into one of Straun's thugs. The look of surprise on the vampire's face turned to one of disbelief as Martin ran him through the throat with the blade to keep him from calling out. Martin knew that given time, even this normally mortal wound would not prove fatal to the vampire. He didn't give him time. Ripping the blade from the others neck, Martin decapitated the vampire in one swift motion. Martin pushed the body aside with his foot, closed the door so that the impending flash wouldn't be seen from below, and started down the stairs. Halfway down a voice drifted up to him from below.

"Hey, Manny, is that you? What was that noise up there, anyway?"

Martin mumbled something about tripping over the doorstep and hoped the other wouldn't notice too much of a difference as he reflected on the fact that for all the physical prowess vampirism provided, it did nothing to improve one's brain power.

"Stupid klutz," came the reply. "I'm done here. I made the call for you," the other voice said moving toward the stairs. Martin didn't answer as he waited just inside the stairwell. "Did you hear me, I said . . . "

The words were still on his lips when his head left his shoulders, a look of mild confusion on his face.

Martin stood and watched as the cannibalistic process took over and the dead vampire's cells consumed themselves. He stepped into the room and turned on the rest of the lights in the lab to try to ascertain what the two had been doing. He felt sure that they were the only ones here or else the others would already have attacked him. Martin wiped the dried ash from his blade and slid it back into it's resting place as he looked around. Nothing seemed to be out of place, yet something wasn't quite right either. He was trying to put his finger on it when he heard the sirens coming down his street and screech to a halt in front of his house. Then it dawned on him. He had thought that the second vampire had been talking about calling Straun. He hadn't. Instead he had called the police. Martin looked around.

There were no windows in the basement and already the police where in the house. He wasn't worried about them finding the bodies in that they had turned to piles of ash and would give the impression that he was not the neatest housekeeper. He also knew that he could more than likely make it out of the house, but then he would be on the run and no closer to finding out who or where Straun was. There was no way he would run out on Julie, either. No, he would have to play this one by ear.

The door at the top of the stairs burst open and the sound of feet pounding down the stairs filled the confined space of the small lab. A body flung itself across the open space and took up position behind a cabinet while two more police provided protective cover from around the corner of the stairwell.

"FREEZE MISTER!"

Martin started to turn with his hands in the air.

"I told you not to move!" came the voice from behind the cabinet.

"Got one here!" a voice bellowed to the other officers from inside the stairwell.

The second officer in the stairwell stepped into the room with his gun leveled at Martin's chest. From above, Martin could hear other officers calling out all-clears. The first officer in the room stepped forward keeping his pistol arm pointed at Martin while he fished out his cuffs with the other. Martin could smell the adrenaline, sweat, and fear permeating the three cops approaching him.

"Listen, officers, there's been some kind of mix up," Martin started.

"Shut up and do exactly as you're told. Now lie

face down on the floor with your arms spread to either side. Now!"

Martin did as he was instructed and laid himself spread-eagle on the floor. As soon as he did, the policeman snapped a cuff on him and pulled his arm behind his back and repeated the process with his free arm. When the officer was satisfied that the cuffs were in place he and one of the others hauled Martin to his feet.

"You are under arrest . . . " the cop started.

Martin didn't even listen to the rest. He was thinking furiously on how or if he was going to make bail before sunup.

" . . . do you understand these rights as they have been read to you?"

"Huh?"

"I said," the cop repeated, "do you understand these rights as they have been read to you?"

"Yes, sure." Martin responded.

The two police were moving him as soon as he said "yes".

"What I don't understand, is what exactly it is that I am being arrested for?"

"You'll be formally booked at the station," the officer said in a very professional voice and then in an aside to another cop who had made their way downstairs, "Like, he would have to ask with all this shit down here. There's probably nothing this guy can't synthesize."

Of course, the police present were unaware of Martin being in on almost every conversation in the house. As they started their way up the stairs the puzzle pieces started coming together.

Straun had tried to kill Martin outright earlier and failed. Martin reasoned that Straun figured he would let the police do the work for him. Plus, this way all the attention would be focused on Martin and away from Straun. Most of the authorities would opt for the quick wrap up and figure that Martin was producing a truck load of just about anything your average junky would want. Martin allowed himself to be led out of the house into a maze of flashing lights to where a police cruiser waited. The one officer opened the back door to the cruiser and turned to Martin, who stood waiting for all the world as if he were in line for an amusement park ride. The cop grabbed his arm roughly and pulled him towards the open door.

"All right, get in and watch your head."

Just as Martin stepped up and started to bow his head, he looked across the top of the cruiser and saw the blue Honda with Julie behind the wheel being waved on by an officer in the street. Martin made eye contact with Julie and with an almost imperceptible nod of his head, motioned her on. All he needed right now was for both of them to be in jail. The cop pushed on the back of his head and he yielded to the pressure and seated himself in the back of the cruiser. He watched out the side window and saw Julie turn down the next street.

"Good girl," he thought as he settled back in the seat. He had no doubt that Julie would be able to get bail for him. It was just a case of getting it in time. It was going to be a close call no matter what. Martin smiled to himself as he thought of all the paper work and what kind of an excuse the sergeant on duty would give for allowing a prisoner of theirs to spontaneously ignite. He had to admit one thing; Straun certainly knew how to set up a snare. Martin would either ignite in jail or escape, possibly getting killed in the process. Either way, Martin would be out of the picture as far as Straun was concerned.

Martin was running all this through his head when the driver's side door opened and a cop who had seen the inside of a doughnut shop a few times too many, fell in behind the wheel.

"Make some good junk today, huh, buddy," the cop said around a mouthful of tobacco.

Martin turned his head to meet the cop's gaze in the rearview mirror. "I don't know what you're talking about."

"Of course you don't," the cop muttered to himself, "you type never do." And punctuated the statement by spitting a mouthful of foul smelling brown liquid out the window.

"You know," Martin said in a matter-of-fact voice, "it would be best if you gave that stuff up now, before it's too late. Mouth cancer is not very pretty."

"Why don't you sit back, shut the fuck up and don't give me any shit," the fat cop snarled. "I don't need the advice of some fuckin' pusher. You got, me?"

"No, problem. It's your mouth." Martin eased back in the seat, closed his eyes and hoped that Julie would be in time. In the back of his mind, he wondered if the jail where completely enclosed. Some of it would be he told himself. But, he didn't know if the cells had windows of some kind. And, even if they didn't. What would happen when he made bail. He couldn't hang around all day. No, there was no doubt about it, he would have to make it to safety before the sun came up.

The fat cop finally came to a stop in front of a set of double doors with an electronic lock and twin surveillance cameras. He switched off the ignition and struggled to undue his seat belt.

"All right scumbag, you're here." The cop made an audible grunt hefting himself to his feet and was out of breath from doing this small amount of activity.

Martin watched the whole thing and thought to himself, "This is what we have protecting our streets. It's nice to know that if he had to chase someone, that he could at least get out of the car before having a heart attack."

The officer waddled around and opened the door to the back of the cruiser. Before he could help Martin out of the back of the car, Martin slid over and was out of the back of the cruiser standing beside him. If the cop had looked pale from lack of sunlight, having worked countless swing and graveyard shifts, and avoiding physical activity whenever possible, the rest of his color drained when Martin turned his head and looked at him. With his back to the camera, Martin let the normal visage of his face drop. For the briefest of moments, his lips curled back in a snarl to reveal two gleaming fangs. The fat man dropped the keys he had been holding and backed away trying to draw his gun.

Martin turned as if there might be something coming up behind him and then faced the cop again with a look of genuine puzzlement on his face. "Are you all right?" Martin asked in his most concerned voice, "What's wrong?"

The cop was definitely fighting for air now and it was his turn to look puzzled.

"Open your mouth," he wheezed.

"Do what?"

"You heard me, dammit! Open your fucking mouth."

"Should I say ahh?" The sarcasm was lost on the

policeman who craned his neck to see inside Martin's mouth. Martin thought about saying boo, but reasoned that that would be carrying it a bit too far.

The policeman's breath was beginning to return to normal, or as normal as his weight would allow. Martin could see the thoughts whirling inside the others head. He knew that if the officer ever said anything, no one would believe him and it would probably get him a trip to the in-house psyche department. Besides, Martin knew that the man wasn't sure if he had really seen anything or not.

"Are you sure you're O.K.?"

That snapped the cop back. "Yea, I'm just fucking fine. Now back up a couple of steps."

As Martin did as he was instructed, the cop bent down to retrieve his keys, which set off another round of labored breathing.

"All right. Turn around and lets head through that door." The officer grabbed Martin by the cuffs and herded him toward the double doors.

Martin could hear Julie now, chastising him for scaring the cop.

Realistically, Martin didn't scare people very often. Just now and then to assholes like this one who deserved it.

The cop buzzed the lock and waited for the officer watching the monitors to unlock the door. The lock made a clunking sound as it disengaged.

"Get the hell in there." The policeman shoved Martin through the open doorway and guided him to the warrant officer.

"He's all yours," he said between heavy breaths. The large policeman couldn't wait to get away from Martin. "Hurry up Hal, I've got paper work running out my butt that I still have to fill out."

The officer behind the desk barely looked up. "Don't we all, so quit your bitchin'."

The fat cop fidgeted as he waited impatiently for Hal to finish what he was doing.

Martin slowly turned his head to stare at the cop, which only served to increase the other's anxiety.

"What are you looking at?" the fat cop spit out.

"Nothing really," Martin replied evenly.

"Well, keep your eyes forward, scumbag."

Martin continued to stare at the other man.

"I said to stop lookin' at me, shit for brains. I mean now!"

The outburst caught the warrant officer's attention. "What's the problem, Stoner?"

"This son-of-a-bitch gives me the creeps."

Martin looked at him again. He could see the beads of perspiration on the other's oily skin and smell the fear emanating from him.

Stoner hissed at Martin. "You look at me one more time and I'm going to crack your skull."

Hal came around from behind his desk. "Back off, Stoner. The guy's just standing there." He stepped between Martin and the fat cop. "Go file your report or whatever else it is you need to do."

Martin calmly stood and gazed over Hal's shoulder at Stoner. He could hear the fat cop's heart thudding in his chest.

Stoner sucked in a heavy breath and pointed a finger at Martin. "Just don't ever let me catch you out on the street."

"Shut up, Stoner. Get out of here before you get another complaint filed on you."

Stoner glared at Martin as he waddled past the pair. Martin turned his head to follow him as he left. Stoner cast one last look back. Martin was out of Hal's line of sight and he made a small biting motion partially revealing his fangs.

Stoner's face blanched and he stumbled over his own feet and crashed into the wall. He recovered and practically sprinted down the hall.

Martin looked back at Hal and shrugged his shoulder. "I think he's been working too hard."

"Just be quiet and let's get this over with."

Martin could tell that although he didn't harbor any mistreatment of the people brought to jail, Hal was all business. Martin didn't attempt to engage him in any more conversation, and did as he was instructed.

After he emptied his pockets of his belongings, was printed and photographed, Hal led him to a holding cell and placed him inside.

The two men in the cell who had been talking loudly, quit their conversation as Martin passed through the doorway. Hal shut the door behind him and turned away without a word. Martin cast a glance at the two men and then took a seat on the bunk in the corner of the cell.

"Hey, buddy." The larger of the two men called out. "Got any smokes we can have?"

"No," Martin answered flatly.

The bear of a man stood up. He was unwashed and unkempt with grime under his fingernails and he smelled of motor oil and sweat. Both arms had a series of tattoos that made their way up to his shoulders and joined across his back. His hair was pulled back into a greasy ponytail and his beard contained stains and parts of past meals. To Martin's senses, the man smelled as if he hadn't bathed in a year, if ever.

"No, what," the big man said, "no, you don't got no smokes, or no, you just won't let us have any?"

Martin looked at the man for a moment and sighed. "I don't smoke, therefore, no, I don't have any for you." Martin leaned his head against the wall and closed his eyes.

The man pulled on his oily beard as he made his way across the cell to where Martin was resting. Martin didn't even open his eyes when the behemoth stopped in front of the bunk.

"Don't cop no attitude with me, sissy boy. I'll rip your fuckin' lungs out, ya hear me?"

The third man in the cell watched with interest as the tension mounted.

"I said, you hear me?" the big man growled, and punctuated the question by kicking Martin in the bottom of the foot.

Martin slowly opened his eyes and looked up the tower of filth in front of him. "Don't go looking for trouble, *friend*, it will find you easy enough on it's own. Now, I am asking you. Please-leave-me-alone." With that he closed his eyes once more.

"I got your trouble right here, sissy boy," the man said hefting his genitals with his right hand as he started to take a step toward the bunk.

Before the man could move, Martin's left hand shot out and grabbed him by the crotch. The big man let out a grunt of pain and grabbed at Martin's hand.

"Don't."

Martin increased the pressure of his grip as beads of sweat broke out on the big man's face. The biker ground his teeth together against the pain in his hand and his gonads. Obeying Martin's order, he moved his other hand away. Martin lifted him ever so slightly off the ground and pitched him backwards. The man crashed to the floor, slid into the bars and came to rest on his side, his face pasty looking through the dirt and matted hair. He immediately started to retch as he continued holding his groin.

"Like I said, leave me alone." Martin turned his gaze to the other man who quickly looked away and took great interest in a spot on the far wall.

Martin slowly stretched out on the bunk. He lay there feeling time slip away and knew it would be daylight all too soon. What would he do then? Even if he managed to get away from the cops and get out of the building, where would he go? There was no place to run too. There were no convenient cellars or warehouses nearby, and it wasn't as if he could walk up to someone's house and say, "Excuse me, I'm a vampire. Could I stay with you today?"

A voice broke through his thoughts.

"Daniels. On your feet. Someone posted your bail. Let's go."

Martin was on his feet instantly.

"That a girl, Jules."

One of the jailers keyed the lock and opened the door. He looked at the biker who sat as far away from Martin as he could get, still cradling his stomach.

"What's with him," the jailer asked as Martin walked past.

"I guess something didn't agree with him."

Martin went to lock-up to retrieve his belongings where the officer in charge took an eternity gathering Martin's package. He watched helplessly as the man moved with the pace of an injured slug down the rows of catalogued items and had to take time out to field a phone call. When at last the officer placed the package on the counter, Martin almost gouged a hole though the clipboard signing his name. He then followed another officer through the door to a well-lit waiting area. There, sitting on a bench waiting for him, was Julie. When she saw him, she sprang to her feet and raced to him, throwing her arms around his neck.

Martin breathed her in, savoring the smell of her hair and the feel of her body pressed to his. He leaned back to look in her face, not ready to let go of her yet. "How did you get bail so fast?"

"I know someone in the business. He's sweet on me and took care of everything. And, no, I didn't sleep with him. At least not yet." She quickly pulled away from him. "I'll fill you in later. We have to go."

He started to check the watch on his wrist and realized it was in the manila folder he was carrying, found the clock on the station wall and swallowed hard. "We don't have time, Jules."

"Trust me on this one. Let's go."

She held his hand and led him through the police station towards the front of the building.

"I don't know exactly how you did it, but I owe you one, Jules," Martin said as he followed along behind her.

Martin pushed the glass doors open that led to the outside and was amazed at how light it was already. He had never been outside his house this late. He didn't need to check his wristwatch again. "There's not enough time." He turned to face Julie, but she wasn't there.

"Over here. Come on, Doc." Julie called.

She had parked her car just down the street and was making for it at a dead run. Martin caught up with her easily and they covered the few remaining yards together. Martin was about to say something when she cut him off.

"Shut up, Martin and listen. Get your skinny butt in the back seat. I've got things covered. So to speak."

Martin wasn't sure what she was driving at, but knew her well enough to go along with it anyway. He opened the back door to find a pair of large packing crate covers.

"Very heavy and impenetrable to light," she said pointing to the covers. She shrugged her shoulders, "It was the only thing I could think of right off the bat."

Martin grabbed her by the face and pulled her to him, kissing her soundly, "I love you, Julie Baxter."

"Hurry, Martin," she said pushing him toward the open door. "I don't want to lose you after hearing those words."

Martin practically dove under the two covers and let Julie tuck them in around him.

As she tucked in the last fold of cloth, she whispered, "I love you too, Martin Daniels."

Trying to shut out the thought of this not working, she closed the door, opened hers and slid behind the wheel. Inserting the keys into the ignition, she paused just before starting the motor. "Martin, just remember, you can't come out from under those covers for anything. Nothing. Not even if I'm getting raped by the whole Hell's Angels gang. Understand?"

There was a pause and then in a muffled but serious voice, "Yes."

Martin knew they were on the expressway, but had lost track of where they were when he heard an, "Oh, shit." from the front seat and felt the car start to slow.

"What is it?" his voice muffled by the heavy cloth.

"Oh, shit. Oh, shit. Oh, shit." Julie braked slowly and started to pull the car to the right.

"What is it? What's going on?"

"Stay down, Martin, and whatever you do, be quiet. It's a cop."

The Highway patrolman approached her window, his eyes inspecting the car as he went. "Could I see your license and registration please," he asked courteously.

Julie handed them to the trooper, having already fished them out of the large satchel she called a purse.

"Mind if I ask where you were going in such a hurry, Ms. Baxter?" the cop asked glancing at her license.

"Yes sir. I'm sorry," she said all milk and honey. "I've been working all night and I was just headed home."

"I see." The officer looked from Julie to her license. "You live at 3365 Glenndale. That's not so far from here," he said with doubt in his voice, "why the rush?"

"Yes sir, I know. It was a long night at work and then this morning a coworker's car wouldn't start, she needed a ride, I was there, and so I took her home and now I'm headed back to my place," Julie said with a look of pure innocence on her face.

The highway patrolman eyed her for a moment and then handed her back her license and registration. "I'm going to believe you this time, Ms. Baxter, and let you go with a verbal warning. Slow the speed down. It doesn't do you any good to be in a hurry if you don't get there at all." The patrolman tipped his hat and started to turn, "By the way, what are you doing with the covers here in the back?"

Martin's heart skipped a beat at the question.

"A friend of mine is moving and knew that my dad had a couple of covers and so she asked if I would ask my dad if she could borrow them. She used them and gave them back to me and I just haven't gotten them to my dad yet."

"Well, it's going to be a beautiful sunny day. Live to enjoy it, all right?"

Julie piloted the car the rest of the way home with no further mishaps. As she neared her neighborhood she suddenly sat bolt upright behind the wheel.

"Oh, God, Martin.

"What now?"

"I just thought of something. I don't have an attached garage. How are we going to get you out of the car?

"We're not," Martin said calmly.

"What do you mean, we're not? You can't stay in the car. You'll die from heat stroke. I could carry you or you could shuffle along 'till we get you inside."

"Right," Martin's voice, muffled by the heavy cloth, didn't loose its edge of cynicism. "It wouldn't be bad enough to raise the neighbor's suspicions, but you drop me halfway there or I trip and the blankets pop open and I end up looking like a Fourth of July fireworks display. Although I truly appreciate the offer, if it's all the same to you, I'll just stay put."

"Well, it's not the same to me. It's too hot. You'll die." Julie pulled onto her street and slowed as she approached her drive. "You need to come up with a different plan."

"No. This will work. Just roll down the windows and I'll be fine."

Julie pulled into her drive and waited while the automatic door opened. Julie sat talking to the bundle of blankets piled up in her back seat. "Isn't there something else I can do for you? I feel so helpless."

"I'll be fine. Really. There's nothing more you can do here. You've been great."

Her head knew he was probably right, but her heart didn't want to listen. "I just feel like there's something I could or should be doing. I . . . "

"Julie, listen to me." The seriousness in his voice carried through the covers. "I owe you my life. You have done more than should be asked of anyone and you've done it without complaining or hesitation. You're exhausted. I know you are. I know how long you've been without sleep."

"No longer than you," she argued.

"But, I'm better equipped to deal with it than you are. I'll lay here and sweat it out while you go get some sleep."

"If I can't change your mind, then I'll at least leave the garage door up for you."

"No. That's a good way to invite someone to rip off your stuff out of the garage, maybe including a pair of heavy covers or the car itself. Please, go ahead and close it."

Frustrated at her inability to provide a better solution, she pushed the button to lower the door. "You're bound and determined to do this the hard way, aren't you?"

"Trust me, Jules. It will be hot, but I won't die. And, I've been in worse predicaments than this. Now go. I'll see you later this evening."

"O.K." was all she could manage as she started out of the garage.

"Julie?" Martin's voice stopped her.
"Yea?"
"Thank you."

Chapter 6

Martin listened as Julie reluctantly closed the side door to the garage. He took a long breath and tried to get as comfortable as possible for what was going to be an exceptionally long day. The temperature steadily rose as the minutes drug past, and his mind began to wonder. The heat and the stuffiness of the thick covers dredged up memories of another time and another place where Martin lay buried much like now to avoid the deadly glare of the sun.

A hundred plus years had come and gone since he had made his way to the hay barn in Jefferson Parish, Louisiana. Lying like he was in the oppressive heat of the thick cloth in the back seat of the Prizm, he could smell the hay and the animal odors. The cloying smell of the hay clogged his nostrils and he could feel the stiff grass as it pricked his skin.

He remembered he had been running most of the night, not really knowing what he was running from or where he was running to. He only knew he had to get away from something. Something that ate at him, that crawled around inside his head like a swarm of maggots, causing everything he heard, saw or touch to take on different, frightening textures;

something that racked his body with pain like none he had ever experienced or knew was humanly possible to endure. A part of his mind wanted to just let go, to get away from the pain. So, he ran.

All the while though, another part of his mind analyzed what was happening to him. Martin had always had a brilliant mind and was well educated for the times. The analytical part of him realized that he should have dropped from exhaustion hours ago. But, he had been able to keep driving his body relentlessly. Now, near dawn, he had come across an old hay barn. As he slowed to survey the situation, the pain overwhelmed him again and he barely stifled a cry as the muscles in his body cramped and contorted, causing his legs to collapse beneath him. He writhed on the ground like a worm on hot rock until the seizures passed. That detached part of his mind told him that he could not afford to be found in the open like this. Summoning his strength and making his body respond by sheer force of will, Martin started forward once more. He stumbled, crawled and clawed his way to the barn. At one time, Martin would have stopped and savored the smells and sounds of the pre-dawn morning, but, now, all that was on his mind was making it to the sanctuary of the barn where he could hide until whatever malady had control of him either passed or killed him.

Martin at last made the door to the weathered structure and clung to the jamb as another wave of pain washed through him. The door, though large enough for a hay wagon to pass through, opened easily when he pulled upon it and he slipped inside. His eyes adjusted immediately to the relative darkness inside the barn and Martin looked around taking in his surroundings. Tiny dust motes floated in the air and the smell of cut grass, mold and animal spoor was everywhere. The old barn was not as solid as a regular livestock barn as Martin could see the outside through gaps in the slats that made up the siding on the structure. There was loose hay strewn all over the floor with bales stacked further back reaching from the floor to the roof. Martin continued towards the back of the barn when he was overcome by a mind-numbing fatigue that emptied every ounce of energy he had. It was if all the activity from the last twenty-four hours caught up to him all at once. Martin forced one foot ahead of the other, the back of the barn receding down a tunnel that grew longer and darker with each passing second. He fought against passing out when a large rat bolted from the hay in front of him. With no conscious thought, he was upon the rat in less than a second, snatching the hapless rodent up in both hands, sinking his teeth into the animals back and neck, ripping the hide and fur away. Without so much as a pause, he tore at the exposed neck with his teeth, severing major blood vessels there and drained the life from the diminutive beast. When there was nothing more to be gained from the rat, Martin released his hold and the carcass fell limp and empty to the floor. Although his limbs still felt like lead shot and his whole being was one huge ache, he realized he still felt better than he had a moment ago. The fact that he had just drank the blood from the rat seemed repulsive and somewhat natural all at once. Martin started once more for the back of the barn when his legs would no longer respond and he sank to the floor, his body weary beyond belief. He lay on the floor, his face covered with blood as dust settled to stick to the wetness there. He was a broken marionette, legs folded under him and arms cast to the sides. He no longer cared if someone found him or not when a shaft of sunlight lanced through an opening in the wall and struck Martin on the hand.

There was no stifling the cry of pain as his arm recoiled from the searing heat. Martin's hand felt as if someone was holding a branding iron to it. He stared in horror as smoke rose from blistered flesh and then just as quickly healed itself. As the sun continued to rise, another beam of light entered the barn catching him in the shoulder. Again, the branding iron touched his flesh and Martin instinctively crabbed backwards to get away from the pain. He cast about and saw that more and more light was coming through the myriad of cracks and knot holes in the walls.

His body responded on pure adrenaline as he leapt to his feet and made for the back of the barn and the bales of hay there. He had thought to hide there to escape detection from anybody passing by, but now realized that that was the least of his worries at the moment. He couldn't explain it, nor did he have time to reflect upon it, but he knew he had to get out of the sunlight. Reaching the stacked bales, Martin started pulling them out with each hand. He tunneled into the stack of hay making for the center of the mound, pulling a bail in behind him like a gopher closing off its hole. He lay panting for a moment in the total darkness and then started to choke on the hay dust he had stirred up. His throat spasmed and he couldn't get any air. There was no room to turn around, and the darkness and confined space closed in upon him like a vice making him try to breathe that much faster which made him suck in more dust depriving him of more air still. Blind panic surged to the top as he drew back his foot to kick the bale he had just drug in behind him. That analytical part of his mind screamed for him to stop, to use his mind to overcome the problem. Martin dropped his foot and then tore off the remainder of his shirt to use as a filter across his mouth and nose. He tied the loose cloth around his head like a kerchief. He lay there gulping breaths to fill air-starved lungs, ignoring the hay that pricked his bare skin. When at last his breathing slowed, he wondered if he was suffocating to death as he passed out from total exhaustion.

Martin woke with a start. As he lay there, his mind tried to separate itself from the nightmare images that still clung to the corners of his consciousness. Vivid dreams of being staked naked beneath a broiling sun, his body engulfed in flames that caused his skin to split and peel away. Suddenly his mind snapped to full attention and he remembered where he was. Martin fought down panic again as thoughts of what had recently happened flooded back in on him. He remembered that in desperation he had buried himself under the hay. Buried. The word rebounded in his mind. What if he couldn't get out? What if the hay collapsed? He could lay there for days or possibly more, unable to move, slowly starving to death. He had heard tales of miners dying in cave-ins and the misery some of them had suffered. He had sworn to himself that that was something that he would never do; work far from the light of day. Yet here he was, beneath tons of hay, lying in a tunnel just as dark as any mineshaft. Panic sought to overwhelm him. He had to get out. Now.

As he started to scramble backwards, his mind asserted itself and he realized that he could still breathe. The air was thick and stale, loaded with hay dust, but it was air nonetheless. Martin wanted nothing more than to scramble from his makeshift tomb, but realized why he was there in the first place. The dreams he had weren't just meaningless visions. He knew now that if he were to venture into the daylight, he would die as surely as he had in this dreams. A seed of an idea started to grow as to why this was happening to him, but seemed so preposterous that he couldn't give it any credit. There were still too many blank spots in the last few days that he couldn't remember. He needed answers. Which brought him back to his present predicament.

He had no idea how long he had been out. It could have been for a few minutes or a few days. The fatigue that had gripped him earlier was gone. He felt of his face and found there was no significant stubble growth on his beard, so he felt safe that he had not been unconscious for more than a day.

The thought of going back into the barn, only to find it filled with sunlight terrified him, but he knew that he couldn't stay where he was forever.

Home. He had to get back home. Home to Emily. She would be worried sick about him. He would get back home and tell her everything was going to be all right now that whatever had been in him was working its way out of his system. That together, they would get through it all.

Now with a plan of action before him, Martin set himself to his chosen path and shoved at the bale in front of him, flooding his cell with fresh air. He grasped the bale in front of him, shielding the opening, ready to pull it back in an instant. With the rush of cool air came the realization that it was early evening, that time of the day when the sun has already set, but night has not truly fallen.

A chorus of crickets and tree frogs could be heard as more and more animals of the night joined the symphony.

Martin shoved the bale one final time and crawled out of the hole. Still crouching next to the wall of hay, he listened for any sign of other humans. Satisfied that there weren't any around, he straightened up and stretched tight muscles. Standing there in the barn as twilight deepened, he realized he was starved. He could only guess at how long he had been unconscious, but it felt as if he hadn't eaten in a week. Not needing his makeshift bandanna any longer, Martin undid the shirt from around his head and donned the tattered remains. As he made his way out of the barn, he smelled something. Actually, he smelled hundreds of things. But, there was one that stood at the forefront of the rest. He sniffed the air again as he walked slowly to the door. He had smelled it before, several times, but couldn't quite place it. His hand reached for the latch when his mind clicked. Venicen. He smelled venicen. Only, there was something different.

This smell was, for no other way to describe it, alive. Martin eased the door open and looked about. There, some hundred yards out from the barn, standing at the edge of the clearing, was a large doe. The wind was blowing towards Martin so the deer wasn't aware of him yet. She had been eating the grass at the edge of the woods, staying close to the relative safety of the trees, and was now standing at attention, testing the area around her, alert to any approaching danger.

With no conscious thought, Martin slipped from the barn and glided silently down the wall of the barn, sticking to the deeper shadows there. He kept moving slowly until he rounded the corner of the barn and passed out of the line of sight of the deer. Once to the edge of the trees, he worked his way deeper into the woods, closing the distance between himself and the doe.

There was an urgency in him now. A compulsion. It was some type of animalistic drive that he couldn't ignore. That part of Martin's mind tried to stop and rationalize what he was doing, but the rest of him refused, as a red film descended over his vision and the deer filled his whole being.

He had cleared to within twenty yards when the deer jerked its head up, sensing something was wrong. Martin pounced with amazing speed. The deer barely had time to turn on its heels before he was upon it. He tackled the deer, driving it to the ground, knocking the air from its lungs. The deer tried to lash out at its attacker with spiked hooves, but Martin was too fast and agile for the deer to be effective. He batted one of the legs out of the way, breaking it in the process. He grabbed the deer by the neck, ripped its throat out and bent his head to gorge himself on the fountain that pumped from the gaping wound.

In less than two minutes the whole thing was over. Martin sat back on his ankles and looked around him. Slowly his mind returned to a state where he knew he had control over his faculties. He sat for some time staring at the deer carcass in front of him. Looking at the dead animal made him remember the rat he had killed earlier. Until now it hadn't crossed his mind. Now, though, he could remember in vivid detail how he had dispatched the rodent and the sweet taste of the blood as it coursed down his throat. Martin noticed that he was covered with blood, dirt and leaves. Staring at himself, he wondered what had just happened to him. He knew that sometimes people who were starving did things they normally wouldn't even think about. But, how had he been able to run down a deer and kill it with his bare hands. At last his original thought of Emily imposed itself on his conscious. Pushing himself up from the ground, Martin left the carcass where it lay and started towards his home once more, then, just as quickly, stopped. He had no idea where home was. He didn't know how long he had run the night before, or in who's barn he had been hiding. Everything from the past few days seemed like a bad dream as images flashed through his mind. Things that he should know but couldn't quite get hold of, danced at the edge of his conscious. Too many questions flitting around in his mind for him to think straight. Too much. Too much had happened. Was happening. Martin grasped the sides of his head and willed himself to think. To remember. He recalled that when he had left his home that he had ran straight from the front of the house. That would mean that he had been running north. Looking up, Martin was thankful it was a cloudless night and quickly located the North Star. Martin now had a general idea as to which direction to travel and set off at a quick trot.

After a short while he came across a small creek and figured that it must be Thompson creek that ran under the bridge on the road to Fayeville. Martin got his bearings and figured that he was some 25 miles away from home by way of the road. He pointed himself in the right direction and took off at a fast walk. At this pace he reasoned he could be home well before dawn. His thinking still wasn't clear, like it was behind some haze that caused him to not want to think at all, to draw in upon himself. There was something lurking just below his conscious thought, something that wanted to be let loose. Martin focused his whole being on this and realized it was the same feelings he had felt while stalking the deer. The thought of losing himself to those urges scared him to the core of his soul.

Martin shook himself loose from that line of thought and concentrated on the terrain before him. He knew he could take to the road, but figured it would be a more direct, not to mention far safer, route cutting across country. Besides, although his mind was still giving him trouble, he realized that his body had stopped aching and in fact, felt good. He could see quite well, but attributed it to the fullness of the moon. Martin picked up the pace and soon found himself running. He practically flew across the ground, reveling in the freedom of his flight, eating up miles in a fraction of the time it normally would have taken him.

Martin slowed once more to a walk as he neared the boundaries of his farm. It was a two-story house painted white, gleaming in the moon light with pillars holding up the second story verandah. Martin sighed and started toward the house where a light could be seen burning in the master bedroom upstairs. He was safe. He was home.

Though the place was modest in appearance, it had never looked so good to him. He had always been proud of it even though his father couldn't understand why he would want to go build a place of his own when he and his wife could live at the big house, especially when he would end up owning it after his folks died. Martin had always been independent and he couldn't make his father understand that he wanted to make something of himself, not live off the family fortune and name.

That and the fact that Martin refused to make any human a slave to another. He would either hire some hands to perform the work in the fields, do it himself, or the work wouldn't get done. Martin loved his father, but couldn't abide by his idea that it was permissible to buy and sell another human being. Though, in all honesty, Martin's wife had argued the same things as his father.

As Martin approached the house, his dog started to bark from her place on the porch. Martin called to her and her tale started to wag as she jumped off the porch to greet him. She was halfway to him when she came to a stop and started a low growl in her throat, her hackles raised.

Martin looked at her for a moment and said, "Sady, what's the matter girl, it's me."

Upon hearing his voice the dog took a couple of more steps toward him and tested the air once more. She was still not entirely convinced this was the person she thought it was and whined plaintively as she fidgeted back and fourth uncertain how to act. To her, this person had her master's voice, but the smell wasn't quite right.

Martin knelt down and patted his leg. "Come here girl, it's all right. I'm home." Satisfied at last that it was indeed her master, she bounded over to him. Martin ruffled her fur, scratched behind her ears and rubbed her belly the way she always enjoyed. When the two finished their greeting, he started once more to the house, the dog trotting beside him as he went. Martin patted the dog once more as they reached the front stoop and then made for the door, which he found, bolted from the inside. Puzzled,

Martin looked around the corner of the house to where the building stood where the hired help slept and thought it odd that there would be no lights on at this time of night. He knocked on the front door and then stepped off the porch a few steps into the front yard.

"Emily, it's me, Martin." he called up to the window, "open the door, I'm home." There was a lengthy pause and he was just about to call again when he saw her shadow against the drapes across the door. Emily slowly opened the glass-paneled doors and stepped onto the verandah overlooking the front yard. She edged her way to the railing, and like a person in a trance, slowly looked down to where Martin stood looking up at her. Instantly her hand went to cover her mouth as she took a step backward and Martin could hear her sharp intake of air.

"Emily, are you all right?" Then he remembered how he must look. "Emily, I'm sorry to frighten you. I'm all right, really. This isn't even my blood, I'm not hurt at . . . "

"No," she began in a choked whisper. "You should not be here. You should be dead, Martin Daniels. You are dead. You're one of the undead! And, you've come back for me!" She was hysterical now.

"Emily, what are you talking about? This is me, your husband."

"You stay away from me," she screamed as she ran back into the house slamming the doors behind her, "just you stay away."

Martin was confused and he felt his anger start to rise. "Emily! You come out here now and stop this nonsense, do you hear me." He kicked the sod in frustration. "Damn." he muttered under his breath. His dog whined from her spot on the porch, but

Martin ignored her. He eyed the verandah for a moment and then on impulse jumped. He caught the top of the ledge and then pulled himself up and over the rail in one motion. Martin opened the twin doors to their bedroom then stepped inside pulling them closed behind him. Emily spun to face him and looked as if she were staring into the face of Death itself.

"What has gotten into you woman," Martin started.

Emily was visibly shaking and backed across the room, "Stay away from me, oh God, please stay away!"

"Emily, you don't understand. The fever broke. I . . . "

"I understand full well. I was there when the fits took you. I was there when they tried to tie you down and you broke the strap leather like yarn." She continued backpedaling until she ran into the dresser on the opposite side of the room. "I saw the fangs that sprouted from your mouth and how you would have taken Amos if Zachary hadn't had a torch there to stop you. You didn't get his blood, but you managed his death anyway, you bastard. His old heart couldn't stand the strain of seeing a demon like you and it quit on him." Her breath was coming in ragged gasps as she fought to verbalize the horrors she had seen. "I knew a Martin Daniels once, and though you might possess his body, you're not him, you monster from hell." With her final statement, she pulled a pistol from the dresser drawer she had been standing in front of and leveled a shaky barrel at Martin's chest. "I don't know what innocents' blood you have spilled on your chest, but you won't have mine."

Martin was dumbfounded. Here was the woman

he thought would have been delighted to see him, holding a gun on him instead.

"Emily, "Martin said as he took a step forward, "please put the gun down."

If Martin was surprised when she pointed the gun at him, he was totally shocked when she pulled the trigger. The bullet caught him in the lower left abdomen. It felt as if someone had kicked him in the stomach and then driven a red-hot poker through him. Martin stumbled for a moment, the realization setting in of what had just happened. Pain and disbelief gave way to primal rage. He looked up at Emily who still had the gun pointed at him.

In a voice he didn't recognize as his own, he growled, "You shot me."

"Why won't you die?!" She fought to pull back the hammer on the pistol again while keeping it leveled at Martin.

With an animalistic snarl, he sprang across the room and ripped the gun from her hand. A red haze fell across his vision as he bent her backward, exposing the long line of her neck that he had so often kissed. Martin moved to rip her throat out when motion in the large dressing mirror caught his attention.

He looked up and froze. There in the mirror, holding his wife, was a person he didn't recognize. The person's clothes were torn, burnt, and blood soaked. The hair matted against his head. But, what caught his attention the most was the pair of white fangs protruding from his mouth that was still caught in the snarl from a moment ago. His mouth. His face. He looked down at Emily who was transfixed with fear, and as she babbled incoherently for mercy, memories flooded his mind. They were a torrent that overwhelmed him. Like waves breaking against an already weakened dike, they crashed against his sanity. They all came back to him now. The woman in the woods that had bitten him. Amos and Zach. The rat in the barn, the deer in the woods and now, Emily. Martin looked into the mirror once more and released his hold on her. He stepped over her and stood staring at his reflection for a moment, muttering to himself that this couldn't be happening, and then drove his fist through his reflection. Martin looked down at Emily and sought understanding, but saw only horror in her eyes.

"Nooooo!" Martin turned with blinding speed and ran through the glass doors, exploding them, sending diamond shards raining into the night. He cleared the balcony in a hurdle, landing twenty feet out in the front yard. The momentum of his jump caused him to pitch forward in a roll. He came to a stop just in front of a number of nervous horses' legs. Martin looked up to find half a dozen mounted riders.

"Hello, Martin," Zachary said.

Martin stared at the riders for a moment trying to get his thoughts into some type of coherent pattern.

Zachary looked at him down the length of a double-barrel shotgun. "Me and some of the boys thought you might just come back here this way."

Martin started to shift his weight.

"Go ahead and do something stupid, Martin, and give me an excuse to shoot you. 'Course, if it were up ta me, I'd kill ya where you stand for what you did to old Amos, you bastard. The sheriff says that under the law you're criminally insane, but we know better. We know a demon from hell when we see one." There was a murmur of assent and Zachary turned in his saddle to look at one of the other riders. "Go look in the house and make sure Miss Emily's all right." The rider nodded and reined his mount out of the group. As he did, everyone's attention was on him for a split second.

Martin used the minute distraction to his fullest advantage. Gathering his legs up, Martin sprang for the horses. He knocked the lead horse off its feet and bolted over the top of it, scattering the other riders in the process. Adding to the confusion was Sadie, which had joined the melee and was helping to spook the horses with her barking. It was a testament to the skill of the riders that they were able to regain control of their mounts as quickly as they did. Still, Martin had gained a considerable head start.

"Somebody shoot that mutt," Zachary bellowed as he wrestled with his horse, Sady nipping at its heels. "Billy, go tell Earnest to get his tail up here with those hounds. Jake go ahead and check on Emily. Damn dog! Somebody shoot it already!"

Martin's arms and legs pumped as he sprinted across the open ground widening the gap between himself and the riders. A shot rang out producing silence where Sady's bark had just been. Hot tears flowed down Martin's cheeks knowing that the dog had given its life to buy him a few more precious moments of time. It was ironic that an animal had stood by him, when his wife and friends had not.

He had just made the woods when he heard the riders coming hard. Martin slowed to make his way through the maze of tangled branches and limbs that snagged and picked at his skin and clothes. He paused for a moment trying to decide on a course of action. For all he knew, he had been running in the direction that they had wanted him to, heading him into an ambush. This was all too much for Martin. He knew these people, had worked in the fields beside them, had gotten drunk with some of them, swapped stories, had gone on hunting parties with them. Now, he was the hunted.

Martin's mind snapped back to focus as he realized that he didn't have time for self-pity. Just then, Martin heard the group of men whoop and holler. Earnest had arrived with the hunting dogs. With a wry smile, Martin knew now what the 'coons and foxes they had hunted must have felt like. He turned and ran as fast and quiet as possible using everything he could to cover his trail.

"Damn," he cursed to himself as the hounds started to bay, signaling that they had his scent and were on the trail. In no time, the riders were to the woods where Martin had entered and were closing fast. They had spread out in an attempt to flush him from hiding and were close enough now that Martin could hear individual voices and smell the sweat and adrenaline radiating off the men. Stealth was no longer viable and he opted for speed, hoping the trees would take out a rider or two. One of the riders heard him break cover and sounded the alarm. Martin ran headlong through the woods, the branches snatching at his face and clothes. He topped a hill and came to a screeching halt. Behind him was the armed group crashing through the woods and closing fast, while ahead lay a wide-open pasture with no cover anywhere. Although he could see near perfect under the full moon that shone overhead, the others, not near as well equipped for night vision, could still make use of the bright orb. He couldn't hope to double back and make it through the picket line the men had set up, and crossing the open field was suicide.

Martin's mind raced looking for options. He looked down the backside of the hill a short ways and saw a fencerow there. There was short grass and sparse brush along the row. Not much, but it was all he had. Martin made for the fence, hurtled it, and was making his way up the row, trying to stay as low as possible, when one of the party spotted him. He immediately bolted. He knew there was no hope of trying to hide.

He left the fence and broke straight across the field, his arms and legs pumping like the pistons on a great steam train. With all the yelping and shouting going on, he knew that they had turned the dogs loose. He was fairly certain that he could outrun the dogs and chanced a glance back. The men in this group were either foolish or desperate or both. Two of the riders had jumped their mounts over the fence and were bearing down on him. Martin put on a burst of speed and would have outrun the horses, but he couldn't outrun a bullet. One of the riders had fired off a shot from a scattergun. The pellets tore through his shirt and ripped into Martin's back, gouging out hunks of flesh as they went. Martin stumbled from the force of the shot, lost his footing in the uneven field and went down in a tangle of arms and legs.

"Yahoo! I got 'em Luke," the rider who had fired the shot whooped in triumph.

Martin rolled to a stop and was amazed that he didn't hurt more than he did. He reasoned to himself that the wound was fatal and that his body was already going into shock, blocking off the worst of the pain. What amazed him more was that he could breathe. He would have figured that anyone shot in the lung like he was should not be able to breathe. All of this flashed through his mind in an instant, and he would have contemplated the situation more, but the dogs were on him immediately.

Ten of the best dogs Jefferson Parish had to offer. Fearless. They had been bred for this job. These dogs had treed everything from coons to cougars and the occasional black bear. Some were old and grizzled and wise to the trail while some were not quite as seasoned, but all of them were a ball of muscle and fangs wrapped in loose hide that allowed them to turn inside their skin if something ever got hold of them.

The dogs never stood a chance.

None of the animals the dogs had faced was anything like what was before them now. Martin simply flung his arm to the side to dislodge the hound that had sunk his teeth into him. The dog flipped end over end and landed twenty yards away. There was an audible crack as the canine plowed in headfirst and laid still. Martin smashed the skull of the one that had him by the leg. Two others he disemboweled; broke the spine of another. In a matter of seconds, it was over. Martin jumped to his feet, covered with blood and gore. Some of it was his, but most wasn't. Seeing what was happening, yet refusing to believe it, the two riders spurred their mounts forward. Martin glanced over his shoulder and realized that the woods were another hundred yards or so. On impulse he picked up a palm sized rock and threw it at the lead. He had hoped to spook the horse and throw the rider, but his aim was off and the missile struck the man square in the chest. The rider appeared as if he had been shot by a buffalo gun, the force of the projectile knocking him backwards out of the saddle.

"Holy shit, Jed! You all right?" The other rider pulled up hard to keep from running over the fallen rider and skidded his horse to a stop. He tumbled from the saddle, landing beside his comrade and cradled the other man's head in his arms while he stared at the hole in his dead friend's chest.

Martin stood dumbfounded for a moment. He hadn't meant to throw the rock that hard. He hadn't meant to hurt anyone. He wanted to see if the man was all right, to say that he was sorry, to let them know it was an accident. But, in his heart he knew that they wouldn't believe him. How could he blame them? He couldn't believe it.

But, he tried anyway.

"I'm sorry, Luke," Martin called to the man who was now sobbing quietly and slowly rocking back and forth. "I didn't mean to. I just picked up the rock."

"You demon bastard, Martin Daniels! You killed him. And, for that I will hunt you till the day I die."

"I . . . I'm sorry." Martin whispered as he turned and sprinted for the woods on the far side of the meadow.

"What are you sorry about," Julie asked as she pulled the heavy cover off of him.

Martin blinked at her, her face silhouetted by the dome light of the car. His clothes were drenched with sweat, though he didn't know if it was caused by the heat of the day or from reliving the nightmare of his past. He sat up, thankful for the twilight once more.

"When I opened the door you said you were sorry. What about?"

"Oh, that. I wasn't talking to you."

Julie raised an eyebrow. "Just who were you talking to then?"

"A ghost."

"Come again."

"A dream. It was a dream." Martin slid out of the car and stood next to Julie in the garage. "And, not a very friendly one I might add."

"I see. I guess. Here, thought you could probably use this," she said as she handed him a glass of cool water from where she had set it on top of the car.

"Thank you, Ma'am." Martin took the glass and drained the clear liquid in one breath. "Good stuff."

"Martin, I feel so bad for you," she said taking hold of his hand.

"No need to." He raised her fingers to his lips. "How about you? How are you doing? Did you get any rest?"

Her face screwed up and she looked up at him from under knitted brows that reminded him of a kid addressing the school principal after having been caught running in the hallway.

"I know I promised to get some sleep, but I couldn't. Not with knowing you were out here. I laid down and rested, sort of. At least I kept the other part of the promise and didn't come check on you. And," she said taking the empty glass from him while shutting the car door, "you don't know how hard that was for me. Anyway, you sure you're all right?"

"Yes, thanks." Martin smiled as they walked out the side door of the garage and headed toward the house. "Although not the funnest day I've spent in a long time, I'm fine."

"If you say so." Julie looked at him with an

appraising eye. "I will say you've looked better. Not to mention that you stink."

"Really?"

Martin, feeling, and smelling, considerably better after his shower, stepped into the living room to finish toweling off.

Julie pinched him on the butt as she passed him on her way to the phone and picked up the message she had written there. "Someone by the name of Bill called while you were in the shower. Said that as soon as you finished preening, to give him a call."

"Super." Martin picked up the handset and dialed the number. "I guess that means you called Bill earlier like I asked."

Julie batted her eyelashes at him.

"Well. It's nice to see you do *something* I ask you to."

"Really?" she said imitating his voice, then snatched the towel from him, popped him with it and ran laughing from the room.

Chapter 7

Shortly after getting off the phone, Martin and Julie backed the Honda out of the garage.

"Who is this guy we're going to see," Julie asked from the passenger side of the car.

"Bill Roper. William actually. Although, that's not the name he goes by today. Known him for years. One of my best friends. Been a vampire longer than I have." Martin looked at Julie and smiled. "We've sort of been our own little support group through the years. When we've had to change identities we still managed to stay in touch. He managed to get a job out here recently. Been nice having him around again. They were some of the nicest people you could ever want to meet."

"They?"

"Bill and Mary. Though Mary's been dead for some time now." Some of the lightness faded from his voice. "Super lady. When she died, Bill went crazy for a while. I didn't know if I would get him back."

"Was she like—you?" Julie asked, still uncomfortable with saying "vampire".

"No. She didn't want it and he wouldn't do it.

He was totally devoted to her. She's the reason he went into the field of hematology."

"Why?"

Martin looked over his shoulder and changed lanes to get past the poking VW in front of them. "She saw him feeding one night. He told me that the look of disgust on her face was stronger than the hunger. He vowed right then to never let her see him eat again and that he would find a substitute for blood.

"Has he had any luck yet?" Julie was really getting into the conversation and finding out about a part of Martin's past she knew nothing about.

"Not really. Although he has made some other interesting discoveries."

"Sort of like you, huh?" Julie poked him in the ribs.

"It's lonely here at the top," Martin said in feigned modesty.

"Pu-lease!" Julie propped her feet on the dash. "How did she die?"

"Like most people. Disease and old age. Her body just quit working." Martin stared at the road ahead and Julie could tell that he was remembering. "He sat holding her hand for two days after she was gone. I left him alone during that time, but we needed to bury the body. And, I was afraid he was going to sit right there and starve to death. He hadn't moved at all in those two days. He just held her hand with his head resting on the pillow next to hers. I remember telling him that it was time to let us take her; that she was gone. I barely heard him say, 'no'. I laid a hand on his shoulder and told him he couldn't stay like this. He had to let her go. He broke several of my ribs and sent me through a wall."

"He hit you?" Julie hadn't been expecting this.

"You could say that."

"I thought you were friends?"

"We were. It's just that his feelings for me were nothing compared to his love for Mary. Besides, he was hurting. You have to admit that we have an animal side to us, and, what happens when an animal gets hurt?" Martin left the question in the air. "I will say it was a shock to our mutual friend that was there. He had no idea about William and me. I didn't wait to mend before I began tracking Bill. I was afraid the stupid lunk was going to get caught and put in the loony bin, like I had been, or worse. I had to find him before daybreak, and I have to admit that it wasn't easy to do."

"Your friend didn't know about you two?" Julie swiveled in her seat to look at Martin, totally engrossed in his story.

"No. It's something you don't go spreading around. He just thought that Bill shoved me really hard. Even back then, people were aware that in times of extreme stress, people are capable of mind boggling physical feats. I didn't see any reason to try to persuade him otherwise."

"That really bothers you, doesn't it? Not being able to tell I mean."

"Leading a double life can be so oppressive," Martin said after a moment's introspection, "sometimes it makes you want to scream. You have this big secret that you can't tell anyone about, but you want to desperately, and then you're scared to death that someone *will* find out and expose you."

Martin fell silent and concentrated on his driving.

"O.K.. Then what?" Julie prodded.

Martin glanced at her. "I found him."

"Don't pull that crap on me, Martin. You know how nosy I am. So, how did you find him?"

Martin's brow lifted as he remembered the events from a lifetime ago. "I tracked him to an alleyway and caught him just in time."

"Was he about to kill himself?"

"No. Someone else. The poor man was too scared to scream. Bill was holding him off the ground and was preparing to bite him when I burst onto the scene. I remember the look on his face and the way he acted like a wild animal.

'He's mine,' he growled, guarding the man like an old bone.

'Bill, wait!'

'I told you he's mine!' he said still holding the man off the ground.

'Mary wouldn't want this,'

'Mary," he asked looking past me. 'Mary . . . is here?'

Then the idea hit me. 'That's right, Bill. Mary's waiting at the end of the alley.'

'Waiting? My Mary?'

Bill slowly lowered the man to the ground and started toward the end of the alley. I let him pass me and then hissed for the man to run while I pulled a small section of pipe loose from the wall. I felt terrible, but I had no choice. If I killed him, I knew that would be a mercy in itself, so I nearly took his head off. I didn't know at the time just how powerful our regenerative powers were, but I had to have time to get him somewhere safe so that hopefully he could work through his madness."

"Since we're going to his house, I take it you were successful."

"Finally. I thought for a while I was going to have to kill him. And, making bonds strong enough to hold him was a trick. I kept him drugged a lot at first. Little by little, he came around more each day until finally out of the blue he looked at me and said, 'You can release me. I know Mary is dead, that she has been for a number of days now and nothing is going to bring her back.' I looked at him for a moment and then nodded. I had one arm released when he grabbed my hand.

'To let you know that I am indeed sane, if this ever happens again, ever, don't hesitate. Kill me. I would rather die than let the madness take me.'

I nodded my head again.

'Promise me, Martin.' There was such agony and conviction in his voice, it broke my heart.

'I promise,' I told him. He lay back on the frame that I had him strapped to.

'Good, then get these restraints off me.'

"That's it. From then till now we've been friends. We've helped each other 'die' when it was needed. And, over the miles and years, we've always been there for each other."

"You two really are close?"

"He knows me better than anyone else," Martin said as he drove on into the night.

Martin steered the Honda up the long winding drive and came to stop in front of an impressive house gleaming like a jewel in the night.

"Bill lives here?" Julie asked, a little awestruck.

"This is it."

"What happened to not wanting to attract attention to yourself?"

Martin chuckled. "Bill likes his creature comforts."

As they got out of the car, Julie surveyed the house and its surroundings. "Although," she looked back the way they had come and couldn't see the road, "driving down the road, you'd never know this place was here."

Martin held her hand as they walked up the front steps and rang the doorbell. It wasn't so much a front door as a huge portal filled by two massive, ornate, oak and iron slabs. Julie ran her hands over the door in appreciation of the craftsmanship.

"How much money does he have?" Julie wondered aloud.

"Enough. The thing is he's had a number of years to accumulate it. It makes it easier to accumulate when you inherit money from yourself."

Julie looked at him sideways. "How much is enough?"

"Almost as much as me."

"Right."

"Do I detect doubt in your voice?" Martin crossed his arms. "You have to remember that I come from old money. Southern plantation holdings and the whole lot."

"You're serious?" Julie looked into Martin's eyes. "You're constantly surprising me Martin Daniels." She kissed him lightly on the mouth, allowing her lips to linger there. "Never a dull moment, eh?"

Martin started to answer and then cocked his head slightly. "He's coming."

"You kill me when you do that. How do you know it's him?"

One of the large doors swung inward and Bill stepped outside.

Martin looked at Julie and raised an eyebrow.

"Show off. How'd you know," she asked, hands on her hips.

"Heard the steps, recognized the walk."

Bill spoke up, "Am I missing something?"

"Nah," Martin said as he walked past not waiting for an invitation to enter.

Bill motioned for Julie to pass. "Please, come inside. I would say that it is nice to meet you, but feel I already know you from Martin's descriptions. Although, I must confess that you are far more lovely than he spoke of."

Julie's face blushed under the compliment. "Thanks."

Julie followed Bill through the doorway. There she stopped and stood gawking at the massive, crystal chandelier hanging from the ceiling in the fourier, each facet like a tiny, captured star. She looked about in awe at the lavish surroundings ablaze with light. The Italian marble flowed from the entryway in three separate directions, cascading down hallways lined with artwork from all periods. Her footsteps echoed off the river of stone and she felt she should be in an art museum instead of someone's home. Bill and Martin's conversation was lost on her as she wound her way through the structure following the pair in front of her. She marveled at the amount and conditions of the antiques filling different parts of the house. Julie wondered how much money Bill had to afford artifacts like these. Then, the thought occurred to her. He wasn't paying collectible prices. He had bought this stuff when it was brand new. These were things that he had acquired down through the decades.

At last they entered a comfortable den, warmly

lit, with a fire burning low in the hearth and strings playing softly in the background.

"I'll say one thing," Julie thought to herself, "this guy certainly knows how to set a mood."

"Please, make yourself comfortable," Bill said to Julie in a voice with no particular outstanding qualities. This was the first time that she had had a chance to really look at Bill and realized that there was nothing outstanding about him. In fact, his looks rather surprised her. She supposed she'd had some preconceived idea about the way vampires should look. Young and virile with dark eyes and dashing, good looks or like something that had just crawled out of the grave. Bill was neither. He appeared to be of European dissent, about 50, thin hair on top with a middle age spread around the waist and dull light brown eyes. He wore a button up cardigan over a knit v-neck with linen trousers and loafers. All in all, a most unassuming appearance. Julie moved to the love seat that Bill indicated and sat down next to Martin. It appeared to Julie that Bill and Martin were opposites, from personal tastes to physique.

Bill leaned back into the stuffed sofa opposite from them and draped an arm across the back. "I haven't talked to you in some time, Martin. What's going on with you?"

"I've got some biiiig problems," Martin began. He laid out the abduction of Julie, the break in at the lab and everything that had transpired since then.

Bill listened intently and then rose to refill the brandy snifter he had drained while listening to Martin. "When I hadn't heard from you I worried that something like this had happened, or worse."

"What do you mean?" Martin looked at his friend and then to Julie.

Bill turned back and looked at the pair over the top of his snifter. "You haven't heard?"

"Haven't heard what?" Julie stopped her gawking and focused on Bill.

"We haven't had time to catch our breath, let alone the news. What's up?"

Bill sat down in a wing-backed chair and twirled the brandy in his glass as he spoke. "In the last month, a handful of other labs have been broken into nationwide. Not necessarily newsworthy and most would suspect industrial espionage. The difference here is that all of the labs broken into, employed people with, how shall I say, our condition. Of course our law enforcement officials don't know this and they've made no connection between the break ins." Bill took a drink of his brandy. "Andy Morris was killed two days ago in what was described as a freak accident."

Martin's brow knitted. "What kind of accident?"

"Gas explosion in his house. Of course they never found the body." Bill drained the glass and set it down on the gold-filigreed table beside the chair.

"What's going on here, Bill?"

"I don't know," he sighed heavily. "I would theorize that someone has become aware of our presence and is attempting to eradicate us."

"Straun," Julie and Martin spoke at the same time.

"Who?"

"Guy named Straun." Martin nodded his head at Julie. "He's the one that got Jules and has made our life a living hell. Why don't you see what you can find out about him?"

"All right." Bill produced a note pad and jotted down the name.

"Just be careful. This guy is bad news."

Bill pulled at his bottom lip. "I've got to tell you Martin, I'm worried about all of this. You know Morris worked in immunology?"

Martin nodded.

"Well, from what I understand, he was this close to providing a cure. There were some whispers that he had already developed a vaccine."

"A vaccine? I didn't know it was this bad."

"Wait," Julie said to Martin, "which bad are we talking about here?"

"The government, Jules. Can you imagine what they'd do if they found out that we do indeed exist? There'd be a government witch-hunt to rid the world of the unholy bloodsuckers while they secretly studied us to use us for they're own agenda. The government would finally get the super soldiers they always wanted. You've seen what Straun can do. Can you imagine if the government had a few hundred thousand like him? Not to mention the field day the press would have with this. You thought O.J. got coverage? And, above all else, the panic it would excite. Anyone who didn't hold down a day job would be under suspicion. Of course, you'd have the right-to-lifers protesting that we had rights too." Martin had been pacing and stopped next to Julie's seat. "It would be like them announcing that Martians are real and they're living next door." Martin's mind kicked into high gear as he addressed Bill. "Was he in contact with any government agency?"

"None that we know of other than the usual channels for grants and such."

"Damn, Bill, I didn't know any of this, but it makes sense. No wonder Straun won't stop hounding us. If he's working for the government then none of us are safe."

"How about his assistants?" Julie spoke up. "Did they know anything about what he was working on?"

"Not that we know of at this time," Bill answered.

"But, he had the cure?" Martin asked wistfully.

"Rumors," said Bill.

Martin fell back into his seat and slumped there for a moment. "No one's found his data and no one else in the field is close?"

Bill shook his head no.

"Damn." Martin steepled his fingers in front of him in thought.

Bill at last broke the silence. "You mentioned that you were in need of lab space."

"Yea, that's right." Martin sat up straight in the chair like he had just remembered the loaf of bread he was supposed to have purchased at the store. "All my data was destroyed. Originals, back up, everything. But," Martin held up a finger for emphasis, "and, it's a big but I think I can duplicate from memory."

Bill turned to Julie, "And, as an assistant, do you have a copy of the data?"

Julie felt uneasy with the way Bill looked at her. "No, I wasn't privy to that information at the time."

"I see. Well then, we'll just have to rely on Martin, won't we? The lab is at your disposal. Let me know what you need and I'll procure it for you."

"Thanks, buddy," Martin said.

Later that evening, Martin and Julie made their way back down the winding drive toward the main road. Julie glanced back at the house receding in the distance and noticed most of the lights had been shut off, obviously set to a timer.

Martin watched her. "What's bothering you?"

"Huh? Oh, nothing's bothering me. I don't understand how, if the virus rewrites your DNA and makes you super strong and stuff, how come Bill is overweight?"

Martin chuckled. "A couple of ways actually. Even though he's off the scale by human standards, vampires can be out of shape like everyone else, and believe me, Bill is out of shape. The main reason is that that's how Bill looked when he was bitten. You're right, the virus rewrites the DNA, but it sort of takes a copy of the original to use as a blueprint for basic construction. Some of that stuff that you see in the movies has a basis. What you see, is what you get. We will all eventually grow older, but the process is so slow that we're basically frozen in time."

"If that's the case, then why are you guys trying so hard to find a cure?"

Martin slumped minutely behind the wheel. When he spoke, his voice was filled with passion.

"Do you know how long it's been since I saw a sunrise or a sunset? One hundred and fifty-seven years," he said not waiting for an answer. "People think living forever would be fantastic, but immortality has its price. The existence is so lonely it's unbelievable. You can't get close to people for fear that they will find out about you. You watch those around you grow old and die while you go on, leaving you lonelier than before. You're forced to move from place to place to make sure your secret stays intact." Martin gripped the steering wheel as his voice grew quiet. "You can't love anyone, because it won't last, it can't, they grow old and leave you."

Julie brushed the side of his face with her hand and then leaned her head on his shoulder. "I won't leave you."

"Yes, you will," he said too low for her to hear.

Chapter 8

Once at Julie's place, Martin excused himself to the bathroom as Julie settled her things and picked up the daily paper. As Martin emerged from the bathroom, he took in the stark expression on Julie's face.

She held the paper out to him. "Oh, God, Martin, I'm so sorry."

"What is it," he asked, taking the paper from her.

"I was scanning the paper and came across the article. They got him, Martin." Julie shook her head. "I can't believe they got him, just like that."

Martin's eyes anxiously scanned the paper in front of him and came to rest on a picture of Pete Hagerston in his guard's uniform. Frantically he flipped to the related article and read how the old man appeared to have been tortured and beaten before his assailants tore the body to pieces. The police were baffled as to a motive for such a hideous crime and had no leads at the present time. Hot tears blurred his vision as he stared at the photo.

Martin looked to Julie for understanding.

"Why? He was harmless. He couldn't have done anything to them." Martin's voice dropped to a whisper. "He did nothing but good for people. I would sometimes go down to his booth and take him to lunch in the cafeteria. We would swap stories. He would tell me tales of his youth, of the Second World War and places he had seen. I told him stories and said they were ones my grandfather had told me from the great depression and such, although they were really mine. We never met outside the company, but next to Bill, that old man was the closest thing to family that I had." Martin rent the paper in half, flinging the pieces into the air and leaned against the doorframe for support. "Those bastards. They killed him for spite. Nothing more. They kill him and they know that I can't even go to the funeral to say good-bye."

Julie held him tenderly. "I'll go to the funeral for you and be your eyes."

"No. It's too dangerous. I won't risk losing you too."

"It's during the day. If you can't be there, neither can they."

"What if they have human operatives? After all, I've got you."

"There is that," she conceded, "but, I had better be more than just an *operative* to you if you know what's good for you." She kissed him on the nose and added more gently, "Besides, if they, whoever *they* are, had humans working for them, then why wouldn't they just bust in and let the sun shine on your shoulders?"

"I don't know." Martin took a deep, steadying breath and wiped at the corners of his eyes. "I've been thinking about that one myself." Suddenly, Martin slapped his forehead. "Oh, geez, how blind can I get? They don't come after us here because they don't know where you live."

"What do you mean? I thought that's why we've been staying gone most of the night, so that just in case they pay a house call, we wouldn't be here."

"You caught on to that, huh?"

She gave him a sardonic look. "Yea."

"I just didn't want to worry you. Sorry."

"But, why wouldn't they know?" Julie leaned her back against the opposite frame and folded her arms in thought. "I mean, Straun had access to the company files."

"That's true. However," Martin held up a finger for emphasis, "you have an unlisted phone number, you've no relatives and did you ever fill out the change of address form at work or the post office?"

"Holy crap. You're right. I wrote to the credit card companies and changed it at the bank and told the people I wanted to have it, but I just kept putting it off at the post office, and, to be real honest, I didn't think about doing it at work. I mean it's not like we're on a company mailing list for Christmas cards or anything." Julie's eyes glinted. "Lucky us, huh? I wondered why the junk mail had been lighter since I moved."

Martin hugged her. "Once again, Jules, you save my hide without even trying. Thanks."

Julie snuggled in closer, enjoying the warmth of his body and the strength of his arms. Suddenly she leaned back.

"The funeral home. You can say good bye to Pete at the funeral home."

Martin slowly shook his head. "No, I can't. They'll be waiting for us." Martin walked to the living room and sank into the couch. "In fact, I believe that's why they killed him. To use as bait." Martin closed his eyes and leaned his head against the back of the couch. "The old man is dead because of me. Just like Amos."

"Wait a minute, Martin. Listen to yourself. Pete is not dead because of you. You didn't kill him. They did. They're the ones that murdered the old man."

"Because I tipped them off that he meant something to me."

"It was an instinct to protect someone you loved. More people should be guilty of it." She rubbed at the tension in the back of his neck. "You realize that you are awfully hard on yourself sometimes."

"Most people only have to live with *one* lifetime of regrets."

Julie knew there was nothing she could say. She wasn't thirty years old yet and could look back on scores of things she would change if she could. She could only imagine what it would be like to have several lifetimes to deal with. So, instead, she continued to rub at the knots of muscle in Martin's neck and shoulders until at last she could feel the tension start to ease there.

"Well, love, what are we going to do now?"

Martin gave a heavy sigh. "Talk to the police. I have to try and get this straightened up before it gets totally out of hand and they want me to appear in court.

I don't think my 'skin condition' will be able to keep me out of the halls of justice during regular business hours. I'm going to have to go down tomorrow night and get this taken care of."

"Don't you mean *we're* going to have to get this straightened out?"

Martin took her hand and kissed her lightly on the fingertips. "Right."

"Thank you, Inspector Tommelson, for taking the time to see us," Martin began as he and Julie seated themselves in the two chairs in front of the inspector's desk.

The inspector pitched the pen he had been using onto the report lying amidst the clutter covering his desk. Tommelson leaned back in his chair and clasped both hands behind his head. He looked at the pair. "How may I help you?"

"My name is Martin Daniels. I was arrested recently for the alleged theft of property belonging to my employer. I have with me . . . "

"Where do you work?" Tommelson interrupted.

"SUNCO, Inc. In the R&D department," Martin brought forth his attaché case and opened it. "As I was saying, I have . . . "

"What do you do there, Mr. Daniels?"

"I'm a chemist," Martin said flatly.

"I see." Tommelson pursed his lips for a moment, thinking. "You're the guy that was busted with the lab setup in his basement."

"That's me." Martin continued before Tommelson could cut him off again. "The thing is, I've got receipts for all the equipment. That's what I've been trying to tell your people. I bought all of the equipment with my own money. And, since that night, I haven't been able to get back into my house to get any of my personal things."

Tommelson leaned forward and rested his arms on the desktop. He studied Martin for a long moment. "Keep the receipts. We transferred your case to narcotics. I'd love to be able to tell you that you scum sucking dope makers deserve everything you get. That, when our boys turn up your goodies, they're going to bust your ass so bad, you'll never see daylight again. That because of all the suffering and kids' lives you've ruined, some big studded bubba will make you his bitch in prison. I'd love to be able to say all that, but I can't, 'cause that would be against the law."

Julie's mouth fell open in shock, her jaw muscles working, as she tried to think of something to say.

Martin stared into the inspector's eyes.

At last, Julie's surprise turned to anger and found voice. "Why you pompous, sanctimonious, self centered . . . "

Martin laid a hand on her arm.

"I want the name of your supervisor," she continued ignoring Martin.

The inspector was unfazed by her outburst. "His office is at the end of this hall. Can't miss it. Go see him, I'm sure he'd love to visit with you."

"Well, don't think I won't"

Martin stood up. "Come on Jules. It won't do us any good." He looked back at the cop. "Guilty until proven innocent, eh, officer?"

"You said it, pal, not me." Tommelson picked up the pen and started work again on the report, effectively dismissing them. Without looking up, he added, "Close the door on your way out."

"You can kiss my ass on the way out," Julie spat at him.

Martin let Julie precede him out of the office and pulled the door closed as he went. As the door came to rest against the doorstop, he pulled it further past the stop, jamming the door in its frame and then twisted off the handle mechanism.

Martin looked at Julie, "I hope our dear inspector doesn't have to go to the bathroom any time soon," and handed her the knob.

Julie grinned wickedly. "I personally hope he busts a bladder."

Martin smiled and put an arm around her. "Did you know you're beautiful when you're angry. Actually you're just beautiful."

Julie gave him a sarcastic look as they started down the hall.

Even at this time of night, there were plain clothed and uniformed cops alike hurrying up and down the halls. The pair made their way through the police officers and assorted clerks running their endless duties.

"I can't believe they can keep you out of your own house like that," Julie fumed as she tromped her way around a corner and headed for a flight of stairs. "I mean, where do they expect you to live?"

"Why, with you of course, my darling."

Totally brushing the humor aside, she continued with her tirade. "Yea, right. But, what if you didn't have me? What then, huh? I mean, do they expect you to live on the street, or pay rent on an apartment while you have to make house payments?" Julie stopped at the top of the stairs to emphasize her point, nearly hitting one officer in the face with her wild arm gestures.

"The way they see it, it's not their problem that I might have chosen to break the law," Martin said taking her hands in his to calm her down.

Julie pulled free and started down the stairs two steps at a time. "But, what if you're found innocent? Do you get any kind of reimbursement? Hell, no!"

"Well, basically you're right." Martin said as he bounded lightly after her.

They were down the stairs and headed toward

the front doors when she whirled to face him. "How do you stay so calm?"

Martin walked past her without stopping. "You change those things you can and accept those that you can't. Besides, who said I was calm?" Then in a bad Scotty imitation, "Cap'n, she canna' take much more of this. She's gonna blow."

"You wish." But, the joke achieved its desired effect and a slight smile spread across her face. "I've gotta get a drink," she said spying a water fountain.

Martin stood with his back to the wall and watched Julie as she drank from the fountain. He was constantly amazed at how sometimes an inconsequential thing could mesmerize him. Martin gazed at the curve of her neck as the water passed her lips and slid down her throat and marveled at the smoothness of her skin.

He came back to himself and talked to Julie as she continued drinking. "To further answer your earlier question, this is one of those times that you have to keep telling yourself that things could always get worse. I. . . . "

The words cut off as Martin's senses snapped to full attention. He looked up and locked gazes with an officer walking past them on the other side of the hallway, the whole scene playing out in slow motion due to his hyper senses.

"Not here, not now," he thought.

Yet, there was no denying the other's presence. The officer slowed his pace but kept walking, his right hand dropping to his side arm, his eyes never leaving Martin's. Martin grabbed Julie by the hand and started once more for the front doors.

"Wait a minute, I'm not finished." Julie mildly protested.

"Yes you are," Martin said, not releasing his grip and quickened his pace.

"Oh, God. Why do I have the feeling that things just got worse?"

"Because they did." Martin looked back over his shoulder to find the cop nowhere in sight.

The two of them hurried as fast as they could without drawing undue attention to themselves. Once clear of the front doors and out of the line of sight of the desk officer, Martin checked the street, extending his senses to their fullest.

"Let's go," he said and picked Julie up in his arms, taking off at a full run. She started to ask what he thought he was doing, but realized that even with carrying her, he was moving much faster than they would have if she were running alongside him. With the extra weight and running full speed, she still couldn't hear his feet hitting the pavement.

"What did you do, study with Kwichang at the monastery," she said to him as he sprinted along.

"Shh. Believe me, he can hear me and I need to be able to hear him," Martin told her as he scanned in all directions.

Julie couldn't resist. "He who?"

"The cop that walked by the fountain."

"Holy shit. A cop?"

Julie wondered when these startling revelations would end. Just how many people did she pass in the course of a day, or actually a night that was a real live vampire? She envisioned her third grade teacher as one of the truly undead. That would explain how she always knew what was being said in the class. But, that wouldn't work because she was out during the day. "Good God, what am I doing thinking about this crap?" she wondered to herself.

"Are you sure?"

"Yes, now be quiet." Martin had stopped just short of the corner of the building and cautiously peered around the corner. He scanned the roofline and saw nothing out of the ordinary. He looked across the street to the parking lot where Julie's burgundy Prizm sat like some piece of gleaming bait waiting to entice him into a trap. Martin had purposely parked directly under a lamp. Not that he needed the light to see by, but rather he hoped that in case Straun or any of his goons wanted to jump him, they might think twice of doing so in a well lit area. As he looked across what seemed like a hundred miles of empty space, he realized that the gesture was futile this late at night and with as little traffic as there was. Julie remained as still as possible so that she wouldn't break his concentration as he looked out over the parking lot. A few days ago, she would have dismissed this as nonsense and insisted that he put her down and quit playing at being such a macho guy. But, now, anything that caused Martin to react this way, she knew was definitely serious. From the look of concentration on his face, she felt as if he were trying to will himself to see through the cars in the lot.

Martin fished the keys out of his pocket and looked once more up and down the street as well as above and behind him. "Well, here goes," he said more to himself than Julie.

Martin took a deep breath and started across the street at a pace that Olympic class sprinters would kill for, closing the gap between them and the Prizm swiftly. Making a beeline for the car, Martin cut diagonally across the lot. Reaching a row of four or five cars, Martin, instead of making his way around them, simply hurdled the cars baring his way. Julie stifled a squeal as Martin's feet left the black top. It gave her a sense of dejavu, reminding her of the flight she had experienced with Straun. Martin hit the pavement on the other side of the Ford Tempo without ever breaking stride. The next two rows of cars were parallel with theirs and Martin sprinted for a gap between two of them like a runaway train headed for a narrow pass. He shot the gap and was about to clear the end of the car when something snaked out, clothes-lined Martin and grabbed at the sleeve of Julie's blouse. Martin's feet flew out from under him like some Saturday morning cartoon character. The sudden deceleration threw Julie from his arms, somersaulting her into a heap in the middle of the lot. With blurred vision, she looked back to see what had happened to Martin and if he was all right from where he had slammed into the ground. But, he wasn't on the ground. She looked around in time to see his body fly through the air and smash through the back glass of a Cougar parked there. She tried to stand, but her vision swam in front of her and then tilted as she slid back to the ground. Julie realized that she must have hit harder than she thought. The other part of her knew that Martin was in real trouble, and although she didn't know just what, she knew that she had to do something. Gritting her teeth, she pushed herself to her knee and willed her eyes to focus. What she saw was not pretty. Whoever their attacker was, ripped the door off the car and dragged Martin out by the throat, smashing his head into the car parked next to it. Julie struggled to her feet and stumbled toward the two grappling bodies.

Martin saw stars explode in his vision when his head hit the parked car. Whoever this guy was, he wasn't giving any quarter and was keeping Martin off balance, never giving him a chance to recover. That, and he was strong. Far stronger than Straun had been. Martin's face slid on the metal, and the gravel tore into his knees as he instinctively tried to get to his feet. From that position, he was struck in both kidneys by twin blows that would have gone completely through a human. As, it was, Martin grunted in pain and tasted his own blood as it flowed from his nose and mouth. Suddenly, massive arms clamped in front and behind his neck hoisting him to his feet. Blood and oxygen were being quickly cut off from his brain. That is, if whoever it was didn't break his neck first. Through a red-gray haze Martin saw the Prizm still sitting there beneath the light waiting for them. He thought that the car would be waiting for him forever when a detached part of his mind realized that he still held the car keys. In an act of desperation, he drove the keys into the leg of his attacker. The man cried out but didn't release his hold on Martin. He did however momentarily relax it. That was all Martin needed. He forced his left arm between his attacker's arms to prevent him from using the choke hold again while at the same time he brought his left foot up and back catching his assailant in the knee. Martin was rewarded with the sound of the other's knee giving way. This time the man did release his hold. Martin pulled the keys free as sugar sweet air poured into his burning lungs. At the same instant, he saw Julie making her way towards him, having recovered much of her equilibrium. Martin pitched the keys at her.

"RUN! Take the car and go. NOW."

Martin turned to face the man who had already gotten to his feet. It was the cop he had seen in the station, just as he expected.

The cop looked from Martin to where Julie was opening the car door. He pushed off from the car and made to go after Julie. "Stop!"

"No. You can't have her." The blood had stopped flowing from his nose but he could feel the bones fighting to mend themselves. His body was one massive ache, but he hurled it at the cop anyway. Martin was trained to fight, but so was this person. Anyone else would have received the kick Martin gave right in the side of the head. Instead, his foot found air. In turn, Martin's inside thigh was hammered by a powerful right hand. He absorbed the pain and instinctively struck down, smashing his attacker in the nose sending a spray of red across the front of his shirt. The force of the blow drove the cop's head down and right into Martin's waiting knee. The other vampire's reflexes were a match for Martin's as he brought both arms up to block the knee and rolled backward with the kick, coming to his feet immediately. The cop crouched preparing to leap at Martin, when the beep of a car horn and the sound of a racing motor caused him to spin just in time to see the backup lights of the Prizm before they smashed into him. The impact hurled him through the air to land against the tailgate of a new Chevy half-ton. Julie gunned the motor for all it was worth crushing him between the two automobiles.

Through the passenger window she yelled to Martin, "Come on, let's go while we can." Julie was impressed and horrified as she looked in the rear view and saw, that despite the man's agony, he was attempting to pull himself free from between the two automobiles and was in fact starting to lift the back of the vehicle.

Martin didn't need to be invited twice. He half-dove, half-fell through the open window into the passenger seat. "Hit it!"

Julie slammed the car into drive.

There was a satisfying squeal of rubber on pavement as the car shot forward breaking away from the cop's grasp leaving him in a crumpled pile. Julie glanced in the rearview just to reassure herself that the vampire wasn't in fact giving chase. She didn't think one could keep up with a speeding automobile, but she wasn't speeding yet, being hemmed in by both rows of cars. She was afraid that if he got back to his legs that he would catch them before they made the relative safety of the street. In the reflection she saw that he was indeed trying to get up, but it was obvious that it was a futile effort. Although she knew that he would heal, it wouldn't be before they made good their escape. Julie rounded the last car in the row, tromped the accelerator, and shot over the curb, fish-tailing into the street.

"Easy partner," Martin said putting a bruised and bloody hand over hers, "we've already got one cop after us, we don't need more." Martin eyed the white knuckle grip she had on the steering wheel. "Ease up, Jules. You're going to break the steering wheel."

Julie looked at her hands for a moment like they belonged to someone else. With a conscious effort, she pulled one hand then the other off the wheel and flexed them to get the circulation going again. Julie sucked in a ragged breath realizing that she had been holding her breath since smashing the cop.

"Holy shit, Martin," she said barely audible above the noise of the air entering the car from the window she had rolled down. "I thought we were gone for sure back there." The adrenaline that her glands had dumped into her system was fading fast and in its wake, Julie felt every muscle in her body reel from the effects. The shaking started in her hands, moved rapidly up her arms and then encompassed her whole body. "I mean, what are we going to do when Straun can get to the cops?" Julie was almost beside herself with fatigue and fear.

"I will say that's one bad boy that Straun's got there, but we'll think of something."

"I hope so," Julie said, her voice, if not her hands, somewhat more steady. "Are you O.K.?"

Martin looked at her from one good eye, the other being a bruised, pulpy mass. "I've been worse. Not much, mind you, but some." Martin's breath caught and sweat stood out on his brow as bones began moving themselves back into their rightful positions. He ground his teeth together as ligaments and tendons pulled dislocated joints back into place sending wave after wave of unbelievable agony coursing through him. "Ah, the price of immortality," he whispered through clenched teeth.

"Huh?"

Martin didn't answer her. He opened his eyes momentarily looking out the window not really seeing anything as the Prizm glided along the near deserted streets.

Julie looked over at him and watched as parts of his body moved of their own volition, "Oh, God, Martin. Are you all right? Is there anything I can do?"

He started to shake his head no when he spied something along the stretch of road they were passing. "Stop the car."

"Do what?" Julie started to protest, "I thought we neede . . . "

"Stop the car," Martin growled.

Julie glanced at him and jammed on the brakes.

Martin's was a frightening visage. His battered face by itself was gruesome to behold, but coupled with the fact that he was now showing his fangs, and the deep shadows of his face made all the deeper by the glow of the dash lights, lent such an eerie appearance it made Julie want to run from the car.

"I will be right back," he said as he slid out the door. "And," Martin's voice floated back through the open window, "don't watch."

Julie's scientific curiosity coupled with her natural brand of nosiness overpowered any warning Martin might have given her and she swiveled in the seat to see what Martin was doing. All she could see at first was him moving away from the car at a quick, silent jog. She noticed that he was favoring his right leg. Then she saw what he was moving towards. It was a large black dog. Well-fed and healthy looking, she realized that he must belong to someone close by in the neighborhood. It appeared to be some type of Labrador mix, so dark that she hadn't even seen it as they passed. The dog finally looked up from where it had been sniffing the ground and saw Martin some twenty yards away. The dog started to react and Martin was instantly upon it, covering the last ten yards in a spectacular leap. Before the animal could yelp, he ripped it's throat out sending a jet of crimson into the night air. Martin held the dog off the ground and gorged himself as the dogs life essence flowed out. Julie sat mesmerized; both fascinated and revolted at the same time. Finally, Martin gently lowered the wrung out carcass to the ground, wiped his mouth on his sleeve and turned back toward the car. Julie still sat wide-eyed as Martin got back into the car.

"I told you not to look," Martin said matter of

factly. "You might want to go, so as not to attract attention."

"Yea, right." Julie looked back at Martin as she pulled the small car back onto the roadway. In those scant minutes, Martin looked exceptionally better. The knot on the side of his face had stopped moving and was almost back to normal. Gone too were the bruises, and the split in his lower lip. Julie piloted the car through the streets and reflected on what she had just witnessed. "Geez, Martin, you just sucked the life right out of that dog."

"I'm aware of that."

"But, he was innocent; so unsuspecting. He didn't deserve that."

"You think about how unsuspecting and innocent that cow was the next time you eat a hamburger or lace up a pair of Reeboks, and then you come talk to me. It was an act born out of necessity. What do you do when you get sick or injured? You eat and get plenty of rest. Well," Martin said massaging the side of his jaw working the stiffness out, "I don't have time for rest, but the meal definitely helps out."

"O.K., O.K.. I can't argue with that. You look a ton better." There was a moment's pause and then Julie back handed Martin on the arm.

"What was that for?"

"You scared the shit out of me! Don't do it again. I mean you looked like you came straight out of Salem's Lot or something."

"I'm sorry, Jules." Martin started to take her hand and then withdrew his. "Please believe me. I didn't mean to."

Julie let go of the wheel and found his hand with hers. "I know Doc. I know you didn't do it on purpose, but you still scared me. I will say this: I'd sure as hell hate to get you pissed off at me."

Martin put his hands together in his lap and stared out the front of the car. "I could never hurt you, Julie. Never."

"Not even if you were starving to death?" Julie said posing the proverbial hypothetical question.

Martin never took his eyes off the road. "Never."

The pair drove on in silence passing out of the inner city streets as they headed for the suburbs where Julie lived; Julie letting her mind sort through all she had just seen and Martin sitting back, letting his body finish healing itself. Julie looked up at the clear crisp sky when they had gotten a little farther from the light pollution of the city. Gazing up at the twinkling orbs on this unusually clear night, she wondered to herself how could the word seem so peaceful with all the turmoil swirling around them. She had always loved the night, even having thoughts of becoming an astronomer at one point in her life. But, her love of chemistry had won out. Although she still kept a telescope that she would take out to the country on some weekends to do some stargazing, she had never regretted her choice of careers. Sure, she told herself, working in R&D for a suntan co. wasn't the most glamorous of careers, but it was a decent living and there was the chance of joining one of the subsidiary branches that dealt in pharmaceuticals. There were the daydreams of finding the cure for AIDS or some other malady, but that would require more schooling. Even now with all that was happening in her life, there were no regrets. For, she thought to herself, if she hadn't gotten on when and where she did, she would never have met Martin. She glanced over at him sitting with a trance-like look on his face, his eyes closed. He could have been asleep, but she knew he wasn't, that he was acutely aware of his surroundings. She figured that he was trying to keep the pain in his body down to a minimum as it put itself back together. From the moment she had seen him she knew there was something special about him. She had always believed in recognition. That ability to know when you met the person that was right for you. That when you saw each other, there was no mistaking that you were meant to be together. She had told herself that that was where so many people went wrong. They didn't have the patience to wait and look for that someone and so wound up marrying the wrong person. Of course she knew the argument that what if the person that was meant for you lived on the other side of the world and you never had the chance to meet them. She had always countered with the notion that coming from two totally different cultures, the likelihood of compatibility was brought to almost nil, and that one had only to broaden one's experience base wide enough that you would eventually find each other. Not that you couldn't be happy with someone else, you just wouldn't be complete the way you would be if you were with your intended.

Julie pulled back from her wool gathering as she turned the car into her neighborhood. As she did, Martin roused from where he was and sat up in the seat.

"Damn. You have an internal chronometer or what?" Julie asked.

Martin looked at her and grinned. "Of course," he said stretching. "Actually, I figured we should be getting close and I peeked."

"Cheater." Julie turned onto her street, the

neighborhood being as sleepy as ever at this time of the morning. "Peaceful, isn't it. It always looks so different from the daytime."

"I'll take your word for it. It's been so long that I've just about forgotten what daytime looks like. I look at pictures or a movie and wonder if that's what a day really looks like. It's kind of like living in a cave." Martin finished the statement with another stretch, looking like a tabby moving off a sunny window ledge.

"I'm sorry, Doc."

"No need to be sorry. Because you're right. It is beautiful. The night has always had a special beauty. Besides, you know me. I like looking at the stars. Kinda hard to do that in the daytime."

Julie slowed to turn into her drive and parked the car directly in front of the garage, put the car in park and turned off the ignition. As she did, a car that had been parked across the street suddenly came to life and pulled in behind them blocking them from escape. As Martin turned to see what was happening, he looked through the front glass of the other car and saw that it was the policeman that he had fought earlier.

"Damn," Martin cursed himself for being so stupid. When Julie had crushed the cop earlier, she gave him an excellent view of her license tag when she had pulled away. All he had had to do was run a make on her tag and he had her address. He'd know from Straun that Martin and Julie were romantically involved. The cop had put two and two together, knew Martin couldn't go back to his place and would come here. All of this flashed through his mind and he told Julie to run for the house.

"Get your gun. Shoot him in the head if he comes for you. That's the only chance you'll have. I'll try to stop him here."

Julie was out of the car in an instant as was Martin, bringing his walking stick with him, drawing the blade as he came. He didn't know how much good he would do since he knew the cop would have at least two guns.

As Julie dashed for the house, the cop stepped out of the car, and instead of leveling a gun at them, said, "Wait, please!"

Martin and Julie both stared for a moment. The cop started to close the door to his car and then stopped when Martin told him to stay where he was. The officer stopped moving, keeping his hands in plain view the whole time.

"You've got to believe me," he said, "I made a mistake earlier. I'm not here after either one of you. I took a real long shot that you'd be here at all. I mean the sun is going to be up in half an hour and there's no way I can get back home before then. I need your help."

Martin stood for several tense moments and then slowly lowered the tip of his blade. Motioning with a nod of his head, he said, "Come inside."

"What?!" Julie looked like the steely inside a pinball machine, as she started first for the house and then towards Martin. "Am I missing something here, Martin? This is the same guy that damn near broke your neck, physically messed up the car, and now you're inviting him inside my house." Julie slapped herself in the forehead, "I really don't understand. I . . . wait a minute." She clapped her hands like someone remembering where it was they left the car keys. "Vampires can't come into your house unless they're invited, right. And, well this is my house, so," she spun to face the cop still standing by his car, "I'm not inviting you. Yea." Julie's voice had risen steadily in pitch and she was starting to look wild out of her eyes.

Martin slid noiselessly next to her and took her by the shoulders. "Jules." At the sound of his voice she looked up to his face. "That crap's just in the movies. Doesn't work in real life. If he wants in, he'll get in. But, I think," Martin looked over his shoulder to where the cop remained and nodded for him to come in, "that it's going to be O.K. I promise."

The fearful looked remained on her face as her eyes darted back and forth between the approaching cop and Martin's face. "Oh, God, Martin. What if he's really with Straun and there's a bunch more waiting inside for us?"

Martin pulled her to him and brushed her hair back with his hand. "If there were more inside, I'd know it and so would he. Besides, why would he stop to chat if he were intent on killing us?"

"To throw us off guard?"

"No, I don't think so." Martin disengaged himself from the hug he had been giving her and touched his forehead to hers. "I really think that he's on our side. Let's all get inside, shall we? It's starting to get light."

Martin looked up at the sky to where false dawn was making itself known and took in a deep breath of the crisp morning air, filling his senses with the smell of honeysuckle, morning glory and azaleas. He glanced at the other man standing there and saw the same expression he felt. A deep longing, almost a desperation, to watch the golden orb climb it's predestined path across the heavens and to behold the magic that only an early morning sunrise can conjure. With a sigh, Martin turned toward the house.

Chapter 9

Martin waited while Julie fished the key out of the small handbag she had been carrying and opened the door. Julie entered first and flipped on the overhead lights. Martin stood to the side and let the other man pass before him.

The policeman didn't really look at Martin as he crossed the threshold into the living room of Julie's modest home. He simply said thanks as he walked by and then with the wary look of a wild animal that has just entered the lair of another, he scanned the room and all he could see with a practiced eye. Having satisfied himself that he was relatively safe, he turned to Julie.

"If you don't mind, I'd like to use your phone. I need to call my wife."

Julie, surprised, asked, "Your wife?"

"Yes," the cop said evenly as he headed towards the phone, "do you mind?"

"No, not at all. Be my guest. After all, you're already inside."

The policeman turned his back on the pair garnering a sense of privacy as Julie mouthed the word, 'wife' to Martin who shrugged his shoulders in response.

Julie walked into the dining room to lay her keys on the tabletop, which was a huge receptacle for all the odds and ends she had around the house. As she walked, she strained to hear what the man was saying, but couldn't hear a bit of his conversation. Julie trusted that Martin, with his superior hearing, was catching every word and would act as an alarm in case the cop was up to no good. Julie decided that if it was a trap there was nothing that she could do about it right now, so there was no need to worry. With that thought in mind, she started for the kitchen to boil some water for coffee.

"Sorry, boys," she said as she went, "I'm all out of O positive, so you'll have to settle for decaf."

"And you told me you went to the store this morning." Martin replied in the easy banter that he and Julie had grown accustomed to.

"So, Grant," Martin said as the policeman hung up the phone, "we seem to be at a disadvantage here. You seem to know more about us than we know about you."

"If that's so," the officer eyed Martin suspiciously, "then how do you know my name?"

"Heard your name mentioned over the phone."

"The phone?" Grant started to look to where he had just placed the receiver, when a look of understanding spread across his face. "I'm not used to someone having hearing like mine."

Julie nudged Martin's arm.

"Thanks," he said taking the steaming cup from her.

The cop nodded his thanks as he took the third cup and leaned against the doorframe of the dining room. He stayed there for a moment breathing in the steam and for the first time, Martin and Julie noticed how tired looking the man was.

"What can I say?" Grant opened his eyes to look at Martin. "I thought that you were going to harm the lady and I couldn't allow that."

"See, a real gentleman," said Julie.

Martin elbowed her in the ribs.

"I don't know why, but the thought never occurred to me that she could be going with you of her own free will. It just gets so tough sometimes and the thought of one of those scumbags hurting someone else; I just couldn't take it."

"Believe me, I know what you're talking about. Why don't you just start at the beginning," Martin said.

Grant stared into his cup for a moment, then looked around the room. "Do you mind if I sit?"

"No. Go ahead," Julie said with a shrug and motioned him into the living room. Grant walked over and melted into the easyboy in the corner of the room.

Julie stirred her coffee, giving Martin an inquisitive look as she followed Grant into the room.

"You haven't . . . eaten since our encounter, have you?" Martin asked still leaning against the doorframe.

"No," Grant said. "I didn't have time."

"I'm sorry, I don't have anything to offer you."

Grant opened his eyes and looked at Martin for a moment. "Thank you," he said, his voice heavy with fatigue. "I definitely misjudged you." He took a sip of his coffee and nodded his appreciation to Julie who sat poised in the ensuing silence expecting something, anything to take place. She glanced at Martin who watched the other vampire over the top of his cup, letting him take his own time to gather his strength and his thoughts.

"This is difficult for me," Grant began at last. "I don't know where to start. First, let me apologize for earlier. I said I misjudged you. I have a question. Actually several questions. First off, how many are there out there?"

"Vampires you mean?"

"Yea."

"Off hand, I'd say thousands," Martin said.

"Here in the city?"

"No, no," Martin replied with a chuckle," I'm talking worldwide. If there were that many in the city, we'd all be in trouble."

"That's one of the things that I need to talk to you about. I've only come across one other vampire, other than the one that bit me, until this past three weeks." Grant stood up and started to pace back and forth. "I've come across four others besides you. The one was just an animal." Grant looked at the couple sitting on the couch, Julie with her head leaning against Martin. "Last week, the little girl they found in the alley over off Broadmoore," Martin and Julie both nodded. "I was the one to initially find her." Grant rubbed at his eyes, his shoulders sagging a little more as he relived the scene again.

Martin gently laid a hand on Grant's shoulder, the other's eyes opening immediately, his whole body going tense. "It's okay. Go ahead and sit. You're out on your feet." Martin steered Grant back to the recliner. "As for what you saw, there's no way I can erase those images; Lord knows I've tried. You just have to tell yourself that you had nothing to do with the attack."

Grant sat there trying to keep control of the

emotions that raged through him. At last the tears came, the drops streaming down his face. "That's just it. I had something to do with the attack. I had come across this smell I had only smelled once before, but I knew immediately what it was. I was off duty and was getting some shopping done when I came across the scent. I thought about ignoring it, but I couldn't. There's so many questions that I wanted answers to and I thought that this might be my chance. I argued with myself over the right course of action to take. Finally, I just started after the person, tracking them like a dog. Not far away I found them." Grant paused for a moment, the words catching in his throat. Julie squeezed Martin's hand and sat in silence, leaving the other man to proceed at his own pace. "It . . . was a . . . woman," Grant started, stopped and started again. "She was straight out of a nightmare. Clothes tattered, covered with gore and blood. It had pulled the little girl's head off and was trying to drain the body all at once. There was blood going everywhere and the thing sat in the middle of her body like a huge parasite." Grant took several deep breaths and wiped his eyes before continuing. "I went nuts. Naturally, even though I'm off duty, I carry a backup gun. I pulled it and charged down the alley. I was fast enough that I was on it before it knew I was there. It turned its head and opened its mouth to snarl at me. I just jammed the barrel into its mouth and pulled the trigger. The thing lay there twitching for a moment or two while it tried to put itself back together. Then without warning, the damned thing caught fire." Grant looked up, "I know it's hard to believe, but it just burst into flame."

"No, not hard to believe at all," Martin told him. "I've seen it a few times myself."

"Spontaneous human combustion," Julie added. "Just think, Grant, you now hold the answer to one of the great mysteries of life." Martin just rolled his eyes and smiled.

"Spontaneous what? I've never heard about it."

"So much for the mysteries of life." Julie got up and headed for the kitchen, "Anyone want some more coffee?"

Martin spoke to her back as she went, "I'd like another please." Then in an aside to Grant, "She's good for helping to relieve the tension of the moment."

"I wish something would," said Grant. "Ever since seeing that, thing, I haven't been able to eat or sleep right. I can't go see the department psychologist, for obvious reasons," he said as he got out of the chair and started pacing again. "If not for Christine, I don't know what I'd do. I had to get out of the alley way because there was no body now to corroborate my story and I had the girl's blood on my shoes and pants, but none of the other's blood. Hell, even it burned up. I had to leave that little girl right there."

"She was dead already," Martin said evenly, "You did all you could do."

"Did I really? If I hadn't argued with myself, I could have saved her. I didn't protect her at all." Grant looked at Martin. "I'm supposed to protect people." At that, he broke down as all the pain he had been holding at bay welled up and flowed out of him. "What scares me most," Grant said covering his face with his hands, "is that I stood looking at the body of that girl and the pile of ashes on the pavement and saw myself."

Martin stepped forward and hugged Grant, letting him cry for a while.

Julie came out of the kitchen to see this hulk of a man crying, being comforted by the man he had tried to kill earlier. As she watched, she was reminded of a scene not too far in the past where she had been the one to provide the comfort. She turned and went back into the kitchen wondering if those that survived the transformation with their sanity intact, were destined to forever teeter on the edge of the abyss.

Eventually, Grant calmed down and returned to the Easy Boy. "Thanks, guys. I mean it. I knew all this was bugging me, I just didn't know how bad. But," he leaned his head against the chair back and took a deep, even breath, "I've still got so many questions."

"Like, how did it all get started? Why did you not succumb to the madness? Is there anything that can change you back to the way you were?" Martin volunteered.

"Like, when do you guys plan to get some rest?" Julie interrupted, stretching as she walked past. "I can't go as long as you guys. I'll see you later."

Martin took her hand briefly raising it to his lips, "Good night, my Lady Fair."

Julie looked at him through bedroom eyes, "God, I love it when you do that," and bent down to kiss him fully on the mouth. "See ya."

Martin watched her go.

"It won't work."

"Do what?"

"You and Julie," Grant said motioning with his chin to the now closed bedroom door. "It won't work."

"I know."

"She called you, Doc. Why? You practice medicine?"

"I have a Ph.D. in chemistry."

"How?" Grant's natural curiosity started to take over.

"Well," Martin said draining his cup, "through the years I've acquired all the training and experience to be able to operate in this field. The diploma itself is, how should we say, questionable."

"You mean you have a false degree?"

"In a certain sense. You've got to admit that a person in our condition would find it extremely difficult to attend day classes and/or take finals."

Grant just shook his head. "How do you do it? It's just been so tough to keep going sometimes. I thought I was the only sane one out there. If it wasn't for Christine, I don't know what I would have done. There I go repeating myself." There was another stretch of silence as Grant twined his fingers together and then looked sideways at Martin. "Christine's always telling me I have a hard time expressing myself and I suppose she's right. It's hard enough with her, let alone a guy I just met. Hell, what I'm trying to say is that I'm glad I found you guys."

Martin smiled in return. "I just wish it could have been under more favorable conditions." Martin perched himself on the edge of the sofa. "I know you're tired, but there's a few questions I need to ask you first. You said you've made some other encounters. Could you tell me about them?"

"It wasn't much actually. What was weird about the whole deal is that there were three of them together. I was at the Fun Fair a few weeks back, working security for extra bucks, you know, a cop's lousy pay and all, when I sensed them. I turned and there they stood across the midway looking straight at me. There was no mistaking their looking at me, because when I turned and stared for a moment, the tallest one smiled. It had to be one of the coldest, pure evil grins I've ever seen in my life."

Martin edged closer to the edge of his seat. "The tall one, did he have a beard?"

"Yeah. A real sharp dresser too."

"Damn." Now it was Martin's turn to pace.

"Why? What is it? What do you know about this guy?"

"His name is Straun." Martin ran a hand through his hair. "I'll give you the Reader's Digest version. Straun is the guy that's responsible for kidnapping Julie, wrecking my lab, my home and basically screwing up my life. And, I don't have a clue why. At first, I thought that I understood. He's into corporate espionage and stole some information from a project that I was working on. Actually he stole the data and then introduced a virus that wiped my hard drive, got my backup disks, broke into my house and got the ones there also. I figured after he got those that that would be the last time I saw him. But, the son-of-a-bitch just keeps coming and I don't know why."

"You're not involved in anything on a national level are you?"

Martin laughed. "No, I'm not that important and I try to keep it that way. I can't afford to have too much attention paid to me. It's too hot as it is now."

"Well, what do you do then?" Grant asked, his curiosity piqued. "What is so interesting about you that someone would want to steal your stuff?"

"I work for a suntan company."

Grant burst out laughing and then covered his mouth casting a glance at Julie's door.

Martin cocked an eyebrow, "Not the most glamorous job, but one with a definite purpose."

"I'm sorry," said Grant waving a hand in Martin's

direction. "I'm not downing your job, man. It just struck me funny. I mean, a real life vampire working for a sun tan company." Grant laughed again.

"Yea, I admit that it sounds strange on the surface, but there's a madness to my method.

"What do you mean?"

"I know several people who suffer from our affliction. We have a viable network among us. The vast majority of them are involved in the science fields. And, most of those work in the medical areas trying to find some cure for what we have, while others work to find a blood substitute. Me personally, I'm trying to find a way for us to carry on a somewhat more normal life and be able to go to the beach in the heat of the day. I'm working on a sunscreen."

Grant blinked. "Wow. I'd have never thought. Sorry, man."

"No need to apologize," Martin said smiling, "Laughter's the best medicine and if a person can't laugh at themselves, they're in a world of hurt." Then Martin turned serious. "But, we do have a real problem."

"What do you mean?"

"All the data that Straun stole by itself is important to my employer, but I have a couple of hidden files in there that up the stakes dramatically." Martin started pacing again. "This man is not stupid and I don't know what resources he has at his disposal, but if he finds those files and is able to unlock them." Martin let the sentence trail off. Martin then filled Grant in on what the files contained and what the information could mean. After he finished they both sat staring at the floor thinking of possible futures.

"Things like this are why I won't involve Christine," Grant said softly. "When we were married I took a vow to love, cherish, honor, and protect her. I take that vow very seriously."

"I took a vow like that once," Martin said with a far away sound to his voice, "but I'm not the one who broke it. Anyway," Martin shook his head slightly to clear his thoughts, "that was ages ago, literally."

"Skipping subjects, did you notify the police about any of this?" Grant asked in a professional tone.

Martin gave him a mock scowl. "You and I both know that the police would be totally ineffective against this guy. Besides, I don't know if that is his real name or not or if he 'died' a century ago and just never resurfaced. No leads, no way to trace him, no witnesses," Martin said with a heavy sigh. He rubbed at the half pound of sand located behind each eyelid. "Even if they could find him and get something to stick, there's no way they could arrest him."

"They got you."

Martin looked out from under his fingers and then let his hand drop to his side, "I let myself be arrested. I didn't want to hurt any innocents. I can assure you that Straun has no such problem."

"That's the other thing," Grant said

Martin turned to look at him, "What thing?"

"The killing of innocents." Grant steepled his hands and looked at them for a moment. "When I killed that *thing* the other night, I had no problem with that and I'd do it again in a moment. But, what about those times that I see a human scumbag beat his wife or kid into a coma or worse. Or, when an innocent bystander gets gunned down in a drive by, and the shooter gets out on bail. Or, the rapist that gets his hand slapped and is put on probation. We bust them, turn around and see these walking cesspools back out on the street again. Sometimes I can't stand it." Grant looked at Martin with eyes longing for understanding. "It would be so easy for me to catch this trash out on bail or whatever and take them out. No more kids hurt, no more families with no father to come home to, and like you said, the police wouldn't be able to touch me."

Martin let the silence hang for a minute and then asked quietly, "Then why don't you do it?"

"I don't know."

"I think you do. You know that if you did, you'd be just as bad as those scumbags you're putting away."

"I suppose."

"Tell you what, let's knock off and since I can't offer you anything to eat, I can at least offer you a place to rest. Crash there in the chair or on the couch and I'll wake you later."

"Sounds good." Grant raised the footrest on the easy boy. "One more thing. You never told me why this guy's got it in for you."

Martin turned back to Grant. "That's the whole thing. I don't know. And, it's not just me. You know that network I told you about earlier. It extends across the U.S. and someone is killing off our members. I can only guess it's Straun. .

"We need to bag this guy," Grant said with finality in his voice. "I'll snoop around and see what I can find out about this butthead. Not only that, I'll check into your case as well."

"Just be careful," Martin's expression was grim. "That could be an awfully big can of worms you're opening up."

Just after sundown Martin woke Grant from where he had slept in the easychair. They stood just inside the open doorway, the fresh air of the evening pouring through the portal.

Grant looked at Martin and then stuck his hand out. "Thank you. I mean it."

"No problem," Martin said shaking the other's hand. "It's a pleasure to know you. By-the-way, I have something for you." Martin pulled a folded slip of paper from his pocket and handed it to Grant. "If anything happens to me or you need to talk to some-one, call one of these people on the list, tell them you know me, your particular *condition*, and they'll help in any way they can." Martin walked him out the door to where Grant's car was parked next to the curb. Martin shut the car door after Grant had climbed behind the wheel. "I'll talk to you soon. Take care."

Grant just nodded as he dropped the car in gear and pulled away from the curb.

Martin watched as the car made it's way down the street and then went to wake Julie.

Chapter 10

They stepped out the door of the small Italian eatery into the cool night air. The restaurant was nestled among a host of other shops, restaurants and pubs in an area popular with locals and tourists alike. Music from several of the establishments could be heard floating on the breeze.

"You know, it's funny. A person starts thinking about some of the things that they don't have and fail to notice the beauty of the things they do," Martin said as he looked up at the twinkling stars dancing above the tops of the buildings, much brighter to his field of visions then hers. "I feel—I feel so alive. Having an almost endless number of years to look forward to had taken the edge off of it. But, now I know I can look to every day with promise, and having had you here has made that possible."

"Wow, thanks." She snuggled closer to his arm she had been holding. "You're not usually this philosophical. What's the occasion?"

"It's just that I want to say thanks for all you've done, for all the time we've had together and I don't know how."

"Whoa, Doc. I mean, you're welcome and all, but you sound like you're leaving or something."

"That's because I am," he said without looking at her. "I've thought long and hard about this, and after talking to Grant, it drove the point home. I have to put a stop to us. Now. While you are still young enough to start over and find someone to spend your whole life with."

"Now wait just a damn minute!" Julie pulled her arm free and spun Martin to face her in the process. "Don't I have any say in this matter?"

"Not really." Martin took her arm and started down the walk once more. The other pedestrians populating the walk hadn't even noticed her outburst. "Besides, what would society think of a beautiful 26 year old living with someone who is old enough to be her great-great-great grandfather?"

"Stuff the humor, Martin." She grabbed his jacket and pulled him into a vacant doorway so that she could look into his face. "Now, tell me you want us to end. Look me right in the eyes and tell me you truly want us to end and I'll walk away from here, turn in my resignation and you'll never see me again."

Martin looked into her eyes and she could see the turmoil there. He started to say something, then spun and smashed his fist into the stone facing of the doorway, knocking out a large chunk.

"That's what I thought," she said. "Now let me see your hand. You probably broke every bone in it."

Martin pulled his hand free. "Not even close. You just don't understand, do you?" Running a hand through his hair he leaned back against the cool stonework. "With all the attention that has been heaped on me lately, Dr. Martin Daniel is going to have to meet a quiet and untimely demise."

"No," she said clasping his hand between her own.

"What with Straun hounding me every other step and the police now in the picture, I can't afford to have my face up everywhere. With the advancement of computers, it's harder and harder to avoid detection. Myself and the others like me, we pop up over and over through history under different names, lead quiet lives, and nobody notices. We do something grand and then everyone and their dog has an inquiring mind and they want to know. As it is, I'm sure the police have started finding discrepancies in my personal file. If everything got shut down today, I don't know that it would do any good." Martin looked down and absently pushed a stone around with the toe of his shoe. "Somebody is going to get real nosy, and want an appearance out of me. And, that would be a grand spectacle, I assure you."

"What do you mean?"

He looked at her sideways, "I never really explained it to you, did I?"

"Explain what?"

"Spontaneous human combustion."

"You were serious about that?"

"Like I said, it's one of those things that stumps modern science, or at least regular modern science. 'Cause the secret to the whole riddle is that it's one of us. The vampire either got careless or just gave up. At any rate, the end result is the same. In the presence of sunlight, cellular activity increases until spontaneous combustion occurs. Not one of the better ways to die, I assure you. Of course, when I finally die or something kills me, basically the same thing will occur in that when my bloodstream stops supplying my cells, they cannibalize themselves and set up the same reaction." Martin pushed away from the wall and stepped back onto the sidewalk. "All that's left is a neat little pile of ash." He looked back over his shoulder at Julie and said with a rueful smile, "I will say the movies got that part right."

"How do you know for sure that that is what happens?" she asked as they started down the walk once more.

"A friend of mine," Martin said trying to sound nonchalant as he pulled a leaf from the Maple tree they were passing under. He twirled the leaf in his fingers as he spoke, not looking at it, but at a different time. "He'd had enough and decided that he couldn't go on any longer." Martin swallowed hard as the memories dredged up emotions from the past. I received a letter in the mail telling me where I would find the camera and the film. He had enough of a scientific mind left to film his own demise in hopes that it would help me and others like himself. It hasn't."

"Ease up, Martin," she said patting his arm, "you can't go around carrying the guilt of the whole world on your shoulder."

He carried on not hearing her, "If nothing else, I will say he was an excellent photographer. The movie footage shows everything in great detail. It's quite spectacular actually. One minute, there appears to be a normal human being, and the next an extremely bright flame where the body was standing that seems to burn in on itself, then a small pile of very fine ash."

"That's all well and good, Martin, but what does it have to do with us?"

"It has everything to do with us. What kind of a life would you have to look forward to? You'd never be able to have friends over during the day. They'd wonder about your antisocial husband. Not to mention the fact that you would have a lot of explaining to do as to why you keep getting older and I look like I just decided to stay on my 29th birthday. I've lost too many people I've cared about to this thing and I won't let you become a part of it. You just don't understand the stakes involved."

"No, Martin, it's you that doesn't understand. I'm pushing thirty and you're the first man I have ever loved. I've dated, I've been around the block so it's not like I'm some wide-eyed doe that doesn't know which end is up. It's just that no one has ever appealed to me until you came along." She stopped him and took his face in her hands. "When I'm with you there's nothing I can't do. Just being around you makes me feel so . . . I don't know . . . so alive. I guess that best describes it. Being with you is just the right place for me and we both know it. You've ruined me, Martin Daniel; I could never be happy with another. There is no one else that could take your place."

"Jules, please don't. This is hard enough, don't make it harder."

"Why does it have to be hard? It could work for us."

"Could it really? It wouldn't be that long and people would start wondering if I had married an older woman. Then they would start to wonder if I was with my mother. We would have to move soon so that people we know wouldn't wonder why I wasn't aging. Listen, I saw what it did to Bill and Mary and I'm telling you, it just won't work!"

Martin paced back and forth on the walk like some restless feline, his heart and conscious warring with each other.

"I have waited this long for you," Julie said, "I'll be damned if I'm going to lose you now."

"That's just it, Jules, you've waited this long; I've waited over a hundred years. Even when I was married before, it was nothing like what I feel for you. It was another time and place unlike this one and I was a different person, yet I still didn't feel the way I do now." He looked at her as tears filled his eyes, "Oh, God, you don't know how hard this is. You've got to leave, Julie. Get out of the city until this thing is over, one way or another. It's me that everyone is after, not you. When it's over I'll send word to you and then when you get back," he closed his eyes against the pain, "I'll be gone."

Julie watched him for a moment and then set her jaw, "There is another way—you could infect me."

Martin's pacing ceased immediately, and his whispered response was barely audible on the evening breeze.

"No."

"Yes, Martin. It would work. I know it would."

"Think about the dog the other night, Julie," Martin said looking her in the eyes. "Remember the one that I drained the life out of and then threw away like a used Dixie cup."

"Look, Martin, I know what you're trying to do. It won't work. And, if I'm willing to take the risk then . . ."

Martin slung his head from side-to-side and turned away from her. "No. No, no, no. Absolutely not. I won't—I can't."

"Why?"

"It's too dangerous. I don't know if you could handle the mutation the way that I did."

"But, that's just it," she said sliding her arms

around his waist, "you'd be there for me every step of the way."

"Yes, I would be there for you," he said turning inside the circle of her arms to face her. He stood for a moment staring into her face, tracing her eyebrows and the line of her jaw with his finger. With a sigh that hinted at the pain that was tearing his heart to pieces he took her hands in his.

"But, there is the chance that you couldn't handle the mutation. That you would become twisted, become something I could no longer reach. Then I would be forced to kill you, and please believe me that I would kill you—just as surely as I would kill myself afterward. I don't won't that kind of responsibility."

With determination in her voice she said, "Whatever the risks. Understand?"

Martin looked at her and then turned and started up the street, a crushed maple leaf falling from his grasp.

She heard someone scream. They screamed again and this time it was closer. When the scream came the third time, Julie realized that it came from her own throat. Martin came bursting through the door expecting to find Straun or his thugs. What he saw made him wish he had. Julie lay in the middle of the bedroom floor, her body contorting this way and that, her muscles no longer obeying her commands. He took in the whole scene in an instant. There, lying on the floor beside her, was the spent hypodermic. Through tear streaked eyes she saw Martin and tried to say something but her jaw would not unclamp. She lay helpless against the onslaught of contractions that racked her body.

"I didn't know it would hurt like this," she cried through clenched teeth.

Chapter 11

Blinding colors flared in her mind and every cell was on fire. The pain was beyond belief. She was burning up from the inside out and there was no escape. As she writhed in agony, something cool touched her forehead and a voice thundered in the distance. She willed her eyes to open, then screamed as white-hot light knifed into her brain. Through her distorted field of vision, she saw someone kneeling beside her, holding the cool thing to her head. His face loomed over her, and she felt she should recognize him. His voice was a distorted baritone rumbling in her ears, causing them to ring and ache unmercifully. And the drums, or whatever that damnable pounding was. It went on and on. A constant pounding that just wouldn't stop! A small part of her mind freed itself from the pain long enough to realize that the pounding was caused by her own heart. But, that wasn't the only sound that assaulted her. She could hear hundreds of creaks and chirps, moans and groans; the settling of the house that made it sound like it was alive. Someone had taken a hundred sound effect tracks, plugged them into her head, and turned them up full volume. And that was only part of the misery. Smells of all types, most that she had never known existed, stormed her olfactory senses all at once causing her to gag and retch. From somewhere, a small draft entered the room and sand blasted her skin making her cry out. Then the pain was back. Starting in the pit of her stomach, it rolled through her body like a tsunami destroying everything in its path. The pain was all-consuming. There was no getting away from it and no part of her that didn't feel it. She wished for death, for anything that would take her away from the pain. Then the booming voice was there again, cutting through the pounding and the rest of the din. She strained to see where the voice was coming from. He was there, swimming in her field of vision. His face expanded and split in two and reformed once more. She recognized that face. She remembered him. She remembered a syringe and then the pain. The PAIN. It was his fault. His!

Julie sought to launch herself at this man who had caused her so much pain. But, it did her no good. Martin had anticipated her reaction and secured her to the bed with reinforced restraints of his own design.

Then something else emerged from the middle of the pain. Something she couldn't identify. An urge. A desire for something. She didn't know what. A desire that grew in intensity until it rivaled the pain.

Suddenly she knew with utter clarity what she wanted. Her eyes widened and rolled to look at Martin like some utterly mad animal. She opened her mouth to emit a snarling hiss and revealed a pair of gleaming white fangs

"My God, Jules, what have you done?"

Martin could only sit and watch helplessly as the disease spread through her body and warped her mind to the breaking point.

"Doc," Julie croaked, her voice little more than a hoarse whisper, "you look like shit."

Martin's eyes snapped open from where he had dozed off. His face spoke volumes as a smile spread across his face.

"I'm sorry, I've been preoccupied lately."

"Ohhh man. You look like I feel," she rasped out. "How long?"

"Shh." He patted her hand. "There will be time enough to talk later. A few thousand years to say the least. To answer you though, it's been a week. You haven't been out the whole time, you just won't remember a lot of it."

"Oh, God, Martin." She reached out a hand to touch the side of his face, but found it still restrained to the bed. She watched as the tissue pulsed and moved like a thing alive on the side of his face, replacing his cheek where it had been ripped off.

"You're stronger than you look. One of the restraints broke. Had a hell of a time getting you back in one."

"I am so sorry, I . . . "

"Don't worry about it. My fault actually. I zigged when I should have zagged. Besides, it should be healed up by morning."

Julie thought to herself how massive a tissue loss Martin must have suffered. She wanted to hug him fiercely. "I could have killed you and then it would have been for not."

"But, you didn't," he said stroking her hair. "No more questions. Here, drink this."

He held a glass to her lips as he propped her head up with the other hand. The liquid was room temperature. It was thick, slightly salty and was the most satisfying drink she had ever had in her life. Her eyes held the unspoken question as she took one more drink from the glass and then lay back against the pillows.

"Yes," Martin told her matter of fact, "It's what you think it is." She could just hear him as she slipped out of consciousness. "It's what you need."

The next time Julie woke, the restraints were gone and she lay on fresh bedding. The room held a pleasant, if somewhat antiseptic, odor. She lay for a while letting her senses stretch beyond the room. She heard the shuffle of sock feet on a tile floor along with the soft clatter of kitchen utensils, and then recognized Martin's footsteps. Odors and sounds assailed her from every direction. But, this time it was different. They didn't seek to overwhelm her as they had earlier. No, this time she was able to sort each one and identify it's source.

"Good morning," Martin said as he carried in a tray loaded with O.J., muffins, poached eggs, and a rose. And, one six-ounce glass of blood. "You look much better."

"Thanks, Martin. I made it pretty rough on you, didn't I?"

He set the tray down and patted her arm. "You had me worried a couple of times. But, you pulled through just fine."

"I'll say you look better, too. The last time I remember seeing you, half your face was gone and the rest of you looked like warmed over death."

"Half is a little exaggerated and I'll take the rest

as a compliment." He fluffed the napkin and placed it in her lap. "Now eat."

She looked at the dark liquid in a clinical fashion. She was a little surprised that the thought of drinking blood didn't nauseate her.

"I think I'll just have the staple. The rest looks good, but not really appetizing, if you know what I mean," she said as she picked up the glass and drank it straight down.

"Eat some of the other. It will help you keep a perspective on life. Besides, it's great for your figure. Heck, this stuff is better than Weight Watchers. You can eat all the usual foodstuffs you want and you won't gain an ounce. In fact, you'll starve to death. Oh, you could eat a really rare steak in a restaurant and gain some nourishment there, but not enough. A bright point though," he said handing her the fork and getting to his feet, "is that food will taste better, or worse, depending on whether or not you liked it in the first place."

Julie was surprised to find that Martin was right. It was as if she had been eating cardboard all her life. She offered him a raised eyebrow in appreciation.

"Glad you like it. As soon as you finish, get your butt out of bed 'cause we got lots 'o work ta do." Martin smiled over his shoulder as he left the room and ducked the English muffin she hurled after him.

"Pretty good reflexes for such an old fart," she said around a mouthful of egg.

Martin laughed as he walked down the hall and thought to himself that after such a long time, it was indeed good to be alive—even in an altered state.

A short while later Julie emerged from the bedroom to find Martin sitting in the living room floor, so engrossed in reading a stack of papers, that he didn't even look up when she came in the room. She stood in the doorway for a minute then went to stand in front of him, finally giving him a loud 'Ahem.'

"Jules," he said waving the papers around, motioning to her, "you're not going to believe this. It's absolutely fantastic."

"You got a refund on your federal this year. I don't know, what?"

"Notes, Jules, notes."

Julie looked at the papers in his hand as what he was saying sank in. "You mean . . . "

"That's exactly what I mean." Martin jumped up and started showing her the hand written notes and computer printouts. "I was going to do some cleaning while you slept and came across a bunch of old papers and stuff. I started to throw them out just now, when the top one caught my eye. I thought that I had transcribed all these and thrown them away. Do you know what this means?" Martin grabbed Julie by the waist and spun her around. "We're back in business."

"Great," said Julie. "Let's head back from wherever here is and get busy."

"Can't do that Jules."

"Why?"

Martin laid the papers down on the end table and took both of her hands in his. "You're no ready yet."

"Don't be silly," she said. "I've never felt better in my life."

"I don't doubt that a bit, but the fact is, you're not ready." Martin gave her a peck on the bridge of her nose. "There's more to it than just feeling good. You have to learn to control your emotions."

"What, you're going to turn me into a Vulcan?" she asked holding up the familiar split V sign.

"Seriously, do you remember the urges you got during the transformation? Those urges will come upon you from time to time and you are going to have to be able to control them. You'll understand more of what I'm talking about later when you start to get hungry or upset."

"Well, you've gotten me this far," Julie leaned forward kissing him lightly on the lips, "so I trust you to take me the rest of the way. And, thanks earlier for the breakfast. It was great. By the way," she asked with a stone serious face, "do I still have to brush my teeth?"

"Only if you don't want halitosis."

Julie laughed and started to pull away when Martin pulled her back. "A couple of other things and these are for real. One: you're used to just leaving the house whenever you please. You can't do that anymore. If you should forget during the day and pop open the front door, it's all over. Also, fire is a very real hazard. Not only can it kill you because of the massive tissue damage it's capable of, but what if the house catches on fire during the day. Your imagination can fill in the blanks. All the exit doors here at the cabin have dead bolts. While you were out, I made up some signs for the doors. Not that you couldn't rip them off their hinges, but they'll act as a reminder before you open the door."

"You really do care about me, don't you?" She punctuated the question with another kiss, this one lingering longer and a bit more full than the last.

Martin looked into her eyes losing himself there.

"More than you'll ever know." When he returned her kiss it was filled with unbridled passion.

As they stood there with their arms wrapped around each other, their lips pressed together, Julie's senses took flight. She could detect the musty odor of Martin's pheromones as he became aroused. She was acutely aware of her own odor as well and realized that she had never become so aroused so fast.

"Oh, God, Martin. I thought that you used to turn me on. This is unbelievable." She shivered as he kissed his way down her neck and her breath was coming in short pants. "I want you inside me so bad I can't stand it."

Martin picked her up in his arms and made his way toward the bedroom. Once in the room he sat her gently on her feet and then took her face in his hands, pulling her to him once more. Julie's hands caressed his back through the fabric of his shirt while Martin slowly sought and unbuttoned each clasp on her shirt. When the last of the buttons gave way, he broke the kiss and slowly slid the shirt off her shoulders letting it flutter to the floor. Martin reached behind her and undid the hook on her brassiere, and achingly slow, slid the straps down her arms and pulled the cups away from her breasts. Julie inhaled sharply as the cool air hit the hot skin of her chest, causing her to shudder.

Martin held out his hand. "Right now, though, we need to get you cleaned up. I washed your face and changed the linen, but the rest of you could use a good scrubbing." He smiled at her. "It's been awhile since you bathed."

Julie wrinkled her nose slightly. "I am kinda rank." She tested the air again. "There's something else. Something I've never smelled before."

"That's you and me."

"What do you mean, you and me?"

"When you're transformed, you acquire a particular odor, just like humans have a particular odor, as do different animals. That's what you're smelling now. All of us smell this way, with slight differences of course. You'll be surprised by what you'll be able to smell. You'll be the best looking bloodhound on the block."

"Thanks. I think."

Martin led the way into the bathroom and started the shower running. "Your bath awaits you, M'Lady." He slid the door open as he made a courtly bow.

As he straightened up, Julie looked into his eyes. "Only if you join me."

"My pleasure," he said moving slowly to her. He cupped her face in his hands and lowered his lips to hers. Julie's breath caught as their lips made contact, igniting the passion once more deep inside her. His hands slid down her neck, to her shoulders, and gently down her arms. Julie shivered in ecstasy and anticipation as he glided his hands over the smooth skin of her breasts. Martin broke contact, shed his clothes, and stepped into the tub pulling her after him. He turned her into the shower, letting the warm stream wash over her. Martin poured a fair amount of shampoo on her hair and worked it into a lather. Julie sighed and let the sensations take her. He rinsed the lather from her hair and then produced a bar of soap and proceeded to wash the rest of her. She was caught in a whirlwind of sensations, torn between the relaxation caused by his massaging hands and the feelings of arousal fanned by his tender caresses. When she thought she would melt, Martin announced she was done.

"On the contrary," she said pressing her body to his, "I'm just getting started."

Julie kissed him fiercely and then stepped out of the tub, urging him to hurry.

"What about toweling off?" he said as she practically drug him from the tub.

"Trust me, you won't need one. As hot as I feel, you'll probably get steam burns."

Once in the bedroom, Martin and Julie fell together, desperate to explore each other. When, at last, he entered her, it was like nothing she had ever experienced in her life. She had made love and had sex in her life, but they were pale comparisons to what she was experiencing now.

Afterwards, they lay together, her head resting on his chest as she idly stroked his skin.

"You are simply amazing," she said softly.

"Like I've said, being a vampire has certain advantages."

"No, that's not what I mean. Yea, you might be able to go longer than the average Joe, but that doesn't give you the insight and the passion or the genuine concern that you have. That comes from you." She lightly kissed his neck. "Thank you."

Martin stroked her hair. "I'm flattered. But, you give me too much credit. It's not me. It's us. We work well together."

She stretched, luxuriating in the afterglow of their lovemaking. "Work is a key word there. I'm going to have to take another shower."

Martin laughed softly. "Tomorrow, or the next day, when you're ready, that's when the real work will start. After we get back." He looked at her and then grew quiet.

"You all right?" she asked after a few moments

Martin smiled and looked away. "It's been such a long time," he said softly, "since I've felt this way."

It had been a long time for Martin; a lifetime ago. He remembered a young woman lying in his arms much like now, hair flowing down her back in an ebony waterfall, the candlelight reflected in her eyes. They had been newlyweds, discovering each other. He thought of the young woman who was now no more than a pile of dust somewhere in a poorly marked grave, while he looked not a day older.

"You look like you're very far away right now. Care to share?" she asked.

"Oh, just musing about the whims of the Fates, and how things work out." He laid his head back and stared at the ceiling. "At one time in my life I thought I was happy and content. I don't know, perhaps I was. But, now, I'm—complete. I have lived several lifetimes and just now know what that feels like. Thank you." Martin ran his hand through her hair and looked into her eyes. "I have been through living hell several times in my existence, but I'd do it all again in a heartbeat to share this moment with you."

Julie hugged him closer. "I love you Martin Daniels."

Martin relaxed with one hand behind his head, the other wrapped around her, staring at nothing as he listened to Julie's breathing become slow and regular. "Maybe things are looking up," he thought as he drifted off to some of the most restful sleep he had experienced in over a hundred years.

Chapter 12

The trip back to the city proved to be an eventful one as they made their way to Julie's house.

Once inside, Martin phoned Bill while Julie went to settle their stuff. Martin was too excited about coming across the notes that he couldn't wait to tell his friend. He fidgeted like a kid needing to go to the restroom as he waited for Bill to pick up the receiver.

"Hello, Bill?"

"Martin, is that you?"

"Yea, buddy, it's me. Long time no hear, huh?" Martin said sheepishly.

"My god, man, where are you and are you all right? Are you safe? Things have taken a turn for the worse, I'm afraid." Bill was frantic in his speech. "They're after you, you know."

"Whoa, slow down," Martin managed to override Bill's deluge of dialogue. "What's bad and who's after me now?"

"The police." Bill spoke as if it were common knowledge. "They've been asking everyone about you and your whereabouts. Julie's too. Is she with you?"

"No," Martin lied. He felt bad about lying to his

friend, but if he said yes, then Bill would start asking questions about her and he just wasn't ready to tell him or anyone else about her yet. "I haven't seen her since I left. I told her it was better if she put distance between us until this whole thing was cleared up." At least that part was the truth. "What do the police want now?"

"Namely, your arrest," Bill said in his matter-of-fact style.

"Do what? They already arrested me and I'm out on bond."

"That was for theft of lab property. This is much more serious. They found narcotics in your lab."

"Bullshit."

"I know, I know. I don't believe it either." Worry for his friend was evident in his voice. "All I do know is that they're after you. They have this idea that you might be running one of the large supply labs in this area."

Martin sat down heavily on the couch. "Cripes. When do I get a break? About the time I think something is going right, I get dumped on again. When did this take place?"

"The police contacted me four days past. I have the feeling that they thought you skipped town." Bill paused for a moment. "I have to admit I was beginning to wonder myself."

"You're kidding!"

"I couldn't believe that you would be mixed up with something like that, but you've got to admit that it looks bad."

"I suppose. I will say that Straun is working overtime with this one. He or someone is intent on taking me out of the picture and I have no idea why." Disgusted, Martin sat for a moment staring at the ceiling, silence on the other end as Bill let him gather his thoughts. "I guess I'd better phone Grant and tell him what's happening and see if there's anything he can do about it."

"Do I know this Grant?"

"I doubt it." Martin sat up and put his arm around Julie as she joined him on the couch. He motioned for her to be quiet. She nodded and then scooted down to lay her head in his lap. "Met the guy recently in a most unusual manner. I thought he was one of Straun's goons working for the P.D. Luckily I was wrong."

Bill's interest perked up. "He's a police officer and he's . . . one of us?"

"Yea. Pretty resourceful guy. Good head on his shoulders. You'll like him."

"I look forward to meeting him."

"But, let me interject a ray of sunshine here. I found a copy of my notes."

"You what?"

"Yea, can you believe it?" Martin's enthusiasm bubbled up. "Came across them and they're an early set, but they're pretty much complete. I get this cop crap straightened up and we're back in business."

"Well, this is most interesting news. When you are ready, let me know. Until then, if there is anything I can do for you, call."

Bill broke the connection and Martin thumbed the switch hook on the receiver and looked down at Julie.

"Do you know how hard it is to carry on a conversation with you lying with your head where it is?"

"No. How 'hard' is it?"

"Pretty hard."

Julie laughed. "You're incredible. You're now

wanted for drug trafficking and you can still take time to get an erection."

"It doesn't take much time where you're concerned. But, you're right. I've got to call Grant."

Martin took his thumb off the receiver and dialed Grant's number.

"I've been expecting you," Grant's voice came over the line.

"What? Is everyone waiting for me to call?"

"That I wouldn't know about," Grant chuckled.

Julie got to her feet and headed out of the room. "I'm just going to leave you boys alone. I have to visit the little girl's room."

"Tell Julie I said, 'Hello.'"

"Grant says hello."

"I heard him," Julie called over her shoulder as she waved a greeting.

Martin paused for a moment collecting his thoughts. "I understand that I'm in it deep with the law—again."

"Maybe you are and maybe you're not."

"Care to elaborate?"

Martin clapped his hands together and danced a little jig after he hung up the phone. Julie came into the room with a puzzled look on her face. Martin grabbed her and spun her around, finishing the move with a deft dip that left his face just inches above hers.

"You just win the lottery," she asked in the middle of the dip.

"Better." He kissed her soundly and then stood her back on her feet. "That Grant is a sweetheart. You know all that 'hard' evidence that they found linking me as a major drug lord? Well, Grant smelled a setup, and all that evidence just happened to disappear from lockup last night."

Julie's eyes widened in surprise. "He took the stuff?"

"He didn't say that. He just let me know that it's missing. And, he says that without it, they'll have to drop the charges. Imagine that."

Martin swaggered into the living room. "It's about time something went our way."

He spun around unexpectedly and almost crashed into Julie who had been tailing him.

"Why don't you grab a couple of things and we'll go on over to my place and see about getting set up. That way we don't have to drive all the way over to Bill's"

"What about the other charges? Won't they have to be settled first?"

"That's the other thing. While we were away, the good D.A.'s office did their job and found that everything was on the up and up. As far as the stolen lab equipment that is." Martin was buzzing with excitement.

"You think that's a good idea? Going to your house and all?" Julie perched on the arm of the couch and pulled her knees up under her chin, looking like a modern gargoyle on a nogahyde edifice. "I hate to be a weenie, but what about Straun?"

Martin paused ever so slightly to ponder the question. "He already tried to get us that route. I don't think we have anything to worry about."

He walked briskly past her.

"Where are you going now?"

"To call Bill again. Tell him the bit of good news."

Chapter 13

A couple of hours later, Martin and Julie pulled into the drive and looked at the dark hulk that was his house. They walked hand in hand to the front door and Martin reached for the police line tape that barricaded the doorway.

"You think that's a good idea?" Julie fidgeted from foot to foot.

Martin gave her a droll look. "What are they going to do, arrest me? If they haven't dropped the charges already it's just a matter of time. Unfortunately, we don't have time to spare." Martin ripped the tape out of the way and inserted his key into the dead lock. He paused for a moment as he turned the locking mechanism. He didn't remember the lock working that smoothly and wondered if it had been locked at all. Martin gave a mental shrug and pushed open the door.

They were immediately assaulted by the ransacked remains of his once tidy house. They gingerly made their way through what was left of the living room on their way to the kitchen. Julie stuck her head into the study and let out a low, steady stream of curses as she looked at where the volumes of antique books and other valuables were strewn across the floor.

Martin appraised the wreckage with a cold eye as he went. "I wonder if all of this was done by the cops or by Straun's men." He pushed some books out of the way with the toe of his shoe.

"I don't know, but I'd like to find out who did it, shove a broom up their ass and let them clean this mess."

Martin smiled in the darkness. Once more, Julie was able to lift his spirits without really trying. Her coarseness when she was angry was one of the things that attracted him to her. That, and the fact that she didn't subscribe to puffed up etiquette and pompous protocol. If she had something to say, she was going to be heard. And, she could be extremely succinct in her delivery.

He made his way across the kitchen without bothering to flip on the lights, not wanting to attract any undue attention.

"I wonder if they confiscated my equipment or just demolished it?" he said to Julie who stood a few feet behind him in the middle of the kitchen with her hands on her hips, her purse slung over her shoulder, a disgusted look on her face. Martin opened the door to the stairwell and was instantly awash in natural gas as it came flooding out of the basement where it had built up.

Martin stood rooted for a moment as the notion of what was happening hit him.

"RUN!"

He turned and bolted for the back door, grabbing Julie as he went, forcing her ahead of him. Time screamed to a halt as each footfall took eons to find it's way to the floor. Martin focused all his being on making the doorway that seemed to be a million miles away. All the while, the jets in the basement pumped out the lethal gas from where they had been opened or knocked completely off. They made it across the kitchen and literally dove through the back door as the gas found an ignition source.

The force of the explosion hurled them through the night air and slammed them into the grassy turf. The blast tore the roof off the house and fractured every wall. Martin and Julie lay stunned, the sound of thunder crashing and reverberating in their skulls.

Martin held his ears, blood running through his fingers from where his eardrums had ruptured from the concussion. He gritted his teeth as his body started to rebuild itself and began to hear a ringing that turned into a chorus of beeps, honks and whistles and realized that he was hearing car alarms from up and down the street.

"Jules," he croaked out, "Jules, we've got to get out of here. Now." He rolled to his stomach and started to rise, then collapsed just as quickly as pain shot through the back of his leg.

Julie shook her head to clear her vision and saw the table leg protruding from the back of Martin's thigh.

"Oh, God, Martin, are you all right?"

"Pull it out. Hurry."

Julie realized the predicament they were in and grabbed the wood with one hand and placed her other on Martin's leg where the wood emerged. She paused for a heart beat, took a deep breath and pulled.

Martin grunted as she yanked the wood from his body. Blood spewed from the hole in his leg. He fought down the blinding pain and pushed himself to his feet, Julie supporting him as they made their way around the burning rubble.

"I suppose that it would have been too much to ask that nothing would have happened to it," Martin said as they slowed to look at the burned out shell of his car.

People poured out of several of the houses while others cautiously slid the drapes aside and peered into the night to see what had rocked their quiet, sheltered world. Martin and Julie blended as best they could as they made their way out of the neighborhood.

"We need to find a pay phone." Martin limped along side Julie as fast as prudently possible, not wanting to attract any undue attention. "This is one time that I wish I owned a cellular."

"Why," Julie asked. "It'd be just as blown up right now as your car."

"Well, there is that."

At the sound of an approaching siren, they turned to face the glow that could be seen in the night sky and acted as if they were headed in that direction until the patrol car sped past.

As they spun back the direction they had been traveling, Martin's gait steadily improved and their hearing returned to normal.

"Martin, what about all your things?"

"Their gone. Not a thing we can do about that right now. At, least the notes are safe. You do have your bag?"

Julie answered by hefting the large satchel.

Martin managed a lopsided grin. "Well, I will say that you were right and that it wasn't a good idea to go to the house. And, yes, I would definitely say Straun had a hand in it."

"But, why?"

"I don't' know, Jules." Martin shrugged. "But, I'm sure a psychologist today would say that it's not his fault." Martin perked up. "I've got it. It was the shock and the trauma of being bitten that make him act out these scenes of aggression. It was that or his mother made him eat all his spinach. All he needs is a little love and understanding."

Julie ignored the attempt at humor. "Bingo. Pay phone dead ahead."

"All right." Martin began fishing for change in his pocket. "We call Bill and tell him to pick us up and then we find out just what the hell is going on around here."

He impatiently waited for the dial tone then fumed as it took forever for the call to go through. Julie watched up and down the street for the police or anyone else that might take an interest in the pair. She glanced back at Martin and saw the look of bewilderment on his face.

"What?"

"I must have keyed the wrong number." He retrieved the change and tried again making certain to hit the right numbers. Martin's brow furrowed in concern. "It says that the number is no longer in service."

"What, he didn't pay his phone bill?" Julie didn't like the sick feeling that was clawing it's way into her guts.

Martin fed the money into the slot for the third time and phoned Bill's lab.

An automated answering service greeted Martin at the other end of the connection and he hastily entered Bill's extension number.

"Hematology, Jenkins."

"Matt, let me talk to Bill, please."

"Martin? Is that you? Oh, geez man, you haven't heard?" Matt's voice was a jumble of words as they fell over each other in their haste to get out.

Martin's stomach fell. "Heard what?"

"He's dead, man. He died today. You didn't hear about it on the news? It was all over the air man."

"I . . . wasn't near a T.V. today. What happened?"

Julie picked up on the conversation and came to stand beside Martin and took his free hand in hers.

"It was an explosion." Matt was almost breathless in his explanation. "His house had a gas leak or something. The whole place blew up. It was just gone, man."

The feeling in Martin's stomach hit bottom and an icy ball started to grow there. "You say that it happened today? What time?"

"About noon. We didn't find out about it until this evening, on the news and all, man. I know you guys were close and I'm really sorry, Martin."

He didn't even hear Matt as he hung the receiver back in its cradle. Martin stared at the phone and slowly became aware of Julie's hand in his.

"I'm sorry, too, Martin. I know what it's like to loose someone."

"I'll be okay. I promise. It's just that there's no hope. He's gone. The house was bombed during the day. If he survived the blast, he died in the light." Martin took a deep breath. "Not only that, the fact that it blew up during the day means that they quite possibly have the formula."

"Oh, shit."

"Exactly."

Martin closed his eyes. His friend was gone. There was no denying it. He felt the realization bare down on him threatening to crush him with the weight of the situation. Bill had been snuffed out today, yet Martin knew that, although brighter than most, Bill had been only one candle in a ball ablaze with light. Martin looked out into the night. Absorbed it. Took in the myriad lights, sounds and smells emanating from the dark. He stood marveling at the amount of life there. From the crickets at his feet to the lights that were mere pinpoints in the distance. As he watched the night, he whispered softly to himself:

*"When, in disgrace with fortune and men's eyes
I all alone beweep my outcast state,
And trouble deaf heaven with my bootless
cries, . . ."*

"Martin? Are you all right," Julie asked softly.

Martin's mind snapped back with clarity. "Just focusing, that's all. My father used to tell me that if you have your health, there's nothing that you can't live through." He bowed his head slightly, remembering and smiled. "Of course, he also said that sometimes it would hurt like a son-of-a-bitch, but you could make it through."

"One of those, whatever doesn't kill you, makes you stronger deals?"

"Something like that. Got another quarter? We're going to need a taxi."

"Where to Kemo Sabe?" Julie asked handing over the coins.

"Your place."

Julie's shoulders slumped. "I got that feeling again."

"I know, but we need some things, transportation among them, and we can't stand out here on the phone all night. We need to meet with Grant and see if we can hole up at his place." Martin glanced at his watch. "And, the clock is running."

Julie took a deep breath. "I trust you."

Martin brushed the side of her cheek gently. "Hey, were both healthy."

Julie and Martin sat together in silence for the few minutes until the taxi arrived. Martin cast a probing look about them before settling into the back of the cab. He continued to look out the window as the taxi started down the street.

"Do you think they're out there?"

"What? No. At least I don't think so. But," he shrugged his shoulders, "you never know."

Julie slid closer to him relishing the warmth and closeness of his body. Her hand found his and squeezed softly with affection.

"Things are real bad, aren't they?"

Martin answered without looking at her. "Yes."

The cab slowed to a stop in front of Julie's house. Before the cabby could quote the fair, Martin laid a hand on his shoulder. "Keep the motor running. I'll only be a minute."

"Sure thing." The cab driver shifted the gear lever to park and settled back in the seat to wait.

Martin stepped out of the cab and stopped Julie as she was about to follow him.

"If I'm not back in two minutes," Martin said in a voice too low for the cabbie to hear, "you leave. Understand? Don't come look for me, don't get out of the cab for any reason. If someone besides me approaches the cab tell the cabby that he's your ex and is out to kill you. In any event, just leave, don't wait for me. If I'm not back in two, chances are there's nothing you could do for me anyway."

Julie just nodded in response and watched tight lipped as Martin cautiously approached the house and stepped through the doorway.

The seconds drug by, time stretching to the breaking point. Julie fidgeted in the seat, unwanted images of Martin's mutilated body heaved their way to the front of her psyche. She looked at her watch once more as the time rapidly approached the two-minute mark. She grabbed the door handle and then released it just as quickly. Julie cursed to herself and grabbed the handle once more. What if he needed her and she didn't know. She pulled the handle and was halfway out the door when a hand stopped the door.

"Going somewhere?" Martin asked smiling at her. He leaned down to pay the fare and threw the cabby an extra ten.

The pair were already in the house before the cabby could pull away from the curb. The driver checked his rearview, stopped the car, and looked around in bewilderment when he didn't see the pair anywhere in sight. The cabby turned in his seat to get a better view, looking up and down the street to see any signs of the pair but saw no one. "Damn, they must have been *real* horny."

Inside the house Martin quickly thumbed through his day planner and found Grant's pager number, phoned him and then replaced the receiver.

"I just hope he can put us up for the night. At any rate, while we're waiting, let's get some things together." Martin followed Julie into the bedroom and retrieved a gym bag out of the closet.

"We definitely need to warn him of the recent turn of events. If they do have the formula, then none of us are safe. And, if he's been sniffing around about Straun, then they could stumble onto his secret as well and he would be in the same boat as us." Martin threw the couple of changes of clothing he kept in Julie's closet, along with his personal articles into the bag and zipped it shut, resting both his hands against the mattress, deep in thought.

Julie was busy doing the same, and they both jumped a foot into the air when the phone rang.

"Damn," Martin grumbled. "I'm as jumpy as a long tailed cat in a room full of rocking chairs." He was to the phone before the second ring and hesitated a moment before picking up the receiver. He held it to his ear without saying anything.

"This is officer Grant Pierce. Who is this?"

The tension washed out of Martin and Julie both.

"Grant, man, am I glad to hear your voice."

"What's going on? Are you two okay? I heard there was an explosion at your place."

"How did you know that?" Suspicion crept into the back of his mind.

"I'm in my cruiser. It came on the air. It was your place then? Are you all right?"

Martin mentally slapped himself for being such a dolt. Of course Grant would have access to information like that before anyone else. Martin wondered if he had any information on Bill's death.

"We're fine, sort of. But, we've got to meet. There's some stuff I need to tell you. Things are bad and they're getting worse. Bills' dead, they just missed us and it appears that they have the formula. I was hoping that we could stay at your place. It'd just be for a day. I've got a little cabin, but I don't want to go there before talking to you and I won't have time to do both."

Martin held his breath at the silence on the other end of the line. Finally Grant spoke again.

"I hate to involve Christine this way, but I also know she'd kill me if she found out that I turned you down. Besides, I kinda like you guys."

"Thanks Grant. Where do you live and we'll meet you there."

"No. We'll meet somewhere else and I'll take you there. It's safer that way."

"You're the expert here," Martin said. "Where and when do we meet?'

Martin jotted down notes as Grant gave directions.

"Can you be there in, say thirty minutes, just below the underpass?"

Martin calculated, "It'll be close, but yeah, I think we can do it."

"I'll see you there."

Martin replaced the receiver. "I've got to use the bathroom and gather the rest of my stuff."

Martin was still in the bathroom when he thought he heard voices. "Did you say something, Jules?"

"No."

Martin washed his face and hands and was toweling off when he was sure he heard Julie's voice and the sound of the receiver being replaced. He gathered his belongings and stepped into the living room to find Julie putting the finishing touches on her bag.

She glanced up as he entered the room and smiled.

"Is everything all right?" He had a very peculiar feeling about the whole situation as he looked at her.

"Yea. Everything is set here."

"O.K. then, let's do it."

They backed out of the drive in Julie's car, the headlights illuminating the front of the house.

"Do you think we'll ever see it again?" she asked.

"The house? I don't know, Jules. I hope so." Martin shifted the car into drive and shot off into the night.

Chapter 14

He glanced at his watch, while weaving in and out of traffic as he made their way to the proper exit ramp.

"We're a little late," Martin said as they came to a stop at the bottom of the ramp. The area was not one of the more savory spots in the city. Trash littered the street and the lamps at the street corners no longer functioned. The few buildings in the area, like the overpass itself were in dire need of repair.

"This place gives me the creeps," Julie said looking around. "Why would he want to meet here?"

"More than likely because it's just off the freeway with easy access and probably in the general direction of his house. Or, maybe he was hungry. But, why not ask him?" Martin pointed to the parked police car that sat in the shadows of the underpass. Martin steered the car towards Grant's cruiser. As they approached, radio traffic could be heard coming from his car. They were upon the cruiser before they realized Grant wasn't sitting behind the wheel and that light smoke was drifting out of the open window. Martin jammed the brakes and sprang from the car with Julie close behind. He crossed to the cruiser and looked inside the driver's window. There, in the burned out front seat and on the floorboard, was a pile of fine white ash with a singed gun belt, badge, and wallet lying amidst the powder.

Martin reached through the window and then abruptly stood up.

"What? What is it?"

"They're here." Martin backed away from the cruiser and started to their car.

"No way," Julie said as she chanced a quick glance inside the police car and blanched. She turned and sprinted to catch up to Martin. As they reached the car, someone fell from the overpass above and landed feet first on the trunk, just as two more vampires landed behind them.

Without hesitation Martin brought up Grant's 9mm and put three slugs into the vampire on the car causing him to flip over backwards.

Julie was as surprised as their attackers at Martin being armed.

Martin didn't hesitate, and turned on the other two before they could react. Julie stood frozen as Martin fired shots on both sides of her. The bullets knocked their attackers off balance and Martin pressed his advantage home as he emptied the clip into the two bodies on the ground making sure they would never rise again. Julie still stood opened mouth as Martin turned and walked back to her car, reached inside and retrieved his walking stick. Unsheathing the blade, he walked around the back of the car to where the first vampire writhed on the ground, a gaping hole in his head that his regenerative system was trying desperately to close. Without hesitation, Martin grabbed him by the hair and pulled him to a sitting position, stepped back and swung the sword with both hands. The blade bit through the other's neck, causing the headless torso to pitch backwards, the head landing in its lap. Martin straightened, wiped the blade on the dead vampire's pant leg and turned to Julie.

"Let's go. We've got to get out of here."

"What about Grant?" Julie asked as she climbed into the car.

"He's gone. They'll think that someone killed him and unsuccessfully tried to torch the car." Martin gunned the motor and shot through the deserted intersection, fishtailing as he went and rocketed up the entrance ramp.

"Where are we going?" Julie hung on to the bar above the door as Martin swerved around a car that wasn't moving fast enough. "We can't go back to my place. How about a motel?"

"The cabin. We still have time. Barely. We can't take the chance on the motels being full. Besides, we need someplace were we can hole up for a couple of days and think some things through. If they can get to Bill and now Grant, then we're in deeper than I thought."

"Oh."

Julie looked out the front window and stared at the white dashes blurring past them.

Martin turned off the asphalt and shot up the gravel access road. The sky was starting to pale as they neared the dirt drive leading to the cabin. Julie held on to the door handle with one hand and the ceiling with the other as Martin slid through the turn.

"Ever think about taking up stunt driving?" Julie said.

"Too boring," Martin said through clenched teeth as the car caught air going over a dip in the road.

Martin made the last curve and stomped the brakes, skidding to a stop in front of the cabin.

Or, what was left of it.

Chapter 15

"Oh, shit." Julie whispered.

Martin sat looking at the burned out remains of the cabin before them, his mind racing furiously. His eyes flicked toward the horizon where the clouds were starting to show the first hint of pink.

"Come on," he ordered as he bolted out of the car. Julie was out of the car in an instant sprinting after him, trying to keep up.

"Where are we going?" she yelled at his back.

"Just come on." Martin raced full out, a blur in the false dawn, winding down a path that led through the forest. Animals were sent scurrying, surprised by the pair's sudden appearance.

"What are we looking for?" she called again.

Martin ignored her. He looked for telltale signs in the grown up brush and weathered trail. Looking ahead as he ran, Martin caught a glimpse of something. He skidded to a stop, using a small tree to help brake his momentum. Julie ran into him as he doubled back on the trail. He looked closer then pulled a bush aside.

"Yes," he whispered as he revealed the opening

to a small cave. "Pull some leafy branches loose. Hurry."

From the dark of the cave came a low menacing growl. Julie looked at Martin as the growl came a second time.

"We don't have time for this," Martin said diving into the cave. From inside there arose a terrible din as fang and claw met inhuman strength and speed. Julie wasn't sure who was louder, Martin or the great cat he was locked in combat with. From inside, there came an audible snap followed by quiet. Martin emerged from the opening covered with blood.

"Oh, god, Martin!" Julie started toward him.

"The branches! Hurry."

Martin raced past her ripping leaf-covered branches off the trees or uprooting saplings as if they were grass. Julie bolted into action following his example. She wasn't used to her newfound strength and almost fell over backward when the sapling turned loose much easier than she expected. Under other circumstances she and Martin would have had a good laugh. But, she knew they were fighting for their lives.

"Come on. These will have to do," he said sprinting back to the cave with his load of timber. Julie was right on his heels as the sun was warming the clouds to a vibrant orange, preparing to crest the horizon.

Martin directed her inside and then started placing the branches in front of the small opening. He left a space to crawl through and pulled a branch after him. The leaves were not lightproof, but he hoped that the cave coupled together with the branches would be enough. The pair crowded together in the back of the cave along with the mountain lion carcass.

"Eat," Martin said flatly. "You're going to need it."

Julie found that she was indeed hungry and tore into one side the cat's neck as Martin took the other.

When they were finished, Julie asked if they could move the thing away from them.

"No," Martin said, "carrion eaters might smell it and come looking. If they tore down the limbs. . . . Also, our smell will help mask it. We should be safe till nightfall. Or as safe as can be expected."

"What's up, Martin?" Julie asked into the dark. "I can understand being stressed, believe me, I can. I'm strung tighter than an eight-day clock. But, I've seen the way you act in tight places and this ain't it. So, what gives?"

Martin was silent for a moment his thoughts in a roil. "No one else knew," he said barely audible.

"Do what? I didn't understand you."

"Nothing. Rest. We're going to need it. Besides, I don't feel like talking right now."

Martin lay in the dark and the thoughts, unbidden, leapt into his mind taking him back once more to when his present existence had begun.

He had escaped from the band of mounted men that been hunting him since they cornered him at his home. And, now, he had made his way to the only person he could think of that could help him. He had made his way through the countryside skirting the roads and farmhouses as he went until he came to another familiar structure. After the incident he had just been through, he was doubly cautious. He had been running for miles and his body and mind were to the breaking point. He knew that it would be morning soon and if he couldn't find help at the house before him, he had nowhere else to turn.

With the quiet of a passing shadow, Martin made his way around the old house looking for signs of armed riders or some other trap. He had become a feral animal starting at every noise, his ears and nose picking up scents denied him before. Satisfied that the place was indeed safe, he made his way to the porch. Glancing over his shoulder at the yard, the details of the layout surprisingly clear to his sight, Martin knocked on the doorframe. The rapping of his knuckles sounded unmercifully loud in his ears, shattering the quiet of the night. Immediately, the rawboned hound inside the door came to life. Martin's anxiety was almost overwhelming as he banged on the door again, this time rattling it in it's frame.

"Paul! It's me, Martin. Open the blasted door."

Martin could see the flare of a match and then the soft glow of an oil lamp as it bobbed its way to the door.

"Dog! Hush. Back up. Go lay down. Lay Down."

Martin could tell that the dog was reluctant to leave its master to what it perceived as a possible threat.

Jean Paul fumbled with the bolt of the door, mumbling all the while. "Hell fire and damnation, Martin. You have no idea what time it ez? Ze cock aren't even off of ze roost yet," the door opened and Paul held the lamp in front of him, the shield protecting his eyes and directing the light towards Martin's face. "All I can say ez this . . . " Paul finally looked at Martin.

"My Lord, Martin," he whispered, "what happened to you, mon ami? I had heard zat you were missing, yes," Jean Paul said as he ushered Martin in the door and headed him toward the kitchen. "How bad are you hurt?"

"I-I don't know. I don't' know what's going on anymore," Martin said lowering himself into the chair that Paul had pulled out for him.

"Why did you not go home instead?"

"I was there earlier tonight. There's nothing for me to go back to," Martin said with tears in his eyes.

"Emily, she is all right? Did anysing happen to her?"

"No, she was okay the last I saw of her."

"Oh," Paul said with a knowing look. "You and her are no more the couple, eh?"

"No, we're not. I'm sorry to disturb you and the family, but I have no place else to turn."

"Nonsense," Paul said starting to remove Martin's shirt. "What kind of a friend would I be if I were not here to help you?" Paul turned and put water on to boil. "Constance! I need you and the boys downstairs."

"No," Martin said starting to get up. "Please, don't disturb them."

"Be still, mon ami. You are at ze end of your rope, yes?" Paul gently pushed him back down.

"Jean Paul? What is going on?" came a voice from the top of the stairs.

"It ez Martin. He ez hurt. I need you to put fresh linen on ze spare bed and tell the boys to see to Martin's horse. Hurry."

"There is no horse," Martin said.

"What do you mean, no horse?" Paul asked as he started to palpate Martin's scalp.

"Just what I said. I came here on foot."

Paul stood up and looked at him with an eye of

doubt and then poured some of the steaming water into a pan he had gotten off one of the hooks.

"All ze way from your place to mine. I find zat hard to believe." Paul started washing the dried blood and dirt from Martin's arms.

"Believe what you want, Paul, it's the truth."

Paul merely grunted as he kept washing. After a minute he stepped back and looked at Martin. "Zere is no scratch one on you."

Martin looked himself over and saw that what Paul said was true. Martin closed his eyes knowing in his heart that what he feared was indeed true.

Paul said softly, "Who's blood ez it, mon ami?"

Martin looked up and sat back in the chair. "It's not Emily's if that's what you're worried about. Or anybody else's."

"Eh." Paul shrugged his shoulders. "Then who's ez it?"

"Not who's. What's." Martin could understand his friend's suspicion. If the tables were turned, he wondered if he would be as understanding. "I killed an animal and that's its blood."

"Papa?"

The pair turned at the sound of one of Paul's son's voice as he came into the house.

"There is no horse, Papa."

Paul looked down at Martin sitting there.

"I tried to tell you."

"So you did."

Constance, Paul's short, pleasantly plump wife came into the kitchen. "I've finished with ze bed."

It was then that she saw Martin. She sat down the lamp she had been carrying and came to give him a closer look. Even though a good deal of the blood and filth had been washed away, he was still a sight.

She covered her mouth with one hand, which made her broken English that much harder to understand, and stretched out the other to his face. "Oh, Martin, you are all right, yes?"

"Yes." He managed half a smile warmed by her compassion. "As well as possible at the moment." It finally registered what she had said earlier. "Listen, thank you very much for the trouble, but I can't really. If I could, just let me sleep in your root cellar."

"I'll not hear of it," Paul said stepping up.

"No, really, I would prefer it."

The pair started to protest anew as Martin held up his hand and took a breath. "Paul, could I talk to you for a moment. In private."

Paul and Constance looked at each other, and then he told her to go on back to bed, that he would be there shortly.

"What ez it my friend zat weighs at your heart?"

Martin looked into his friend's eyes for a moment and then turned away. "It's not that I don't want to sleep in the room, Paul, I can't."

Paul spread his hands. "I don't understand."

"I know. Neither do I." Martin sighed and rubbed at the fatigue that creased his brow. "You are my friend, Paul."

"But, of course."

Martin lifted a hand so he could finish. "I am about to tell you something and I am putting my life in your hands. My own wife could not handle it and tried to kill me." Martin could smell the nervousness emanating from his friend. "I've tried to reason out what is going on, but the only conclusion that I can come to is that I am a vampire. That is why I must sleep in the root cellar."

Martin turned and looked at his friend who stood

rooted staring wide eyed at him. It was obvious that he was at a loss as to what to do.

"I-I can't believe zat, my friend. You were wise to ask Constance to leave as superstitious as she is, but zose are just tales, Martin. Stories to frighten the children on a dark night, yes? Zay are not real."

Martin hung his head. "I didn't believe in them either. Until now."

Paul put a hand on Martin's shoulder. "Are you sure you didn't hit your head in all of zis?"

Martin looked him in the eyes. "I know it sounds crazy to you. Hell it sounds crazy to me and I'm the one saying it. I didn't want to believe it, but I have to, and so do you. Look," Martin grabbed the lamp off the table and held it closer to his body. "I was shot tonight and mauled by a pack of dogs. Do you see any bullet holes or bite marks? Go on, look."

Jean Paul's gaze slowly left Martin's face and looked to where he held the lamp. "I do not know what to say, Martin."

"You can say that you believe me and let me stay in the cellar today. Please, Jean Paul. I don't have much time. The sun will be coming up soon." Martin's eyes searched Paul's, pleading for understanding.

Paul let the air slowly escape between his lips. "Okay. You sleep with ze other potatoes."

"Thank you, Jean Paul. You are a true friend."

"What are friends for, eh?"

Jean Paul went to fetch the linen from the room his wife had prepared. When he returned, Martin had already lifted the trap door located in the kitchen and was waiting for him in the cellar. Paul took the bedding down with him.

Jean Paul looked at his friend as Martin took the blankets from him.

"Martin," Paul said slowly, "why don't you go with me today to see ze doctor. I'm sure zere's something he could do for you. If you sleep till noon, we could probably make it by nightfall.

Martin shifted the load to one arm and placed his hand on Paul's shoulder. "Paul, don't you understand? I can't. I can't go out during the day or I will die. It's that simple." Martin sighed and measured his friend for a moment. "You and I have known each other for years. You and I have shared things I never told my folks or my wife, so you know I've never lied to you. I'm not lying now. I don't understand it, you and the family are in no danger, but I am no longer what I was. Something happened. I can hear sounds, see things, and smell smells that I shouldn't be able to. I've been gunshot and attacked by animals and I don't have a scratch. The fact is, I'm a vampire and things are never going to be the same again."

Tears welled up in Paul's eyes as he stood looking at Martin.

At last Martin spoke, "I'll be okay. I just need to rest here today and then I'll move on tonight. Thank you, my friend."

Paul just nodded, sat the lamp down and turned to leave.

"Good night," Martin called after him.

"Ourviore," Paul said and then climbed the steps shutting the trap door after him.

Martin came to as rough hands laid hold of him. In the dim light of the oil lamp he could plainly see several large men dressed in white jackets attempting to bind his hands and feet. Martin broke the shackles they had put on his wrists and was attempting to stand when he was struck in the head with a Billy

185

club by one of the orderlies. Stars flared in his vision and he pitched forward to his hands and knees. Through the haze of pain that obscured his vision, Martin looked up to see Jean Paul standing on the stairs. Someone put a rag over his nose and mouth. A sickening, sweet smell filled his nostrils and his vision blurred further. Martin tried to get to his feet, but his legs wouldn't respond as the ether took effect. The last thing he could think of was, "Why?"

Time took on no meaning as Martin drifted in and out of consciousness, his system fighting the effects of the ether.

"I've used up more than half the blasted bottle," one of the orderlies said to the others.

The words buzzed inside Martin's head, flitting this way and that, not making any sense in their flight.

"Just make sure them shackles are good and tight. If he wakes up, I don't want him gettin' loose." The man massaged the swollen, discolored side of his jaw from where Martin had clubbed him earlier. "Just keep an eye on him," he told the two in the back of the reinforced wagon, "this one's a brute." The driver slid shut the panel that allowed people driving the rig to talk to those in the rear. The driver was very experienced and knew well how dangerous and strong the insane could be. It was this experience that led the driver to believe they could handle this or any other situation. Still, he didn't want to get caught out in the dark with a crazy like this one. He urged the horses to a faster pace.

Martin woke sprawled on a straw tic to the sounds of wailing, tormented souls. His first thought was that he had died and been condemned to hell. His senses swam once more and then sprang to clarity as his system rid his body of the effects of the drug. He lay motionless for a couple of minutes just in case the person with the ether was close at hand. The stench of the place was overpowering, but he couldn't hear anyone breathing in the room with him, so he slowly opened his eyes. A quick glance around showed plain stone walls and a heavy looking metal door set into a reinforced frame. Basically, he was in a dungeon cell. From the sounds and smells and the looks of this room, Martin knew right where he was; the Sanitarium for the insane. Paul had thought him crazy and summoned them himself. Martin couldn't be angry with his friend. He only thought he was helping Martin. Educated the way he was, Martin had heard about such places as this, but had never seen the inside of one. He had a feeling that the stories weren't going to compare to the reality. Martin sat up and took further stock of his surroundings. The room was a small cubicle, barely six feet by eight, containing nothing but the makeshift mattress he had been laying upon. The room was windowless, which was a small blessing since he had no idea what time of day it was or how long he had been out. Martin heard the faint sound of grating metal and whirled to see part of a face looking back at him through the grate set in the door. The person called out and Martin heard three others moving towards his room at a trot followed by the sound of a key turning in the lock.

"Well, I really thought we'd find you out like a newborn," the person in charge said as he swung the door open and stepped inside flanked by two large orderlies. "I guess William and the boys weren't kidding when they said you come around fast. No matter. The Doc wants to see you, so we're going to move you."

Martin finally noticed the straight jacket the man was carrying and automatically backed up a step.

"Listen," the man's voice dropped a menacing note, "the Doc canceled a dinner engagement when he heard that they had brought you in. He wants to see you, so we're going to deliver you." He looked to the large goon on his right. "Why am I bothering talking to him? He probably doesn't understand a word I'm saying anyway."

"I understand you perfectly well," Martin said evenly.

"Well, what d'ya know? This one actually speaks. And, proper at that. Well, Mr. Proper," he said looking back at Martin, "if you understand me perfectly well, then understand this: We're going to move you. To do that, we're goin' to put you in this jacket. It helps to keep you from thrashing around. You have the choice. You can make it hard or easy on yourself. Totally up to you, 'cause one way or another you're goin' in the jacket."

Martin's mind raced and then caught on something the guard had said. This doctor, whoever he was, broke a dinner engagement. That meant there was darkness outside and a chance of escape. Martin's eyes flicked across the faces of the three men standing there. They wore the faces of men who liked their work. He had seen that look before on the faces of those that had beaten slaves or raised a violent hand to wife and children. At last, Martin simply nodded his head.

"See, I told you not all crazies were stupid," the leader said and stepped forward with the jacket.

"Right," the goon on the left said and then spit a

mouth full of tobacco juice in the corner. He and the other orderly helped secure the straps on the jacket, pulling them so tight that they dug into Martin's flesh and made it hard to breathe. "There, just like a Christmas present. Let's go."

"What time is it?" Martin asked.

"Why? You got an appointment somewhere?" This brought a laugh from the others, including the one that was standing guard outside the door. "Just shut up and come on."

"All I want to know is the time."

"You heard 'em. Shut up."

Without warning, one of the orderlies pulled his billy and caught Martin across the back of the legs, sending him to his knees. "From now on, don't open yer yap unless we ask you a question." He punctuated the sentence with the club across Martin's face.

"Please, don't," Martin said spitting blood. "You don't understand."

"I told you to shut up." The guard kicked Martin viciously in the ribs as the other one stomped Martin's right leg. The orderlies continued to beat him as Martin tried in vain to protect himself, his arms bound by the heavy canvas.

"Please, stop," Martin pleaded. "I don't want to hurt anyone."

This brought another laugh from the lead orderly. "Hear that, boys? He doesn't want to hurt anybody."

"You know," the other guard said, gritting his teeth as he kicked Martin in the face once more, "you don't listen very good. He told you to shut up."

"And, I told you to stop." The voice coming from the crumpled figure on the floor was no longer recognizable as Martin's.

The same red haze that had taken him when he killed the deer fell over his eyes. Martin struggled to keep control of himself, but it was impossible. With a snarl, Martin was on his feet in an instant, all pain blocked out by the animalistic urges and adrenaline coursing through his veins. Martin leaned forward, flexed his back and straightened his arms, bursting the heavy leather straps and shredding the canvas like paper and string. The guards stood motionless, looks of utter shock forever frozen on their face. Martin ripped the throat out of the orderly that had first struck him and broke the neck of the second. Martin grabbed the lead orderly and bent him like a rag doll, breaking his back in the process. It was over so fast that the guard at the door, looking through the grate, didn't have time to sound an alarm. Martin turned and ran straight at the door knocking it out of its frame in a cascade of rock and mortar dust. The guard didn't even have time to scream as the heavy metal slab bore him into the opposite wall leaving a crimson stain where his head had hit the stone.

Martin whirled, looking up the hallway through the haze of dust and the dull red film that still shrouded his vision. His senses stretched out in all directions testing his surroundings. He paused for a moment and then started up the hall.

As he trotted silently past the rows of locked doors, Martin tried to calm himself. He stopped at the bottom of a flight of stairs and took stock of his situation.

He had killed those men. As easily as he had killed the pack of dogs. Four bodies lay at the end of the hall because of him. His mind threatened to run away from him. He really was the monster his wife had called him. Perhaps it would be best if he gave himself up now and ended the whole thing. Martin didn't know if it was self-preservation or simply the voice of lunacy that argued against the other voices in his head.

"I asked them to stop and they wouldn't." he said to himself.

If Martin had been a witness to the event before his transformation, he would have thought the guards got just what they deserved. But, it was hard to see things in that light when it was his own hand that had taken their lives. Once more, the analytical portion of his mind took control. He didn't know exactly how this had happened to him, but he was going to find out and discover a way to rectify the situation and to do that, he was going to what he needed to get out of this mad house alive. Martin's breathing approached normal and the urge to kill was gone.

He was discovering certain advantages to his condition. The stairwell and the hall where he stood were poorly lit with only a few sporadic lamps burning low, yet he could see perfectly well. Martin had no idea where he was, but the hall led up, so he followed the steps to the top of the stairs. At the top, his way was barred by another heavy door that was locked from the other side. Martin listened for a moment and then pushed the slide panel out of its tracks so that he could get a view of the other side. Satisfied that the hall beyond was clear, he braced his feet and then began a steady push against the door. This one was heavier and more sturdy than the one to his cell, designed to hold back several people instead of just one. Nonetheless, as Martin kept up his pressure, he could feel the lock starting to give. The metal inside the door started to groan in protest. Martin shoved hard and the lock broke, shattering the catch. It sounded like a small explosion to his ears. He stepped through the opening, closing the door behind him, ready to face another round of guards. The hallway stood empty, save for several large rats that made a dash for holes they had burrowed in the walls. Martin closed his eyes. He could smell the vermin, their scent everywhere mixing with the smell of filth, sweat and dried urine that permeated the place. He could hear their scurrying in the walls. Hundreds of them. And, he could hear something else. A faint jingling, growing louder, getting closer. Then he heard the footsteps that accompanied the jingling of keys and realized that another guard was coming. This part of the hall was just like the one he had just left, except it ended in a T some ten yards ahead of him. He realized he couldn't make the junction in time because the guard would be around the corner any second.

The guard rounded the corner and headed straight toward the metal door. He stopped and reached for the ring of keys that hung from his belt.

From where he hung suspended across the hallway near the ceiling using his hands and feet to brace himself, Martin saw the odds of his escape go up a couple of notches. He dropped to the floor and grabbed the key ring just before the guard. The guard's fingers closed around Martin's as Martin's closed around the keys. The man jumped like a cat, spinning in mid air to land with his back to the door. Looking back at the incident, Martin realized he probably looked like a ghoul from hell with his matted hair, bloody torn clothing, and remnants of the jacket still hanging from him. The poor man wet himself, made a gurgling sound in his throat and slid down the door, unconscious.

Martin hefted the keys and started up the hall once more. Even though it was evening time and Martin would have thought that most of the patients interned here would be settling down for the night, he could hear wails, crying, and laughter coming from the floor above him. Martin found the next-door, thumbed through the keys, and unlocked the heavy door. He slipped through the opening and quietly closed the door behind him. Once inside the room, the sounds and smells almost overwhelmed him. He was the one that was supposed to be the monster, yet he felt he was the one trapped in some land of horrors. The stench made him retch, and the forgotten humans stuck behind the myriad doors sounded like giant versions of the rats he had heard earlier. At the far end of the hall there was a large open ward. Martin spotted a guard sitting at a table with a low burning lamp, located just outside the barrier enclosing the ward. Looking closer, he noticed the guard was asleep where he was sitting, his chin resting against his chest. Martin stole up to the guard and stared at him for a moment. He thought about breaking his neck, but couldn't bring himself to kill this innocent man. Instead, Martin cocked his fist and struck the man in the jaw, catching him before he could fall to the floor. He propped the guard back in his chair and glanced at the barred window behind the guard and cursed to himself. He was on the second floor. He hadn't noticed a door before the last set of stairs and had wound up on an upper floor. Cursing to himself for having to backtrack, Martin started back towards the door when he heard a key being inserted in the other side of the lock. Martin froze as the door swung open and a man in a stylish suit stepped through followed by three others wearing hospital garb. Instantly the whole world narrowed to the man at the end of the hall. Martin felt the hairs rise on the back of his neck. His eyes locked with those of the man standing there, and he had to fight down an urge to rush down the hall and split the man in half. Though he didn't know how, Martin knew he was facing someone like himself. The other man started forward, as one of the others grabbed his arm.

"Doctor, be careful!"

"Doctor?" Martin thought. "This thing is a doctor?"

He took a step forward, feeling once more the urge to rush headlong to where the other was slowly making his way up the hall. Instead of giving in to the urge, he turned and bolted past the unconscious guard to where half inch steel bars blocked his path. Martin grabbed a bar in each hand and pulled. The world around him exploded in a flurry of motion as the doctor realized what he was about to do. Martin yanked the door off its hinges, the metal shrieking as it came apart. This, along with the yelling of the guards brought all the patients awake. Not pausing, Martin threw the door at the doctor who was almost upon him, catching him in the stomach, which sent the other vampire skidding down the hall. Martin ran headlong into the open ward yelling for the inmates to run, that they were free.

Spotting the open doorway, half the crowd rushed in mass towards the opening. The three orderlies turned tail and ran for the other doorway, inmates hot on their heels. The doctor simply brushed aside any inmate that tried to accost him as he made his way toward Martin.

Martin made the other side of the ward, grabbed the bars covering the window and pulled them loose in one motion. He looked out the window, saw an open courtyard below and jumped, sending a spray of glass glittering through the night air. He landed in a crouch and then sprang to his feet looking for the best way out of there.

"Martin, wait! Don't go," the doctor yelled down from the window.

Martin froze at the sound of his name, wondering how the other would know him and then just as quick felt foolish realizing that of course the other would have information on him. After all, it was a hospital; sort of.

"I can help you." The doctor leaned out the window, supporting himself against the broken frame. "Please, believe me."

"Just like Paul helped me," Martin yelled back and then more quietly, "or my wife?"

"They didn't understand. I do. You know I do."

There were so many questions Martin wanted answered, but he had been hunted, harassed, beaten, and left for dead. He had been betrayed by every friend he had ever counted on and there was no way he was going back into that living hell.

"Maybe next time, Doc, but not today."

Martin turned and cleared the hedges that closed in the courtyard, disappearing into the night.

"God's speed, Martin," the doctor said to the night air and turned from the window.

The sanitarium came alive as all available help mobilized to deal with the escaped inmates and Martin made it unnoticed over the wall surrounding the grounds. As he ran, all Martin could think about was Jean Paul. "Why?" The thought tumbled over and over in his head. "Why did you do it?"

"Why did I do what?" Julie asked from far away. "Martin, you asked me why I did it. What did I do?"

Martin opened his eyes, no longer in the Louisiana countryside. Slowly, he realized he had been dreaming and where he was came back to him. Along with those thoughts came the memories of why he was here.

"Are you going to tell me or do I have to play 20 questions?" Julie's voice came once more from the dark of the cramped cave.

"I trusted you," Martin hissed, "just like all the others. Why did you do it? What did Straun promise you?"

"What the Hell are you talking about?" Julie said sitting up as straight as she could in the cramped space.

"Don't play stupid with me, Julie. The phone call at your place. You were the only one to know where the cabin was located. You just happen to make a call and then we get here and the cabin is gone. You didn't plan on that though, did you? He used you, Jules. You were just a tool to get to me. He sucked you in and then threw you away. Were you two together in this from the very beginning?"

Julie reached out in the dark, found Martin's face and then slapped him with everything she had, the sound echoing in the small cave.

"I knew something was bothering you, but did it ever occur to you to talk to me about it, instead of letting your imagination run away with you? How could you think that I would ever be hooked up with Straun?"

The slap on the face and her words jarred Martin, but the thoughts of Jean Paul and his first wife were still fresh in his mind. Martin pressed his palms to his eyes. "I want to believe you, but how else could he have known about the cabin or where to find my backups, or where to look for the hidden files? How, Julie?" His voice rose in frustration. "You're the only one."

"I don't know how he knew," she said, her voice matching his, "but I do know that I love you and would sooner die than hurt you like that. Even if we weren't together, I'd never get in bed with a snake like Straun. You want to know who I called on the phone? A florist. That's right, a stinking flower shop. I knew that you'd been having a rough go of it lately. I also knew that we had enough time for me to make the order. There's a 24-hour service that I know about and ordered some flowers to be waiting at the cabin when you arrived. Cost me a pretty penny, but I thought you were worth it."

"A flower shop?" A lot of the tension left Martin's body.

"That's right. Why, is that so hard to believe?"

"Yes," Martin said quietly. "When everyone you've ever really trusted turns on you or gets killed, you get gun shy." Martin told Julie about his wife and Jean-Paul and how hard it was to trust anyone. "And, now, I thought it was happening all over again."

Julie sighed and took Martin's hand in hers noting the tension there. "I'm sorry for what they did to you, I really am, but you've got to realize, I'm not them." They sat in silence for a while. Julie stared toward the opening. "It'll be dark soon and then we can go." She paused again. "You still don't believe me, do you?"

Martin closed his eyes. "I want to."

"I can understand the way you feel. All I can do is tell you the truth, and either you'll believe me or you won't," Julie said and pulled her hand from his. They sat that way until the sun had fallen below the horizon.

"I'm sorry," Martin said softly, "I was just kind of at my wits end. I let the past get in the way. Bad thing to do and I apologize." Martin sighed deeply. "Fact of the matter is, I love you enough that if you were involved with Straun, I'd just be doomed. I said that I could never hurt you, and I meant it. I would walk into the sun because there would be nothing left."

"What about all that stuff, ' . . . if you have your health, you can get through anything?'"

"I wouldn't have my health. I would have a broken spirit."

Julie couldn't see his face, but she could hear the emotion in his voice. "To be so smart, you can sure be stupid sometimes. I love you, Martin Daniels. Don't ever forget that. And, I'm sorry for slapping you."

"I deserved worse." Martin patted her leg softly. "Let's go. I don't want to be around here if they come back," he said and started for the front of the cave. Martin shoved the barrier aside and stepped into the cool, country air followed by Julie. Martin touched the side of her face as she stood next to him. "I do love you, Jules."

"I'm glad. I'd be in a world of hurt if you didn't," she said bringing his hand to her lips. "So, does this mean that you won't trade me off?"

"Not for blood nor money."

Julie looked at him sideways in the rising moonlight. "Don't you mean, "Love nor money?"

Martin gave her a wry look. "I think in our situation, it takes on a special meaning."

"Good point."

"Thank you," he said kissing her lightly. "You ready?"

"Not really, but let's do it anyway."

Together they made the trek back the way they had come earlier that morning, albeit a much slower pace. Although they weren't running headlong down the barely visible path again, the trip was just as nerve-wracking knowing that Straun or some of his goons could be stalking them right then. Before they cleared the edge of the woods, Martin motioned Julie to silence. Together they made their way to where the trees stopped growing, forming a rough circle around the cabin. Martin and Julie stood motion-less, blending with the shadows of the trees and un-derbrush. They stood that way for several minutes testing their surroundings with hyper acute senses. The Prizm was still where they had left it, as was the burned out husk of the cabin, although it was no longer smoking. Martin and Julie started slowly for-ward, their eyes scanning the semi-darkness as they went. As they made their way, something seemed out of place to Martin. He stopped, trying to put his finger on it. Julie cast an inquisitive look his way. Martin stood for a moment and then the alarms went off in his head. He quickly gave Julie a set of hand signals and then made his way to a chest style freezer sitting in the front yard. It had been powered by so-lar panels and storage batteries when he was at the cabin. But, the batteries and panels were just part of the rubble pile like everything else. What Martin couldn't figure out was why the freezer itself was outside the cabin. Martin stole cautiously up to the freezer. Stretching out a hand, he started to open the lid when it burst open and a double-barrel 12 gauge was shoved in his face.

"Hi ya, Doc. I was beginning to think that you weren't going to show up." The vampire stood up unfolding his lanky frame and motioned Martin to step back. "Hot damn! It's warm in there."

He wiped his brow and ran a hand through sweat soaked hair. The vampire kept the shotgun leveled at Martin as he put one leg over the side of the box followed by the other, reminding Martin of a spider unfolding from the center of it's web.

"You know you got more lives than an alley cat. I tried to tell 'em there was no way you were going to survive, but they wanted to be sure, so I got stuck in the box. I heard you when you pulled up this mornin', but I couldn't be sure it was you or if it was daylight yet, so I sat it out all day long. You know, it's a shame your lady friend won't ever know what happened to you, especially after she went to the trouble of sending you these. They were on the porch when we showed up last night." The vampire reached behind him into the freezer and pulled out a half crushed bouquet of flowers. "But, don't worry none though. When we find her, we're going to make her feel real loved and then make her one of us." It was all Martin could do to resist testing the other's reflexes and grab for the gun.

"Listen," Martin said, "whatever it is that Straun promised you is a lie."

"Right." The vampire sniffed the flowers in his hand. "I'd love to say and chat, but I've got a job to do." He straightened his arm holding the shotgun, pointing it right at Martin's head. "I've got to admit that although it was hotter than hell in there, it was worth it just to see the surprise on your face."

The vampire jerked slightly as a red covered blade suddenly appeared out of his chest. The vampire looked from the blade to Martin with an uncomprehending expression. Martin reached out and calmly took the gun from the other man.

"Those are for me," Martin said taking the flowers from his slack grasp. Martin leveled the twin barrels at the side of the vampire's neck and pulled both triggers. The tissue between the vampire's head and trunk disintegrated, sending the head rolling in a bloody spray. Martin pulled the blade free as the body pitched forward and then looked to where Julie was perched atop the freezer lid.

"Oh, geez, Martin. I killed that guy," Julie said staring at the body.

"No, Jules. I killed him. You just stabbed him," Martin said trying to take some of the sting out of it. "Jules, it was him or us."

Julie drew a ragged breath. "I know. I'm just not used to it." She sat down heavily on the lid, her feet dangling just above the dirt, looking like a little girl on an oversized stool.

Martin laid the gun and blade atop the freezer and put his arm around her. "You never get used to it. If you did, then I'd worry about you."

Julie looked into his face and managed a slight smile and then turned back to the body lying there.

"Holy shit."

As she watched, the vampire's body began to smoke and the clothes caught fire filling the air with the stench of burnt cloth and flesh. As she sat mesmerized, there was the slight whooshing sound of air being pulled in as the body's cells totally consumed themselves in a brilliant flare. A moment later when her eyes had once more adjusted, she looked to see a pile of ashes where the body had been along with a smaller pile where the head had rested.

"That was what you were talking about, huh?"

"That was it," Martin replied.

Julie shook her head. "I keep expecting some director to yell 'cut,' or the show to break for a commercial." Julie slid off the lid. "This is the kind of crap that happens in movies."

"I wish I could make this all go away for you," Martin said with bowed head. "I hope I can. But, it's going to take me awhile. If it ever gets to be too much or you want out, let me know."

"Martin. Love of my life, sunshine of my existence," she said as they started for the car, "give me a break. For starters, it's you and me. And, I knew what I was getting into when I became like you. Well," she looked over her shoulder at the two piles of ashes, "for the most part I knew. Now then, if it's okay with you, I'd like to go now. I figure that since they left someone, when that guy doesn't check in, they're going to come checking and I don't want to have to experience that again anytime soon."

Martin opened her door for her before crossing to his side.

"By the way," he leaned over and kissed her lightly, "thanks for the flowers."

Chapter 16

Julie reclined the seat back part way and adjusted her lap belt as she watched the passing pines speed by in the night. She was content to let the wind ruffle her hair and savor the scents and sounds of the forest. She had already put the thought of killing another living being in the back of her mind. As it was, it seemed like a dream or something that had happened in another lifetime. If anything, she had the ability to be practical about a situation.

They drove on in the comfortable silence between them, Martin watching the road front and back, and Julie watching the moon dance between the trees. Julie took her eyes from the brilliant orb and rolled her head over to look at Martin. She watched his intensity and knew his brain was running full steam. She reached out her hand, placing it on the back of his neck and began rubbing out the tension there.

"You're hired," Martin said gratefully.

"Thanks, but you couldn't afford me," she said continuing to rub his neck. "By the way, Doc, where are we going and what are we going to do once we get there? I mean, I can practically hear the gears turning in your head."

"I don't know about you, but I'm tired of waiting around wondering where these bastards are going to ambush us next. So, we're going to Christine's.

"Christine's?"

"Yes," he said checking his rearview again. "We're going to see if Grant found out anything that might help us. I had hoped that Straun would forget about us, or at least give us some breathing room. Maybe give me a chance to check my notes and resynthesize the sunscreen. I was going over some of the notes earlier and I think there may be a discrepancy there. I've also been thinking . . . "

"Obviously," she interrupted.

"I've been thinking," he said ignoring her, "as to how they could have found out about the cabin. They could have someone in the cop shop or Phone Company tracking calls, but that would take too long, so the obvious means is that they have the phones bugged."

"Get out of town. How could he do that?" she asked setting up in the seat.

"With his knowledge and the contacts he has, it would be a snap. The thing is," Martin said instinctively dodging as a lightning bug plowed into the windshield, leaving a luminescent swath on the glass, "we have a network of our own and we're about to put it to use. It's obvious that he's not going to leave us alone, so we're going after him." Martin found her hand and wrapped his fingers around hers. "This is going to get real nasty, real quick. There's the probability that we're going to get hurt, maybe real bad and the possibility that we'll get killed. Do you want to take that chance?"

"Hell, you take a major chance every time you crawl behind the wheel to drive. Besides, you want to live forever?" Then she added more seriously, "I don't like the thought of killing someone, but believe me, I like the thought of dying a whole lot less. I'll do what it takes to stay alive." She looked straight into the night before them, "Let's go kick some ass."

Martin and Julie found Grant's house easy enough from Grant's driver's license. It was nearly midnight when they pulled into the drive and walked to the front door. Martin hesitated a moment then knocked sharply on the doorframe. There was a slight pause and then the pair could hear someone moving about inside as they made their way to the door. There was another pause and Martin knew that they were being scrutinized through the peephole. The chain latch on the other side of the door made clattering sounds that brought forth images of Marley's ghost to Julie's mind. At last, the door swung open to reveal an older looking woman framed by the dim glow of the table lamp in the living room.

"Hello. Please come in," she said before Martin had a chance to open his mouth to speak. "You two must be Martin and Julie," she added never missing a beat.

Martin and Julie exchanged glances. He then moved aside for Julie, to let her enter. As he passed the woman, he stopped just inside the doorway.

"You're wondering how I knew who you were," she said answering the unspoken question.

Martin inclined his head and said, "You're absolutely correct."

"Christine Brewer," she said extending her hand. Martin was only mildly surprised, where as Julie, who made it a habit never to play poker, gaped at her.

Christine released Martin's hand and shook Julie's in turn. "I can see by your surprise, I'm not what you expected." She patted Julie's hand and said, "Don't worry, you're not alone." With a reaffirming squeeze she let go of Julie and started farther into the house, where several wreaths and plants, sent in sympathy, lined the room. "A lot of people wonder if I'm Grant's older sister or worse," she turned and smiled at Julie, "his mother. I cover the gray, but that only hides so much. Doesn't do much for the lines in your face, you know." She eased her self into the overstuffed chair, wincing as she sat. "Please, make yourselves at home. Can I offer you something to drink? If you're hungry, there's a bottle that Grant kept in the back of the refrigerator. There's not a lot there," she said matter-of-factly, "but it will help out if you need to eat."

Julie wanted to jump for the refrigerator. Instead, she followed Martin's lead.

"Thank you very much," Martin said, "It's too kind of you. First, we would like to tell you how sorry we are about Grant. We didn't know him long, but he seemed to be an outstanding individual."

"Yes, he was. And not just to me." Christine motioned around the room with her hand. "These came in earlier. And, I just found out about him today," her eyes misted over and she fought the lump in her throat, "so, yes, I think you could say he was well liked." She looked away for a moment and then added softly, "When he didn't come home this morning without calling, I knew. They didn't have to tell me. I already knew. They showed up at my door to tell me personally. It was one of those calls that every cop's wife dreads. Sure, he was *special,* not like other people, other cops, but he was still a cop and we both knew that this could happen." Christine sniffed slightly and looked at the pair again. "Forgive me for going on. Are you sure there is nothing I can get you?"

"No, thank you. And, I realize this is not the time, but I need to ask you a few questions. Like how did you know it was us?"

"I was married to a cop," Christine chided good-naturedly. "Grant was excellent in his observations and descriptions. You look exactly as he described you. Right down to the small mole by your left eye, Miss Baxter." She used Julie's last name to let them know she knew about them as well as what they looked like.

Martin smiled genuinely. He liked this woman. The modest, well kept appearance of the house, coupled with her own non-showy attire, told Martin here was a down-to-earth person who appreciated the creature comforts, but refused all the glittery trappings.

Christine waved a hand covered with small bruises, "I'm rattling. I don't suspect this to be a so-cial call, so how can I help you?"

"You're right again," Martin nodded. "We apolo-gize for seeming so insensitive, but, we need to know if your husband told you anything about vampire ac-tivity in the area. Other than ours, of course."

It was Christine's turn to smile. "Yes, he spoke of an increase in the number of vampires," she said having trouble with the word. Her countenance be-came severe. "Do you think it was one of them that killed Grant?"

"Yes, I know it was. And," Martin took a deep

breath, "It was probably because of his involvement with us. I'm sorry."

Christine shushed him. "You're innocent. And, that was Grant's job, to protect the innocent. He took that job very seriously." Christine's voice became ominous. "If you think he was murdered, then I'll do everything I can to help you get the son-of-a-bitch that did it."

"Anything you have will be greatly appreciated," Julie added from where she had been sitting. "We're very sorry about Grant. He really helped us out when it counted. I just hope we can repay a small portion of that debt now."

Christine sat in silence and looked at the pair for several moments. "Grant said that I would like you folks, that you were good people. He was right. If you'll wait for a few moments, I'll go get his personal log."

Christine pushed herself out of the chair and grimaced as she stood up.

"Are you all right," Martin asked stepping forward.

She held up a hand and waved him off. "I'm fine, thank you." She looked at him with a pained smile, "I'll be right back."

Martin and Julie watched as Christine turned a corner into the hallway. Martin glanced at Julie, a worried look on his face, his brows knit in concentration.

"What is it?" Julie asked.

"I don't know for sure. There's something wrong with her. She's in pain."

"Maybe she's got a bad back."

"No," Martin said absently. "It's something else."

Martin's subconscious had been working on it since they had entered the house. "That smell."

"What sme . . . " Julie stopped, aware, now that Martin had brought it to her attention, of a peculiar odor.

Christine came back into the living room carrying a small journal. She walked slowly over to Martin and handed him the book. "I hope this will help you in some way."

"Thank you very much." Martin watched her intently as she made her way back to her seat. "Tell me, Christine, how long have you had cancer?"

Christine looked at Martin sharply and then softened as she lowered herself into the chair. "It's hard to hide anything from you people. I wasn't able to keep anything from Grant. If I whispered in the next room he would hear me. I couldn't sneak up on him. I used to ask him if he had x-ray vision," she laughed dryly. Looking at Martin she said, "To answer your question, I don't know for sure. Grant knew before I even suspected that anything was wrong. I had been a little tired and thought I was working too hard. Working in the public school system can do that to you. We had been making love one night, rather passionately," she said wistfully. "After we were through, we lay there together sweating like a couple of teenagers, when Grant sat up quickly. I asked him what was wrong. He sat that way for a moment, testing the air like a wolf or something. Then he looked down at me, or more like he was looking through me. 'What is it?' I asked him. He had been transformed years ago, but it was still unsettling when he looked at me like that."

Julie remembered the intensity of Martin's gaze and sympathized with her.

"'I thought I smelled something. Nothing major,' he told me and we laid back down together. Nothing major," she said with an edge to her voice. "Just big enough that it changed our lives forever."

Christine was sitting trance-like, recalling the story as if she were peering into some secret screen that she couldn't take her eyes from. Martin and Julie sat still, not wanting to break the spell as Christine continued with her tale.

"The next morning over breakfast he told me I needed to go to the doctor."

'Why?'

He sat his fork down and pushed his plate back.

'You have something wrong with you. I don't know what, but,' he swallowed hard, 'but, something is wrong.'

I stopped chewing for a moment to see if he were kidding. 'When did you get your Ph.D.? Besides, I can't go to the doctor today. I've got tests to prepare.'

'All right then. Promise me you'll go tomorrow or sometime this week.'

'I don't know where you get this notion. I'm fine,' I told him. 'If you're worried about my fatigue it's just that I've been busy at school.'

'It's not that,' he told me.

'Then what?'

'You smell different.'

I didn't know if I should laugh or be offended. Then a thought snuck into my mind as I remembered that wild animals can smell disease in others. I looked at Grant, and an icy ball of fear formed in the pit of my stomach. As usual, he read me like an open book and reached across the table to hold my hand.

'It's probably nothing, and more than likely I'm

out in left field on this,' he said. 'But, it's better to be safe than sorry. So, if you could indulge your over-protective husband, I would appreciate it.'"

The three of them sat without moving, the steady thrum of the air conditioner the only noise present.

"He was right, of course," she said softly. "I was diagnosed with bone cancer. Nasty stuff, cancer. Your body eating itself up. But, I think it was harder on poor Grant. He couldn't be there for some of the treatments and that killed him. Of course, none of the radiation or chemotherapy worked. Oh, it slowed it down. Killed it here and then it would pop up there. After the last time, I told them I'd had enough, and that I was going home." Christine paused for a moment. When she spoke again it was barely audible. "I hated him sometimes because he wouldn't infect me, to be like him." Martin watched as a tear rolled down her cheek. "And, now, I can't thank him enough. The thought of living forever without him is something I couldn't endure."

Martin had come to stand beside her chair and placed a hand lightly on her shoulder. "I'm sorry. Believe me, I understand."

She took a shuttering breath, "At least I don't have that much longer. It was apparent that Grant was going to far outlive me. Even before the cancer, I had told him to leave me. He told me that he'd sooner tear out his eyes. He wasn't the most articu-late man, but he could be extremely passionate. He told me that when I died, on that day he would kill himself, so that we would spend no time apart. Even after I got sick, and we couldn't have a physical rela-tionship any longer, he never strayed, even though I gave him my blessings." She gave another long sigh and said more to herself than to Martin and Julie, "It wasn't supposed to end this way. I wasn't supposed to outlive him. But, you came here looking for help, not to listen to someone bemoan their condition." Christine looked up into Martin's face for a long moment, "I don't have Grant's strength or courage."

Martin saw a longing there and patted her shoulder. "We'll talk more about that later." He gave her arm a small squeeze. "I promise."

Martin stood upright and examined the book cover. "We'll look this over and then get it back to you."

"You keep it. It will do you more good than me. Besides, you're not going are you? There's plenty of room here."

"Thank you very much, but there's some things we need to take care of." Martin tipped the journal at her, "You've already been a huge help."

"Well, if you need them, Grant had some other items you might find useful. Guns and such. Police stuff."

Julie's ears perked up. She like the idea of having a gun or something to help even the odds. She looked at Martin and raised an eyebrow.

Martin glanced at his watch. "It's late and we'd better be going. We'll keep your offer in mind. Thanks again, Christine."

Julie knelt down in front of her chair. "We'll keep you posted. I promise." She patted Christine's hand and then joined Martin on his way to the car.

Chapter 17

Julie piloted the Prizm while Martin thumbed through the journal looking for any inferences to vampires.

"So, how goes it, Kemosabe," Julie asked after a couple of minutes.

"Well, it's not nightstand material, but I will say he was good at keeping notes." Martin thumbed ahead, glancing at the pages as he went, stopping now and then to check something a little closer. "I haven't read everything of course, but I keep seeing references to a nightclub on the East side. Seems that a few of them like to hang out there together." Martin rubbed his chin in thought and glanced at his watch. "Hmm. Too late tonight."

"What? What's too late? You thinking of going to this place or something?" Julie asked, her voice rising a little.

"But, of course, Dear Watson," he said in a bad British accent.

"That's what I love about you, Martin," Julie said as she accelerated onto the interstate, "if you don't have trouble beating down your door, or landing in your lap, you go looking for some." She looked out the front window at the lines passing beneath the car as Martin continued scanning the journal. "I hate to bother you, Love," Julie said, "but, we do need a place to stay and I really am getting hungry."

"Hmm? Oh. Right. Well, let's see. I believe there's a Denny's up ahead." Martin quipped.

"Right. I'd like two O positives to go, please. One with no ice. Next suggestion. You *are* a little more experienced at this than I am."

Martin closed the book on his finger to mark his place and then surveyed his surroundings.

"Take the next exit," he said placing the book on the console between them. "At the bottom of the ramp, turn left. We'll find something there."

"Exit here?" Julie checked to make sure she had heard him correctly.

"That's right."

Julie slowed to let a car pass and then moved into the exit lane. "This is not one of the best parts of town if you know what I mean."

"Which is what makes it so much more advanta- geous for us. Stuff happens here that no one no- tices, or if they do, they don't care. A sad commen- tary on our society, but the truth. Besides, there's lots of stray animals here that no one will miss." Mar- tin sat forward in the seat, getting his bearings. "Turn right at the next light and slow down."

Julie steered the car through the intersection and slowed to the prescribed 25 mph. Not that there were any cops around to give her a ticket she mused to herself. She looked around at the buildings bur- ied beneath years of neglect and decay. People stood or sat just inside some of the doorways staring hun- grily at the car as it slowly passed. Dull, dingy lights shown through some of the panes while others were boarded up.

"Depressing, isn't it," Martin said reading her expression. The sounds of music blared from one of the structures ahead and voices drifted to them on the night air. Julie made another right as Martin directed her through what she thought of as a hunting ground.

"That, is what is really depressing," he said motioning to the three youngsters ahead. They ranged in age from six to twelve years old and were kicking a can and testing doors as they went. "They'll grow up only knowing this. And, then, perpetuate it to their children."

Julie's thoughts were shattered when several people stepped into the street blocking her path. She had been passing between rows of cars on either side of the street when the group had stepped out. Julie instantly thought of backing up, but stopped when she saw the other group step up behind the car and realized that they had been purposefully trapped. Her heart hammered in her chest and she dropped the car back into drive preparing to run over those in front of her when Martin's hand closed over hers.

"Relax," he said, "These are just street punks."

Just street punks she thought to herself. One thing for sure, Martin didn't lead a dull life.

Martin lowered the window and nonchalantly propped his elbow on the car door as the group closed in around the car. From where she sat, Julie could see that they were mostly male, late teens, and early twenties. Most stood in a menacing fashion, trying to intimidate the pair, while she did notice a couple of them were carrying pipes, and one of them stood by Martin's window and made a show of cleaning his fingernails with a butterfly knife. If she would have been alone, she would have been scared spit less. Having Martin there made her feel a little better. A little.

One of the punks, who Julie took for the leader, made his way over to Martin's open window.

"Hey, man. You got any idea where you are?"

Martin's face gave an expression of deep concentration. "L.A.?"

"Where at in L.A., bright boy?" the leader leaned both arms next to Martin's and looked around the inside of the car.

"On a street?"

"No, Holmes, you're on a toll road."

"That's funny. I wasn't aware the city owned any toll roads. Particularly outside the interstate system."

"That's the thing, Holmes. This don't belong to the fuckin' city, or the state or anyone else. You see, it belongs to us." he said motioning to himself and the others, "This here's our fuckin' toll road and if you want to pass, then you're going to have to pay toll."

"Oh. Well, in that case, we'll just go back the way we came," Martin said with mock naiveté.

"Oh, well, you see, Holmes, that's our toll road too." This brought a series of snickers from the mob.

"So, let me get this straight," Martin said, "we're going to have to pay to get out of here?"

"Hey," the leader stood laughing and looked around at his gang, "this pretty boy catches on fast."

"Isn't this sort of behavior illegal?" Martin asked still playing the dolt.

Another round of laughter and the leader said, "That depends, Holmes, on who's laws you're talkin' 'bout. And, it's our laws we're talkin' 'bout, so you don't have a problem with that, do you?"

"Oh, no, of course not. I was just wondering, though, how much is the toll?"

"Well, now. Let's see," he said as he squatted down to look eye-to-eye with Martin. Speaking calmly as if quoting rate fares, he said, "This stretch of road at this time of day is going to cost you a hundred bucks. Or," he looked past Martin to where Julie sat with her hands still clutching the steering wheel, "you could just leave the bitch here. Me and Manny and the boys could show her a good time." One of the men standing at the front of the car grabbed his crotch and howled.

"Believe me," Martin pitched his voice so that they all could hear, "you're not man enough for her."

This brought loud jeering from the gang and caused the leader to turn a deep red.

"Oh, great," Julie thought. "Things aren't bad enough as they are, he has to antagonize them."

"Hey, Hector," one of the gang members goaded the leader, "he says you got a little dick! He been lookin' in your pants?"

"Hey, Mother Fucker," a switch blade materialized in Hector's hand, "I'm going . . . "

" . . . to listen to me," Martin finished his sentence for him. Martin's hand flashed out the window and closed around Hector's knife hand. Holding the handle, Martin pushed against the flat of the blade with his thumb, snapping the knife like a pencil. Before Hector or any of the others could react, Martin pulled him through the window. Some of the others started to move forward.

"Don't." Martin's voice carried to where everyone in the crowd could hear him.

The gang stopped where they were at Martin's command. Martin held Hector off balance with his legs sticking out the window. He maintained a tight grip on Hector's arm.

"I hate to lower myself to your standard, but if violence is the only thing you understand, then so be it. Tell your people to back off or I'm going to start breaking things, starting with your arm."

From where Martin held him, Hector turned his head to look at Martin.

"Fuck you!" He spit in Martin's face.

Instantly there was the sound of snapping bone followed by a high pitched wail as Hector looked at his arm where it now formed a right angle.

The crowd surged like an ocean wave, pushing forward and falling back on itself.

Martin covered the gang leader's mouth. "Listen to me. Since your leader is too stupid, I'm going to speak to you instead. If you don't back up now and get out of our way, I'm going to hand him out this window to you one piece at a time."

To drive home the point, Martin moved his hand off the other's mouth and twisted his arm slightly.

"Ahhhh! Shit, man! Do what he says. Back the fuck up!"

The crowd moved back and Julie instantly floored the accelerator, clearing the end of the row of cars. Martin told her to stop and stepped out of the car holding Hector off the ground in front of him.

"Listen up, people. You don't need to follow assholes like this. Be your own person, with your own ideas. Band together, yes, but to help each other, not hunt others." Martin slowly surveyed the crowd, still holding Hector in the air. "I don't want to hear of you people doing this again. Because if I do,"

Martin's voice dropped to a growl, "I won't stop with an arm." Martin flung the gang leader through the air like a rag doll causing him to land in a pile of garbage.

"Let's go," he said sliding back into the car.

Julie tromped the accelerator again and sped off down the street, swirling trash and dirt in her wake. She looked at Martin who sat stone-faced scanning the area ahead.

"Yea, we won't attract any attention. I can see that," she said.

"What? You think they're going to go to the cops? Not likely. I just hate that mentality. They think they can just take what they want without working for it." Martin shook his head, "I suppose it's not all their fault."

"Bull crap!" Julie replied. "Yea, there's some that get warped for some reason or another. But, ultimately, everyone is responsible for themselves. With TV as prevalent as it is today, people know that there's something better out there and that they can go for it. I mean, how is it that foreigners can come to this country after living in abject poverty and make a good life for themselves? If you want something bad enough, you'll work for it. It's just too easy to put the blame on someone else and not take responsibility for your own actions. I tell you, a lot, not everybody, but a lot of people in this country just need a swift kick to get them off their lazy asses!"

"Need a bigger soap box, dear," Martin asked.

"No, this one's just fine, thank you."

"Ever think about going on the speakers' circuit? You'd be a natural." Martin leaned over and kissed her cheek. "I've got to admit, I love you, lady."

Julie relaxed a little. "See, that's the difference

between you and me. You stay so calm and I just get wired for sound. Me, I don't think I could have stopped with his arm." She gave a slight shiver. "He was such a slime ball. How do you do it?"

"I've had a hundred more years than you to practice." Martin glanced out the window. "Pull over here."

Julie pulled the car over to the curb. "What? I don't see anything."

"I thought I saw . . . yes. In that lot between the buildings. Just a minute and you'll see them.

Julie looked into a lot overgrown with weeds and covered with rubble and trash. Her eyes pierced the dark that others wouldn't have been able to see through. She was about to say something when the first member of a wild dog pack came into view. Immediately her mouth began to water.

"You know," she said, the excitement thick in her voice, "I used to be opposed to hunting. All hunters were Bambi killers." As she spoke, her eyes never left the pack of dogs rummaging through the lot. "But, right now, I have to admit, I'm wired."

"It's a little different when you're doing it for self-preservation, hmm?"

"Yea, I guess it is. So, what's the plan?"

"You've never hunted before, so you do as I do." Martin opened the glove box and pushed the button to pop the trunk lid. He looked out the window to see if the noise had alerted the pack, and then chided himself because he realized there was noise going on all around them. "Dinner is served," he said, and stepped out of the car. As he walked to the back of the car, he told her, "Push come to shove, we could rip their throats out, but that's real messy, so," he opened the trunk lid and pulled out a large hunting knife. "This is faster and a whole lot cleaner." Martin looked directly into Julie's eyes. "This is one of the drawbacks I warned you about. You have to take them alive. Otherwise there's nothing to move the blood. Remember the cougar? We didn't get much out of that. I've developed some more "humane" methods, but we're still sucking the life out of them. I wish I could provide for you all the time, but that's not going to be possible. If you're ever out by yourself or something happens to me, you need to know how to do this." Martin brushed a stray hair out of her face. "O.K.?"

Julie didn't blink when she answered him. "I knew what I was getting into when I did this. You should know by now that when it comes to survival, I can be very practical minded."

Martin traced the outline of her jaw and said, "In that case, Miss Practical, let's go get some supper."

Martin quietly shut the trunk lid and moved off the street to the side of the building with Julie in tow. "We're in luck," he whispered in her ear, "they're slowly making their way in our direction, and the wind is with us. We can see better than them, but they will be able to hear us coming and some will have just as good a sense of smell. If we spook them and they run, it turns into a foot race. We're far faster, but they have four legs and know the terrain."

Julie knew that Martin wasn't just giving her a play by play, but was teaching her to size up any situation and know your opponents strengths and weaknesses. She nodded to indicate she understood.

"We'll move on down the wall and wait for them. When you grab one, it's not like it used to be, you'll be far stronger and faster than it is. Hang on to it. If it manages to bite you, ignore the pain. It will go away soon enough. Cut off it's air and I'll be there with the knife. Believe me, these dogs aren't somebody's pet. They would eat you for breakfast given the chance." He paused a moment. "Ready?"

She nodded again and melted into the shadows along with Martin. They moved slowly, using the piles of rubble for cover as they went. Julie marveled at Martin's stealth. She was moving as quietly as she could and each step sounded like someone stomping through a midnight house. Even with her acute hearing, Martin's passing made no noise. If some of the other vampires down through the ages had been as good as Martin, which she was sure they were, she could understand where the legends and superstitions came from. As quietly as he was moving, it would be easy to believe that he could transform into mist, because you'd never hear him coming.

They were about halfway into the lot when Martin motioned for her to stop. There were several 55-gallon drums scattered next to the building. They settled in behind these and waited. They crouched there, looking between the barrels when the pack came into view. They both could hear the snuffling and panting as the pack worked it's way toward them.

Martin estimated twelve to fifteen in the group. They were mostly mongrels with one notable exception. There was a huge Rottewieler present. It appeared to weigh around 175 lbs. With an enormous squared head and jaws that could break a human's leg. From the look of things, it appeared to be the dominant member. The group swirled and eddied, moving toward the opening in the wall behind them. The pack was almost upon them and Julie felt Martin's muscles tense against her.

Then the pack was around them, not knowing Julie and Martin were there until it was too late.

Martin sprang up just as the Rottewieler trotted past.

"Get the big one!"

Julie acted without thinking, launching herself onto the back of the huge animal. It went down under the impact of her body, grunting as it went, but instinctively rolling with the blow. The dog was a mass of muscle and lightning-like reflexes from living in the urban jungle. From flat on its back, the thing sank its teeth into Julie's shoulder, shaking its massive head back and forth. Red-hot pain shot through her arm and blood welled from the wound. Julie cursed against the pain and wrenched her shoulder free grabbing the dog's throat with her left hand. Quickly shifting her weight, she hoisted the dog off the ground, holding it in front of her. The rotteweiler tried to break her iron grasp, clawing and scratching her arm as she slowly choked the life out of it. It was a futile attempt. Julie shook the dog, her fangs a mirror of the snarl on the dog's face.

As the dog's body went limp, she became aware of her surroundings again. She heard growling and turned her head to see where Martin was engaged with half a dozen dogs, two already dead on the ground. The dogs weren't used to these two new animals that looked like humans, but smelled different and moved faster than anything they had encountered. Even so, they realized the threat to the pack and moved to protect it.

Martin hated to kill needlessly and tried to dissuade the dogs. Unfortunately for some of them, they didn't dissuade easily. Martin caught one dog as it leapt at him and used it for a club against the others.

When the fourth dog fell, the rest of the pack lost nerve, broke ranks, and ran. Martin dropped the battered carcass and joined Julie who was still holding the rotteweiler.

"Son-of-a-bitch tried to chew my shoulder off," she spit out.

"I'm sorry you got bit, sweetheart. It's usually not this rough. But, then again, these aren't the average neighborhood dogs either." Martin looked at her shoulder as he took the dog from her. The bleeding had already stopped. "You'll be all right."

"It hurts like hell," she said feeling the tissue mend itself.

"This will help," Martin said laying the dogs head back feeling for the carotid artery. Julie realized the blade was as sharp as a scalpel as he made an incision across the skin of the neck and peeled it back to expose the tissue beneath.

"When I make the cut, you drink," he said and moved the blade across the dog's throat.

Martin drove them out of the neighborhood and found a comfortable motel for them to stay in until the next night. He opened the glove box and retrieved a roll of duck tape and upholstery tacks he had placed there.

Julie raised an inquisitive eyebrow.

"To hold the blanket in place that we're going to put over the window."

"Good thinking. You have been around longer than me."

Standing beside Martin, Julie said, "Did anyone ever tell you that you're a messy eater?"

"Huh?"

"A messy eater," she said indicating the blood stains on his shirt.

"In that case, you know what you can get me for Christmas then," he said making his way across the parking lot.

"Yea. A bib. Which, by the way," she added, "what's for dessert?"

"I don't know if we have time to go get anything and I doubt they have room service."

"We don't have to go anywhere if you're on the menu," she purred taking the room key from him and opening the door.

Julie woke late in the afternoon, stretched and checked the time on her wristwatch. She rolled over to find Martin sitting up in bed, reading the journal. She moved closer and laid her head in his lap. Looking up, she said, "Have I told you lately just how good in bed you are?"

"No," he said running a hand through her hair.

"Well," she stretched again, "that's probably because we haven't *been* in bed lately. She propped herself up next to him against the headboard. "Anything new and interesting?"

"According to Grant," Martin said slowly reading the last page of the journal, "there's been a definite increase in the number and the activities of the vampire community." He read the last entry and shut the book with a snap. "This guy was good at surveillance. I wish he were still here. For more reasons than one." Thinking of Christine made him realize just how much he loved Julie. "Anyway, he could have busted these guys half a dozen times, but looked to the big picture and tried to find out what they were up to. It seems our blood-sucking friends, and there are quite a few of them, have banded together under a common flag."

"Straun," she said flatly.

"That's the most logical assumption. Grant has been tracking them for about six months or so and they specialize in industrial sites. Somebody is bankrolling these guys, or there are a lot of businesses out there desperate to find out what the competition is doing. And, Straun, it appears, just happens to be one of the best in the business." Martin got out of bed and started to pace back and forth. "It stands to reason he can't work alone, so why not have people in your organization with the same abilities as your own. Somehow this scumbag is managing to bring a large number of people through the transformation intact. And, Lord knows, there are a number of the criminal element that would jump at the opportunity to become like us."

"Question is, why," Julie asked from her spot on the bed. "I mean is this all for money? What if this guy starts working for international terrorists?"

Martin stopped pacing and spread his hands in front of him. "I don't know what motivates him. This guy is just plain bad to the bone. He's not above murder and rape, so we can expect him to do anything. Since we can't figure the cause, let's go for the source."

Martin picked up the handset and started to dial.

"Who're you calling?"

"Christine. Our car is too visible. I'm going to see if we can use hers." Martin finished dialing the number and waited. At last Christine's voice came over the other end of the line.

"Hello, Christine. Martin Daniels here."

"Well, well. I didn't expect to hear from you so soon." Her voice was filled with warmth as her words made their way to Martin. "What can I do for you?"

Martin explained the situation to her.

"Hell, Martin, you can have the bloody thing. I can't use it anymore."

"Thanks, but if we could borrow it, that would be sufficient."

"All right then. I'll see you after dark. I'll fix a small supper, but you have to bring the wine."

Chapter 18

Martin and Julie showed up a little after eight. They waited as the front door slowly opened and Christine hobbled to one side to allow them to enter. As they passed through the front door, Martin produced a bottle from under his jacket.

"I didn't know what you were serving, so I went with a light rosé."

Christine laughed. "I wasn't serious, but I'll sure help you drink it. Please come to the dining room and we'll talk there."

Martin offered her his arm, which she took with a grateful smile. He helped her to the table and eased her into the chair, while she gritted her teeth against the pain. Martin looked over the modest fair spread before them and realized what a toll it must have exacted from her to prepare the meal.

Martin and Julie sat down, a worried expression on their faces.

"I'm fine now, thank you," Christine said as she caught her breath. "The pain killers take the edge off, but getting up and down is the worse."

"I'm sorry, Christine. I didn't think about your medication when I bought the wine."

"Nonsense. If I got looped on alcohol and pain-killers, it would be a welcome relief. Please, eat. I'm just thankful to have you young people here."

Martin smiled inwardly as the thought crossed his mind that he was actually older than Christine and Julie combined. "Thank you," was all he said.

He poured the wine for Christine and then noticed the extra glasses sitting in front of his and Julie's settings. Julie had noticed them also and looked to Christine.

Christine settled further into her padded chair. "I took care of Grant, he was my husband. I'm from the old school and felt that I should cook for him. When his—tastes changed—I still took it upon myself to prepare his meals for him." She indicated the two glasses of blood sitting in front of them. "We raised rabbits out back. Once I drained them, we could still use the meat. I've had that in the freezer. I hope it's still good."

Martin gained an appreciation of just how deep Christine's love for Grant had been. He raised his wine glass and inclined his head toward her. "To a most endearing host, thank you."

For a moment Martin saw a small twinkle in her sad eyes.

The next hour was spent swapping tales and passing information that might prove to be useful. At last, Martin looked at this watch.

"Thank you so much for a wonderful dinner. Unfortunately, we have to go. It's imperative we find these men, take them out, and retrieve the formula."

"I understand." She reached into her pocket and pulled out a set of keys. "Besides, it is I who should be thanking you two for helping to make Grant's death not so meaningless. Here." She laid the keys on the table.

"Thanks again," Martin said. He took the keys from her, but before he could pull away, she covered his hand with hers.

"I'm very happy to be able to help in any way I can. I was just hoping that you could do something for me."

"Whatever's possible."

Christine took a deep breath and glanced at Julie and then looked Martin in the eyes. "I want you to kill me."

"Are you sure," Martin asked evenly.

"Do what?" Julie, who had been sitting passively, sprang to life. "Wait a minute. You can't be serious?"

Christine smiled ruefully at the younger woman. "I told you, I don't have Grant's strength. I am in constant pain and I don't know which is worse, the cancer or being alone. I can't end it by myself, but I know he can help me." She looked at Martin. "You know the kind of loneliness I'm talking about. If I had my health, it might be different. But, I don't. I'm asking you, begging you, help me end it."

Martin looked at her for a long minute while Julie held her breath. "All right. If you're sure that's what you want."

Julie's mouth dropped open and she stared at Martin.

"I'm going to give you a couple of days to think about it. If at that time you're still sure, then I will help you."

She squeezed his hand and whispered a quiet thanks.

Julie sat dumbfounded, staring at the two of them. Martin started to rise.

"Just a minute," Julie headed him off. "Christine, life can be the pits sometimes but that's no reason to kill yourself. Think of all the people you'll be leaving behind. How will it affect them?"

"It won't. I have no family to speak of. My folks have long been dead and I've no brothers or sisters." She folded her hands in front of her. "Besides, we all leave sometime. Even you two."

"But, life is so precious. How can you waste it?'

Christine looked at Julie with eyes that held nothing but kindness. "Please don't let my words sting you, but who's life is it? And, don't think that I haven't thought of all you're saying." She shifted in her chair and tried to hide the pain caused by her movements. "You are absolutely right. Life is precious. But, what kind of life do I have?" She looked around the room. "I'm a prisoner in my own home. I can't get out. It hurts to move. And soon, I won't," she struggled to fight back the tears, "I won't be able to stay here. I won't be able to take care of myself. There's already a nurse that stops by two or three times a week." She looked down at the placemat in front of her seeing a different scene than the Norman Rockwell picture painted there. "All I have to look forward to is lying in a bed in a room somewhere, breathing air that reeks of urine, listening to the moans of others whose deaths are being prolonged because life is so precious. In ancient societies, old people were revered for their wisdom. When they could no longer contribute, then they were allowed to leave this world on their own. Not kept alive by a machine and a host of drugs."

Julie sat stock still for a moment longer and then slowly pushed the chair back. She walked to where

Christine sat crying softly. She gently hugged her. "I'm so sorry. I didn't mean to upset you."

Christine sniffed as she wiped at her eyes, "There's nothing to be sorry about." She looked Julie in the face, "I was just feeling sorry for myself, that's all. We all have to play the hand that life deals us. Mine's just going to be a shorter game than the one you're playing. But," she searched Julie's eyes for understanding, "even in card games we have the chance to fold our hand."

Julie simply nodded and stood up. "Thank you again for the meal. I'll wait for you in the car," she said to Martin and headed for the garage.

"You're lady friend doesn't agree with my ideals," Christine said to Martin.

"Perhaps, it's because she hasn't lived as long as we have. Or," Martin stood slowly and pushed his chair in, "maybe she honestly feels that no matter what, life should run its own course. Either way, it doesn't matter because it's your life, your choice. I said I would give you a couple of days to think about it and then I would help you, and I will." Martin jingled the keys in his palm. "Thanks for the loan."

Christine waved a hand at him. "Ah, keep the damn thing. I've no use for it. Somebody might as well get some good out of it. Besides, you'll find a few nifty add-ons."

"Thanks," Martin said smiling and headed for the door.

"Oh, Martin, wait," Christine said. "I can't believe I almost forgot. There on top of the hutch is an envelope. I think you'll find it useful. I was going through the rest of Grant's police things and found those."

Martin crossed to the antique hutch set against

the dining room wall, his mind flashing to a time when this style had been commonplace. He retrieved the envelope and opened the flap. Inside were several photographs. Thumbing through them he found a short description on the back of each one. Martin leafed through them all and then looked at Christine. "You are an angel without wings." He put them back in the envelope. "He really was good at what he did, wasn't he?"

"Yes, he was." She looked at him sideways and said, "At least it's not like television. You guys really do show up in photographs."

Martin narrowed his eyes and wagged a finger at her. "See you soon."

"Now, this guy was practical," Martin said as he steered the black on black Chevy 1/2 ton pickup through traffic. "I've got to admit, I never expected a pickup truck."

"That's not all," Julie said propping her feet on the dash. "You need to check out the camper shell. It's sealed, has a bed, hint hint, and even has a secret compartment that we could hide in if need be."

"If it's so secret, how did you find it?"

"Are you kidding? You're talking to a woman and a natural born snoop." She gave him a condescending look. "It also helps that Christine left a note on the dash." She waved the piece of paper at him.

"Hmmph." Martin flipped the envelope at her. "Check that out."

"What is it?"

"A short cut."

Martin pulled the truck into the parking lot of Club Enhanced, found a space toward the back and shut off the engine. They scanned the parking lot and the immediate area. Martin reached into the bag he had taken out of the Prizm and brought out two pair of field glasses.

"Well, Grant was right again. One of them works as a bouncer here. Perfect job for these scumbags. No one off the street can touch them and they get the ego boost of being able to whip up on someone. More importantly, they can screen the clientele against people like you and me."

"So what are we going to do?"

"Wait." Martin lowered the glasses and looked at Julie, "Even a vampire has to take a leak sometime."

A couple of hours passed as the pair sat and watched the front door.

"You sure know how to wow a girl on a date," Julie said.

Martin stretched. "Kind of takes the glamour out of PI work doesn't it?"

They waited for another hour when Julie called Martin's attention to the door.

"Isn't that another one of them?" she asked.

"Where?"

"The one that just walked up to the bouncer. The little weaselly looking dude," she said thumbing through the pictures. "Yea, this guy!"

Martin looked from the eyepiece of the glasses to the picture Julie held up. "Nice job, lady. It looks like we might actually get a break tonight. We don't have to go inside looking for answers. They're coming to us. You drive."

They watched which direction the smaller vampire was walking, letting him get farther away from the door and then Julie eased the pickup out of its slot and headed that way. Julie slowed as she passed him going the opposite direction, then braked to a quick stop. Just as the vampire cleared the tailgate, Martin burst out of the back of the camper. In the span of a heartbeat and using the truck for cover, Martin clamped a hand over the other's mouth and ran him through with the heavy hunting knife. The vampire jerked in response as Martin withdrew the blade and plunged it through him again. Martin yanked the smaller man off his feet and drug him into the back of the truck.

"Let's go!"

Julie eased the truck forward again and out of the parking lot, noticing that the bouncer was none the wiser. In the back of the truck, the other vampire was lying on his back, perspiring with a shocky appearance as his body put itself back together.

"Where to, Doc?" Julie called out to him through the boot between the cab and camper.

"Hit the interstate." Martin looked down at the low-life lying on the floor. "No one can hear him scream there."

The smaller man's eyes widened in panic and he bared his fangs with an audible hiss and reached for Martin's throat.

Martin brought the blade down square in the middle of the other's right lung and twisted the heavy blade.

The vampire screamed, a bloody froth forming on his lips, and released Martin, grabbing the blade instead.

"Being immortal can be a real bitch sometimes," Martin growled at the other and twisted the blade again.

The smaller man clutched at the blade, cutting his fingers, the blood running down the blade to mix with that welling from his chest. Martin wrenched the knife out of the vampire's chest and wiped the blade on the other's shirt. He sat back a moment and waited for the other's body to stem the flow of blood.

When most of the bleeding had stopped, Martin tapped him with the tip of the blade, "You with us yet?

"Fuck, man, what do you want?" he whined.

"I need some answers and you're the most likely source."

"I don't know nuthin'. Besides, what makes you think I'm going to help you?" he stammered.

"You don't even know what I'm going to ask, Chucky old boy," Martin said imitating Straun's voice. "Surprised, Chucky? We know a lot about you and your friends. I just don't know if I know everything and that's where you come in. And, don't think about holding out on us, because what Straun will do to you is nothing compared to what we will do." Martin punctuated the statement by driving the knife into Chucky's shoulder, separating the joint. The smaller man screamed repeatedly as Julie drove down I-5. "I think you realize that we mean business." Martin pulled the blade out once more and leaned closer to Chucky. "Do you know who I am?"

Chucky gritted his teeth against the pain and shook his head yes, drops of sweat running off his face.

"So, who am I?"

"You're some fuckin' chemist, man, that Straun wants to whack."

"Why?"

"How the fuck should I know?" he spat out.

"Chucky," Martin's voice lowered menacingly,

"don't lie to me. Have you ever been injected with hydrochloric acid? It will eat you up from the inside out. Every cell will be on fire. It will be like going through the transformation all over again, only this time there won't be an end to it."

The whites of the small man's eyes gleamed in the light coming through the front windshield.

"We feed you and control the flow of acid and you'll never die from it. You will lie there and suffer for years. Think about it Chuck. Years. Centuries if we choose." He paused for a second to let all he had said sink in. "Did you bring the syringes?" he called out to Julie.

Julie, having listened to the whole conversation never missed a beat.

"Right here," she said patting the seat beside her. "Do you want them now?"

"Nooo!" Chucky tried to sit up but was pushed back down by the heel of Martin's hand. "Please don't." He tried to crane his neck to see what Julie was doing in the front of the truck. "I swear man, I don't know. Straun just said that his employer wanted you dead and that it was his responsibility to see that it gets done. That's all I know, man, I swear."

Martin absorbed what he said. "How many of you are there?"

"Twenty or thirty. I don't know. I haven't met everybody."

"Where is Straun operating from?"

"Oh, shit man." The fear in his voice threatened to close off his windpipe as he sucked for air. "Straun will kill me."

"He might. That is, if he ever finds you." Martin's eyes turned to stone. "He *might* kill you. I won't."

Chucky wiped at his face with his good hand. "He

has a penthouse. You take I-5 like you're headed to Burbank. It's in the Weston Tower. He also goes to some lab."

"Where?"

"I don't know man. I can't remember?"

"Think, Chucky."

"It's..it's not far from the penthouse. On King Street, I think."

"Do you mean King Avenue?"

"Yea, that's the place."

"Why?"

"Computers or something. I heard some of the other guys talkin'. I've never been there myself. High tech shit. The guys some kind of freakin' computer whiz or somethin'."

"Anything else you want to share with us?"

Chucky glared at Martin for a moment and spat out, "Just that he's goin' to rip your fuckin' lungs out and I hope that I'm there to see it."

"Be careful what you wish for, you just might get it. And, then he's goin' to wonder just how I found him." Martin fixed the little man with an icy stare.

Chucky's complexion blanched even further as the implications of Martin's statement sank in.

"Chucky, you're as good as dead if Straun ever finds you. On the other hand, if *I* see you again or hear about you preying on humans, well, you know what I'll do." Martin yanked him to his knees. "Go away. Get a job. A night job. And, lead as normal a life as your existence will permit you." Over his shoulder he called to Julie, "Is there anyone behind us?"

"No," Julie said checking the side mirror.

"See ya, Chuck." Martin kicked open the door to the camper.

"Wait. No!" Chucky wailed as Martin pitched him

out of the truck. His body hit the pavement with a sickening thud, rolling and flopping like a rag doll. Martin watched as the tumbling figure finally skidded to a stop on the shoulder of the highway. He closed up the camper again and slipped back through the boot to sit beside Julie.

"Damn, Doc. Did you use to work for the Inquisition? You give one hell of an interrogation. I just want to know where your bright light and Joe Friday accent were."

"I'm just trying to follow Sun Tzu's words of wisdom."

"Who?"

"Sun Tzu. Art of War. 'Know thyself—Know thy enemy. Well, I know myself. I don't know enough about our enemy and he knows way too much about us. One thing Sun really advocated was the use of spies. I believe him. You've seen the effects of Straun's network and the help that has come out of Grant's work. And now, the info from Chuck there is invaluable." Martin drew a long breath and let it out slowly as he ran his hands through his hair. "Mr. Tzu also said that if one is going to make war on someone, do it full out, no holding back. Make it so that they can't possibly retaliate. It's time to take it to Straun. Let's head back to Christine's."

"O.K.." Julie gave him an appreciative glance. "By the way, good bluff with the acid and all. Nice touch."

"Who says I was bluffing?"

"Nonsense. I won't hear of you leaving," Christine said to Julie as they sat together in her living room. "It's too close to dawn for you to find some other place."

"We had planned on spending the day in the camper."

"In that stuffy old thing? No, you'll stay right here with me."

Julie very gently patted her hand. "Thanks Christine. Really, but it's too dangerous. The more we're here, the more likely it is that Straun will find out and that will put you right in the middle of things. Martin will be through gathering up the stuff in a minute and then we can jet out of here."

As if on cue, Martin came in carrying the two large duffel bags loaded with gear. "Did he used to be a boy scout? This guy was prepared for anything."

Christine chuckled. "That's what he used to say all the time. 'Be a boy scout.'"

"You sure you don't mind us using this stuff?" Martin indicated the bags in his hands. "You could sell it for quite a bit of money."

"I'm quite sure. I can't use it and very soon I'm not going to need money."

Martin's gaze turned serious.

"Anyway, let's not be glum." she motioned for Martin to sit in the chair across from her. "You were raised to respect your elders, so have a seat young man."

Martin sat the bags down and crossed the floor to the chair. As he sat, he said with a mock official air, "I feel that I must point out that I am the senior member of this group."

"Just in years, not countenance. So, don't argue with me." Christine waved him off. "Besides, I'll appeal to your logic. You need to ready yourself if you're thinking of storming this place, wherever it is. I have resources you can exploit. A base of operation if you will. I also have a phone and food.

You said it yourself, be prepared. Why go off half cocked at this stage and get yourself and your young lady killed?"

Martin looked from Christine to Julie who hunched her shoulders in response.

"You really do put up a convincing argument." Martin said submitting to her logic.

"Of course I do. Now, first things first. Do you need to eat? If so, there is blood in the freezer. Also, do you need to sleep?"

"Not just yet. We're fine."

"I forget how long you people can go on a little sleep," Christine said off hand. "I wonder where the legends came up with that crap of having to sleep in your coffins during the day?" She cocked her head sideways at the pair. "How does it feel to be the stuff of legends?"

"Misunderstood?'

Julie nodded in agreement and then added, "Legend or not, I am getting hungry."

Christine started to rise and then settled back into the chair, her breath escaping between her teeth as she fought off the pain. "Perhaps you'd best get it yourself. I'm not very spry today."

Julie placed a hand on the older woman's shoulder. "I'll get it. No problem. Martin?"

"Please." To Christine he added, "And, then, we might actually catch a couple of winks until regular business hours. I know the lab Chuck told us about. Place called Mem-Tech. Not only that, but I know someone employed there. This could definitely work for us. I need to make a handful of other calls and if everything works out, a couple of days from now we'll go in and get all our information back. I can only surmise that they haven't been able to get into the

241

files yet or they're unable to synthesize the formula. Hopefully the former."

Martin heard Julie running hot water in the sink to thaw out their meal as she called out from the kitchen. "You said you knew someone at the lab. Who?"

"A gentleman by the name of Thurston Myers. A real scholarly type, goes with the name. Good friend, middle aged and quite human."

Julie stuck her head around the corner. "You mean he knows about you?"

"Why? Does that surprise you?"

"I thought you said that you only told two people besides me?"

"That's true. I have only told two people. I mentioned he was the scholarly type. That's putting it mildly. That and he's extremely observant. He figured it out, asked me about it, and accepted things the way they are. The difference is that you're bull headed enough that you did something about it."

"Good point. Soups on," she said ducking back into the kitchen.

"We'll be right back," Martin spoke to Christine excusing himself.

"Take your time. I'm not going anywhere."

A couple of minutes later, Martin and Julie returned to the living room where Christine sat with a look of amusement on her face.

"I will say that having a liquid diet definitely speeds up the dining process." Her eyes sparkled as Martin stopped to look down at her.

"It just depends on whether you have to catch it or not," Martin quipped. "In the mean time, Julie and I are going to turn in for a short while." Martin knelt beside the stuffed chair and took her hand lightly in his. "Is there anything we can do for you?"

"Not right now," she said looking into his eyes.

Martin nodded and headed toward the guest room with Julie.

A few hours later, Julie handed the receiver to Martin.

"Hello, Thurston. Martin here."

"Martin? I thought you were dead. I'd heard that you were involved with the police and I haven't heard from you. What in Hades is going on and above all else, how are you?"

"I'm fine, thanks. For now. Sorry for all the cloak and dagger stuff and having Julie tell you to call me from a pay phone, but I'm dealing with some real heavy hitters here and for all I know they have your phone bugged as well." Martin drew in a deep breath, "It's the same bunch that killed Bill."

"No."

"Yea. I told you when it happened that it wasn't an accident and now we know for sure. That, and they set me up on drug charges and have tried to take Julie and me out of the picture several times. A couple of times they almost succeeded. They also killed a very good police officer we knew."

"I am very sorry that this has come about, Martin, but how does this concern me since it obviously does or you wouldn't have presented the subterfuge?"

Julie raised an eyebrow.

"I told you he was sharp." Martin said. Then to Thurston, "Julie is listening in on the conversation."

"She is? I did not hear her on the extension."

"She's not." Martin looked at Julie who gave a saccharin smile. "She's just listening in."

"You mean that . . ."

"Yes."

"You didn't . . . "

"No."

"Don't you guys ever talk in complete sentences?" Julie asked.

Martin ignored her. "She infected herself and I helped her through it."

"I see," Thurston said, "but, still, how do I fit into all of this?"

"I've received information that the person ramrodding this whole affair uses or works at your facility. I was hoping that you could confirm it. It's a guy that goes by the name of Straun. I don't know if that's first, middle, or last or if that's even his real name."

"The name doesn't strike a chord. What does he look like?"

Martin described Straun to his friend.

"Wait a moment. Yes, I believe I have seen this one when I was working late on a couple of occasions. His eyes are cold black, like those of a, ah, a shark."

"That's our man," Julie said from where she was sitting.

"You hit that one right on the head," Martin told Thurston, "this guy is a shark."

"I will do some digging around then and find out what department he is with or who it is he is seeing. I don't know of any other of your inkling that works here."

"No! Stay away from this guy, Thurston. You don't know what you're dealing with."

"Nonsense. And, what kind of a friend would I

be if I left you to your own devices, especially after all you've done for me?"

"A live one. Please, I've lost too many people to this guy. If you really want to do something for me, then stay put. The information you just gave me is invaluable. Let me ask you a couple of more questions about the layout and we'll call it even. O.K.?"

"No, it is not O.K.. But, if this person is as ruthless as you make him out to be, then I have no desire to meet him. I have heard that the eyes are the window to the soul. If that is the case, then this man's soul is as black as pitch. I will do as you ask. Now tell me what it is that you would like to know."

"Well, first I need to know if . . . " Martin continued talking to him for the better part of an hour. At last, Martin felt he had as much information as he could use. "Thank you, Thurston. You don't how much of a help you've been. You shouldn't encounter him if you leave during regular hours. If you do see him during the day, by all means stay away from him and let me know immediately. Oh, Thurston, one more thing. I need the name of somewhere I can go and use their facilities to work on the formula."

"The formula, you perfected it?"

"Yes, I believe so, and there's the catch. If Straun and his bunch crack my file, then they'll have the formula too and we'll be in deep stuff. If they synthesize it before us, all they would have to do is find where we are, wait for daylight, kick open the door and we're toast."

"I see your problem. I will do my utmost to solve it."

"Thanks, Thurston. Call tomorrow or sooner if you find anything." Martin slowly replaced the receiver and turned back to the pair of women sitting together talking quietly. "Thurston gave us the layout of the building. I remember the place pretty well, but, of course, I haven't been everywhere." Martin looked up from the carpet where he had been staring. "Let's start getting our stuff together, 'cause we're going to pay Mr. Straun a visit tonight. Julie, call that one cyber junky friend of yours and see if you can persuade him to give you the nastiest, most fast acting virus he has. We'll make a present for Straun."

Julie looked at Martin. "Although he collects them, they're not something you just go passing around. Besides, what makes you think he's going to hand over something like that to me?"

"Because you tell him the truth."

Julie raised an eyebrow in surprise.

"Not that you're a vampire, dear. That you've stumbled onto someone heavy into industrial espionage and they've cost you your job and you're wanting pay back. It's the kind of thing he won't be able to resist. Besides," Martin pulled her to him, "you're irresistible. You could convince the Pope that he's Baptist, and not only that, the guy's got a crush on you."

"Phhhh. Right."

"Hey, I just call 'em like I see 'em." Martin kissed her on the nose and released her. "But, you tell him not to get his hopes up, because you're with me."

"See. He loves me," Julie said to Christine who had been taking in the exchange.

"No. You're just better on the computer than I am," Martin said dancing out of the room.

Chapter 19

Nightfall found them in the cab of the truck once more headed across town.

Julie took a deep breath and blew it out slowly, trying to calm herself. "You want to tell me again why we're doing this?"

"I believe that Straun thinks we're dead or else he doesn't know how to find us. We, on the other hand, know how to find him."

"That's fine and dandy, but what do we do when we find him?" Julie fidgeted in her seat.

"Like I told you earlier," Martin said flatly, "we kill him. We make sure he's nothing more than a pile of ash when we leave."

"Yea, I've been thinking about that part and I just want you to know that revenge is not a healthy thing."

Martin squinted against the glare of the oncoming traffic. "This isn't about revenge, Jules, and you know it." He looked across the cab at her. "I won't lie to you. Sure, I want to see Straun dead, no doubt, and I will gladly pull the trigger given the chance, though he deserves a lot worse for all the people he's hurt and killed and the things he's done. But, this goes way beyond all that. Whatever is happening with this guy is about to get real big, real quick, unless we can do something about it."

Julie sat across from him for a moment staring at the stern expression on his face.

"Aren't you scared?"

"Shitless," Martin said, his face softening a little as a slight smile crept to one corner of his mouth.

"What does that commercial say, 'Never let them see you sweat.'?"

"Then you better put on your deodorant, Babe, we're here."

Martin cruised the truck past the front of the high rise and turned left at the corner, circumnavigating the building. Looking for the best way into the building, he made one more pass around the structure.

"Why not try the front door?" Julie asked innocently. "You know, a lot of people use them now days. Unless of course, you plan to scale the walls. Although," Julie said laying a finger along the side of her face in mock thoughtfulness, "I don't think that would work. You come closer to qualifying as Batman, not Spiderman."

"Hey, if Adam West can do it," he said not looking at her, "so can I."

Martin turned right at the corner this time and cruised down the street until he found a pay parking lot. He pulled the truck into the indicated space after paying the attendant and turned off the ignition. He looked out the window at the city around them.

"Even though I've lived in the city for years, all this just doesn't feel right. I'd be much more comfortable if this were a wooded hillside instead of all this concrete. You know, have them on my turf."

"Seems like the last time we were in the country they almost cooked us." Julie undid her seatbelt and swiveled to look straight at Martin.

"But they didn't," he told her. "Anyway, it's a mute point. We're here and so are they. Let's go get 'em."

Martin hefted one of the duffel bags lying between the seats and unzipped it.

"Here, spray yourself again."

"Why," Julie said taking the spray bottle from him. "Do you smell me?"

"No, I don't. In fact I haven't caught a whiff of you since you put the stuff on, but I just want to be sure."

Martin took the bottle from Julie when she had finished and began spraying himself. When he was through, he opened the door and poured the remainder of the liquid on the ground.

"What are you doing?" she asked in disbelief. "You go to all the trouble, not to mention danger, of producing that scent mask and then you simply pour it out?"

"Just in case we can't get back to the truck and they tie it to us, I don't want them to get their hands on this stuff. We need every edge we can muster."

"Oh."

"Well. It's show time." Martin took out a ratty looking jacket and floppy hat and put them on. Julie picked up the other duffel and took out similar garb. She put makeup on her face to simulate dirt and tied a scarf around her head.

"All I need now is a shopping cart," Julie said checking her appearance in the rearview mirror.

"You'll just have to settle for the bag." Martin stuffed the duffel into a shabby, oversized tote bag.

Martin and Julie exited the truck making sure that the attendant wasn't watching and headed toward the back of the lot. There they vaulted the eight-foot chain link fence and headed towards Straun's apartment. While not as common as in Hollywood, street people could still be found here, and the pair blended with their surroundings. They were within a stones throw of the building, slowly making their way when Martin stopped and bent over to pickup a can. As he slowly put it into the knapsack, he asked Julie if she smelled anything.

"No-wait a minute. Yes. It comes and goes." she whispered. "Where?"

"Over there, close to the front," Martin motioned slightly with his head, "the one with the close cropped black hair and Armante suite. That's one of Straun's goons. I wondered about him earlier. Thought he looked too much like he was standing guard. Now I'm sure of it."

The pair shuffled across the street and slowly up the sidewalk until they were even with the vampire standing guard. Martin acted as if they would pass by the guard, then turned and spoke to him.

"Excuse me," Martin slurred, "you wouldn't happen to have a ten spot so that the Mrs. and I might get a bite to eat?"

"Piss off, you bum," the other said giving a disgusted look at the filthy pair of vagrants in front of him.

"Perhaps your pocket change then. Anything, really."

The vampire folded the paper he had been reading, tucked it under his arm and jabbed a finger at

Martin. "Get the hell out of here before I have you run in."

"Please, sir," Martin begged, "we haven't eaten in such a long time. We've no one to turn to here. We've no family or friends and we're at our end. Surely you know what it's like to be hungry?"

"You don't have any family?" he asked the pair.

"No. None." Martin could see the hunger well up in the other's eyes.

"Maybe I was a little too hard on you there," he said sickeningly sweet. "I do know what it's like to go hungry, so, I tell you what I'm going to do." The vampire looked up and down the street making sure the situation was to his liking. "I can't do anything for you here." He put an arm around each of their shoulders, heading them down the side-walk. "See, I actually work security for the building, but I know the manager of the restaurant, and I think I can help you out." As he talked, he squeezed Julie's shoulder through the rags she was wearing and looked down at her with only a half-veiled leer. "Yea, I think I can do something for you."

Julie felt the bile rise in the back of her throat at the thought of this cretin having his hands on her.

"We just need to go around to the side entrance and I'll take care of you there."

The vampire steered the couple around the corner and down the alleyway. About halfway down, he suddenly slammed the pair into the brick wall.

Julie twisted her neck where the other man held her to the wall, struggling to get the words past the fingers that were closing off her wind. "What are you doing?"

"This is the end of the line, kiddies." The vampire

laughed, revealing a set of gleaming fangs. "Soups on."

"I don't think so," Martin said effortlessly prying the hand off his throat. Before the vampire could react, a switchblade appeared in Martin's other hand from where it had been concealed under his sleeve. In one motion, Martin thumbed open the blade and drove it just under the other's sternum. The vampire's eyes widened in surprise. He made a feeble attempt to grab at Martin's hand. Martin twisted the blade causing the vampire to slump to his knees on the filthy pavement.

"Wh-who are you?" he rasped out, his face ashen gray from the blood he was losing. His face twisted in agony as Martin pulled the blade free.

"Doesn't matter who I am. The only thing you need to know is that I'm going to ask you some questions. If you answer them truthfully, I might let you live. If not, I'll kill you right here." Martin, closing the knife, returned it to its place in his sleeve. He then fetched his cane from the knapsack, unlocked it, and pulled out the blade with an audible hiss. The vampire stared at the point of the blade barely an inch from his nose.

"Now," the other's eyes flicked to Martin's face, "which room is Straun in and is he there now?"

"I don't know what you're talking about," he said holding his stomach, waiting for his body to repair itself.

"I won't ask you again." Martin's voice took on the finality of the tomb. "We know he's here. We just don't know where, but you're going to tell us. Now."

The man shifted slightly, the gravel digging into his knees as he looked from the blade to Martin and back. He swallowed hard against the pain that was churning his insides as they rearranged themselves, closing off arteries and reattaching muscles where Martin had severed them.

"You don't know what you're dealing with here, man."

"I think we do," Martin said revealing fangs of his own. The wounded vampire looked from Martin to Julie who had been keeping an eye out for foot traffic. She smiled sweetly and inclined her head, her fangs in sharp contrast to her other teeth.

"Oh, shit," the vampire looked back to Martin, recognition setting in.

"Live or die." Martin laid the blade against the other's neck.

"Fifteenth floor. West side."

"Thank you," Martin said leaving the blade where it was. "Is he there now?"

The vampire glared at Martin and thought about not answering, but was persuaded other wise by the blade pressing into his neck.

"I-don't-know," he said, acid dripping from the word.

Martin ignored the other's attitude. "When are you expected back?"

"I'm not. I was supposed to hang out and watch for anything unusual. Everybody thinks you're dead except for maybe Straun. He never saw your body so there was the possibility that you were still alive. He's the real cautious type. That's why you'll never make it."

"Don't worry, we're not going to take the elevator."

"Doesn't matter. He's got video in the building and extra muscle both inside and out of the apartment."

Martin could see the color starting to come back to the vampire's features and could hear the strength returning to his voice and speeded up the questioning.

"Is he at the lab?"

"How do you know about…?"

Martin drug the blade across the skin of the vampire's neck, causing blood to run freely down the metal. "Is he there?"

"I don't know. I'm telling you. He could be anywhere. I was told to stay out front. That's it man. Take it or leave it."

Martin pitched his voice for Julie. "Is it clear?"

She nodded her head, not taking her eyes off the entrance to the alley.

Quicker than the human eye could follow, Martin drew back the blade and then brought it forward again cleaving through the other's neck. The head made a dull thudding noise as it hit the pavement and rolled to a stop against a dumpster.

Julie walked to where Martin was standing. "I thought you said you weren't going to kill him?"

"I said, 'might'. I decided against it."

Julie looked down at the body already starting to smolder. "I noticed."

Martin shucked out of the shabby coat and tossed it in the dumpster.

"Just realize that any of the scumbags we encounter tonight are every bit as ruthless as Straun, just not as intelligent. They won't hesitate to kill you. You've heard the old expression, fighting fire with fire; that's what we're doing now."

Martin pulled the black duffel out of the knapsack and slipped it across his shoulders. As he settled it, his features were momentarily highlighted by the flare of the body as it ignited.

Julie looked to the mouth of the alley to see if the light had grabbed anyone's attention. She glanced back to where the body had been. "I'll say one thing. You don't have to worry about hiding the corpse."

Julie's disguise joined Martin's in the dumpster and she accepted the 9mm automatic that he held out to her. She checked the chamber, flicked on the safety and slipped it into the holster she wore on her right leg. She already wore a utility belt that held extra clips, a kubaton and pepper spray. On her other leg, tucked in its scabbard was a 12-inch stiletto.

Martin carried the same gear plus 150 feet of climbing rope and karabiners, as well as a few other devices in the duffel bag.

Julie hitched at her belt one last time and looked at Martin as he settled his gear in place. "Why do I feel like Rambo?"

Martin cocked an eyebrow at her, "Rambo? I don't think so. You're much better looking." Martin looked at her in the pale light of the alleyway and then pulled her to him and kissed her fiercely.

He slowly released her. "Let's go do this thing."

"Lead on, McBeth," she said falling in behind him as he made his way farther up the alley.

Martin stopped and scanned the side of the building. "What do you think?"

Julie appraised the situation. "Looks as good as anything."

Martin ran his hands over the surface of the brick structure gauging the depth of the joints there. Julie watched as he adhered himself to the side of the building and started up.

"Maybe you are more like Spiderman," Julie said to herself.

She gave Martin a slight lead and then started up after him. Julie had been rock climbing several times in her life, but she would never have tackled a naked brick wall. She was amazed at how she could cling to the tiny crevices between each brick. She was glad that they had procured climbing shoes in that they aided their ascent dramatically.

The building was not well lit on this side and their presence would be blocked by the building next to it for half the climb. They could move quicker on this side although Martin doubted that anyone from the street would notice them anyway. He was counting on the fact that, unlike their animal counterparts, humans are basically unaware of their environment.

They cleared the top of the neighboring building and were now visible to anyone looking up from the street. They avoided the windows that now dotted the side of the building and made their way to the 18th floor. Martin perched himself precariously on the window ledge like a gargoyle overlooking the city. He fished inside the duffel and brought out a high tech glasscutter and attached it to the window. Martin scored the glass deeply and then shoved, taking out a piece of glass large enough to crawl through. Martin pushed the duffel bag through and followed after it. He waited by the elevators until Julie was through the window. He grasped the sliding doors, forcing his fingers into the seam and pulled them apart. He drew a screwdriver from his utility belt and jammed the door open. Martin looked at Julie and nodded. She took a deep breath pulling on a pair of gloves and stepped up to the opening. Martin grasped the cable first and started to descend the three floors between them and Straun's men. Martin stepped quietly onto the ledge by the elevator doors and waited for Julie to get into place. He held up one finger, then two. By the time he got to the third finger she had the flash-bang out and armed. Martin grabbed the doors and heaved them apart. As he did, Julie saw the four armed men standing in the hallway outside Straun's door and slid the flash-bang in the middle of them. Julie remembered Martin's instructions to cover her eyes as soon as she threw it, and ducked her head.

Reflex took over three of the four vampires and they looked down to see what was on the floor. The fourth tried to turn, but was not fast enough. The device went off with a brilliant flash, blinding the four. Martin knew the effect would last only a few seconds and jumped up from the prone position he had been in, pulling the 9mm as he rose. From one knee, Martin fired four rounds, placing one in each of the heads of the vampires. Shouts rose from inside the room as the door leading into Straun's apartment burst open. The first one through the door tripped on one of the bodies sprawled there and caught a round in the throat from Julie as she swung through the opening to the elevators. The vampire staggered backwards into the one following him. Julie followed Martin's lead and fired several rounds into both.

The hallway was a small corner of hell, filled with the sounds of men screaming, the flash of gunfire and the acrid smell of sulfur. The body of the first vampire to fall started to smolder as it prepared to consume itself. Martin closed the distance to the other three and point blank shot them in the head.

Martin dropped his spent clip, jacked a fresh one into the handle and dove through the still open doorway rolling to one knee. He came up facing half a dozen armed men, two with automatic weapons. Martin shot one before they could react and caught another as he tried for the bedroom. The other four opened up. Julie watched in horror as Martin went down in a hail of bullets, the force of the impacts slamming him to the floor. Just as quickly, Martin was back on his feet and head shot one of the vampires using a machine gun.

"He's wearing armor! Shoot him in the head," screamed one of the remaining three.

"Martin! Eyes!" Julie yelled above the chaos going on around them. Martin reacted instantly squatting down with his back to the others and clutched his head just as the flash-bang went off. Martin whirled back around and took out two as Julie dispatched the third.

"Oh shit, Martin!" Julie exclaimed, her hands shaking violently. "Are you all right?"

"I'll be okay," he said, blood showing through his shirt. "Let's see what we can find. There's going to be cops, fire department, and more people than we care to mention, real quick."

"More goons like these?" Julie asked plaintively.

"You can count on it," Martin said casting about the room. Martin spied Straun's P.C. in a study off the bedroom. "Jules! In here." He began searching for the place Straun kept all of his disks. "Turn that virus loose on him and let's get out of here."

"Martin, he's probably tied into the main frame at Mem-Tech. If I turn this loose, it might fry everything there before they can stop it."

"I know that, but we'll just have to chance it."

"Man, oh man." Julie reached for the pocket containing the floppy with the virus when a bullet ripped through the outside of her arm, exploding the hard drive in front of her. She screamed and rolled out of the chair to her right as several more shots riddled the monitor and the remains of the hard drive, scattering shards of plastic, glass and circuit board around the room. Martin had collected the automatic weapons earlier and turned and sprayed the doorway.

Julie leapt to her feet to get out of the line of fire.

"The balcony, Jules! We're out that way." Martin put several rounds into a hapless vampire that tried to storm the doorway.

Julie ripped open the duffel that was hanging on Martin's back and retrieved the rope, beaners, and the harnesses. Trusting that Martin could keep the bogeymen at bay, she kicked open the French doors that led to the small, semi-enclosed balcony overlooking the city below and surveyed her possible anchor points. She found them lacking. She tested the tubular railing, gave it a sharp shove, and knew that it would have to hold or they were going to get a really quick ride to the street. She thanked her lucky stars that they had tied a beaner to one end of the rope before ever starting this little escapade. She looped the line over the rail and clipped the beaner to it, letting the rest of the rope play out to empty space below.

"God," she said to herself as she quickly slipped into the harness and clipped a D-ring through the belt, "my instructor would have a cow."

"Martin! Let's go!"

Martin backed toward the French doors keeping up sporadic fire as he went.

"I've got your harness here," she said holding it out to him.

"No time. Hook in."

"Do what?"

"You've got more experience on the ropes than I do. You repel, I'll ride on your back."

Martin splintered the door facing with a shot that missed the hand that had snaked around the frame to squeeze off a couple of rounds.

"What if you fall," she protested as she slipped the rope through the speed eight and clipped that into the beaner on the front of her harness.

"Then I fall. We don't have time, and someone has to keep them from shooting us on the way down." He instinctively ducked as sheetrock and plaster exploded over his head from twin shotgun blasts. "You ready?"

"No. Yes!"

Martin climbed over the rail and then fired one of the automatics into the doorway and through the wall. He didn't know for certain, but from the sounds of the cursing, he figured he hit at least one of them. The firing pin clicked empty and he pitched the weapon aside as he climbed onto her back. "Let's go!"

Julie took a deep breath and kicked back from the ledge into open air. The line went taut and the rail groaned under the strain, but held. She let the rope play through her gloved hands in a barely controlled free fall. She ignored the pain as the friction burned her hands through the gloves as they picked up speed.

Martin had been right. As soon as the armed group realized that the pair had gone over the rail, they were there in an instant. A rather squatty vampire was the first to the rail and was greeted with several shells from Martin. He had leaned out over the rail for a clear view when the shells ripped a path through his head and upper torso. The body convulsed from the impact of the shells, slumped, flipped over the rail and almost struck Martin and Julie as it overtook them on the way down. They were over two thirds of the way down when Martin caught a glimpse of others at the rail. He took aim and squeezed the trigger of the other machine gun he had taken from the apartment and was rewarded with the click of an empty chamber.

"Damn." Martin cursed as bullets began bouncing off the wall in front of them. In one motion, he slung the automatic rifle over his shoulder, drew the 9mm at his side and returned the fire from above.

Suddenly there was a jerk on the line and a moment later the pair realized they were being hauled back up. They had been scarcely twenty feet off the ground and were now double that already. Martin drew his boot knife and slashed through the rope.

Julie's mind registered what he was doing a split second before they went hurtling into empty space, headed for the pavement below.

"Martiiiiin!"

He let go of his hold on her as the pair crashed into the pavement amidst the din of Julie's curses and the clatter of hardware. They didn't give anyone a chance to get a clear look or a clean shot at them as they jumped to their feet and dashed around the corner and down the alleyway. They raced back to the dumpster where they had stashed their disguises and retrieved them from the smelly interior. They hastily put them on as Martin stuffed the machine gun and duffel back into the knapsack.

He picked up a nearly empty beer bottle from the dumpster, poured the remainder of the contents on himself, and kept the bottle for effect. They could already hear the sirens rapidly approaching and started shuffling their way up to the mouth of the alley. As they walked passed it, Martin scattered the pile of ash that had been the vampire he had killed earlier.

They were out on the street when the first police cruiser showed up, its tires protesting loudly as it slid to a stop in front of the building. The first car was joined by several others and the fire department could be heard rapidly approaching. A crowd had already gathered and Martin and Julie melted into it.

Along the way to the truck they ditched the overcoats and quickly stuffed the body armor and black fatigues into the duffel bags. To the world, they looked like a typical pair of west coast yuppie health enthusiasts in shorts and tank tops. They made their way back to the truck, unlocked it and climbed inside the darkened cab. Once inside the cab, Martin slammed his fist against his leg in frustration.

"Damn. We were that close. I can't believe we missed."

"I'm just glad they missed." Julie fingered the hole in her shirtsleeve. "And it's not like we didn't take out his PC. Or I should say they did for us. Not exactly the way you had in mind, but it worked."

"I was hoping that Straun would be there. I also didn't have time to look for any backup disks." Martin started the engine and put the truck in gear. "The virus, do you still have it?"

Julie fished in her duffel bag for her fatigues, popped open the pocket and produced the floppy still in one piece. "Right where I left it."

Martin sighed. He drove out of the parking lot and turned left, away from the commotion that was taking place further down the street in the other direction. They could see in their mirrors the flashing lights reflecting off the buildings. "We've got to go to the lab, you know."

Julie propped her feet on the dash and rubbed the back of her neck trying to loosen the stressed muscles there. "How'd I know you were going to say that?"

"Sorry, Jules. If he's at the lab, then you can guess what he's working on. We need to get the formula away from him. If we're lucky, maybe we can kill him."

"Well, one consolation is that at least this time he's the one that's going to have fun explaining stuff to the cops." Julie continued to work her shoulders. "It'd deserve the scumbag right if they gave him a cell with a nice ocean view."

"I doubt it," said Martin. "Two gunmen bust in, shoot up the place. A couple of crazies probably hopped up on drugs. There's no casualties on their side. None that the cops will ever find anyway. They probably had a damage control team in there as soon as we left, to make sure nothing would implicate any of them. For all we know, the place isn't even in Straun's name." Martin's face was grim in the light from the dashboard. "The son-of-a-bitch got off again."

"Oh, I don't know about that." Julie said innocently.

Martin cut his eyes at her. "What do you mean?"

"You know when I picked up the floppy from that certain cyber friend of mine? Well, Tad likes to partake of certain, how shall we say, mind expanding substances from time to time."

A smile started across Martin's face. "You didn't?"

"Didn't I. Turn about is fair play and I doubt seriously that Straun's goons are going to notice a few small baggies around the room before the cops get there. But, you can bet the cops will when they start poking around."

"You're awfully full of yourself, aren't you?"

"Extremely," Julie said raising an eyebrow and lacing her fingers behind her head.

Chapter 20

"What do you mean someone stormed the penthouse," the voice on the cellular asked menacingly. "Are you telling me that someone broke into my home and they're not dead?"

"Yes, sir. But, I think they were vampires, Mr. Straun."

"You think? Were they or not? And if so, who were they?" Straun's impatience poured through the line. "They weren't one of ours?"

"I don't know for sure," the voice on the other end said rapidly. "We couldn't smell them, but they acted like vampires, you know?"

"No, I don't know. Enlighten me."

"I mean they were wearing body armor, but they moved fast like us. Or, at least the big one did. We shot him a couple dozen times and he came back for more."

"The bigger one?" Straun's mind started putting pieces together. "How many were there?"

"Two." The voice spoke hesitantly.

"Two? Two!" Straun almost crushed the handset he was holding, the plastic crackling as it neared its breaking point. "There were only two of them, and they took out nine of your men?" Straun paused in his tirade for a moment as a thought occurred to him. "Could the second one have been a woman?"

The vampire on the other end of the line spoke slowly as he considered the idea. "I didn't get a look at the face, it being covered and all, but I suppose so, yea."

Straun floored the accelerator on the black JXL. "Daniels."

"'Scuse me, Mr. Straun?"

"It was Daniels, you idiot," Straun spit out.

"But, you said they were dead."

"Obviously I was wrong. Have the police shown up yet?"

"They're outside the building now, sir."

"I trust you have secured the scene?" Straun's voice implied volumes.

"Yes sir. We've taken care of everything. We threw the ashes in the fire place, and . . ."

"Shut up and let me think. Damn. The man is like a bloody cockroach." Straun was silent for a moment and the person on the other end knew better than to interrupt. Suddenly, Straun slammed the receiver down in the cradle, switched it to speaker phone and whipped the Jag into a convenience store parking lot, almost running down a couple of pedestrians in the process. He wheeled the car around and headed back the direction he had come from.

"Tony," Straun said into the speakerphone, "I will leave the scene in your capable hands. I have a hunch as to where our little cockroaches are going to show up next. And, Tony," Straun said with finality, "don't screw this up."

He paused for a reply.

"Did you hear me, you imbecile."

Straun ripped the handset out of the cradle and fairly screamed into the receiver. "Did you hear me?" Straun listened but received only silence. The abuse the handset had received in the last few minutes proved too much for it.

"Damn," Straun pulverized the cellular phone, pitching the remains out the window in disgust.

Tony gave the other four vampires in front of him a grave look as he closed the handset and waited for the police to arrive.

Martin used the ID card he had acquired from Thurston and flashed it at the gate security guard who waved them past. Thurston was proving to be a friend indeed. He had done his homework and provided Martin and Julie with invaluable information. He had instructed Martin where there was a small dead spot in the surveillance camera's sweep of the parking lot where he could park the pickup.

Martin shut off the ignition and stared at the expansive, three story structure in front of them.

"Thurston's really putting his butt on the line for us," Julie said quietly as if someone in the building could hear them speak.

"Not really," he said off hand. "He'll report his card missing tomorrow morning. Then when they tell him they were raided, he'll be in the clear because his stuff got wiped like everyone else's. That, and the fact that he will be seen at a highly visible establishment at the time of the purported crime will keep him the clear. There's no way his employers can hold him responsible."

"I wasn't talking about his bosses. What if Straun and his goons find out?"

Martin sighed. "There is that."

She laid a hand on his. "You really are worried about him, aren't you?"

"Good friends are hard to find. And, he's not quite as resilient as we are." Martin glanced at his watch. "He said that the power would go down at 12:42. The back up will fail approximately 30 seconds later. Once we're to the building, we can use his access card. The building is on a separate backup system than the parking lot, so the video inside will be operational. Do you see the door halfway down the building?"

Julie looked and could just make out a doorway from the angle they were looking from. "Yea. I see it."

"That's a security entrance. Everyone else is supposed to use the front. We'll go through there. Thurston's card will get us inside. He also made a loop of the west stairwell tape so we can use the stairs without being seen by security."

"You've gotta be kidding me?" Julie looked flabbergasted. "How did he set all of this up?"

"I told you he was an electronics genius. If I knew how, I wouldn't have needed his help. Although, having him on the inside makes life a whole lot simpler."

Julie sat back in her seat. "Why do I feel like I'm in some James Bond flick?"

Martin looked at his watch once more. "Any second now."

Right on cue, the lights in the parking lot went out, only to be replaced by the dimmer backup lights.

"The man is punctual," Julie said checking the pocket of her fatigues for the fourth time since she had put them back on.

"I take it the disk hasn't crawled out of your

pocket since the last time you checked it two minutes ago," Martin teased.

"Hey, if I'm going to be risking my butt, not to mention the rest of me, I want to make sure I've got the damn thing."

Martin smiled. "I don't think it's going to be as dangerous as the penthouse. Just a little trickier to get into, that's all."

"Then why didn't we come here first?"

"Because it is harder to get into. We can't storm the place like we did the penthouse. There's a lot more people involved here. Most of them innocent. Then, there was the chance that we could have caught Straun at home and killed him there. Also, we could have wiped the computer at the apartment and the company could have perhaps shut down the virus before it got everyone. As it is now, we're going to have to take out the whole system."

"You know, the more I'm around you, the more I get the impression that you've done this sort of thing before." Julie looked at him across the cab of the truck as he watched the timer on his wrist. "Am I right?"

"Let's just say I've done my share of breaking into and out of places during my somewhat lengthy stay on this realm. So, no, I'm not a total novice at this. But, believe me, this is not the movies. Bad guys can win. So, stay sharp."

Just then, the backup system failed and plunged the parking lot into total darkness.

"Ready," Martin asked as he stepped out of the truck.

"Ready," Julie said checking her pocket again.

Under the cover of the blackout, Martin and Julie, twin blurs in the dark, raced across the parking lot, covering the distance far faster than humanly possible. They checked their speed, halting in front of the door. They paused for a moment, listening for movement on the other side of the door. Martin slid the card key through the reader and waited a moment as the latching mechanisms retracted, unlocking the door. The pair slid inside, quietly closing the door behind them. Without hesitating, they ducked into the stairwell and made their way to the third floor. Martin looked at his watch, waited for a little over a half minute, then opened the door and raced down the hall with Julie in tow. She noticed the camera near the ceiling in the middle of the hall pointing in the opposite direction. They stopped in front of Thurston's office, which in turn led to his lab. Martin brought the card up and caught it on the doorknob, knocking it out of his hands. Julie watched in horror as the camera stopped its pan of the opposite end of the hall and started back.

"Oh, shit, Martin," she hissed, "Hurry.!"

Martin grabbed the key off the floor and slid it through the mechanism. Martin started to sweat as nothing happened the second time he ran it through. A thousand possibilities raced through Martin's mind with one thought sticking out above the rest. He wondered if Straun had somehow found out about them being at the lab, allowed them inside and was just now springing the trap.

"Turn it around," Julie urged.

He switched the orientation of the card and tried it again. This time the lock mechanism clicked, and Martin pushed the handle, practically falling into the room with Julie on his heels, closing the door swiftly but quietly behind them. To anyone watching the monitors, nothing would seem out of the ordinary.

"Damn. That was too close," Julie panted as she leaned against the back of the door. "Can vampires have heart attacks?"

"I don't think so." Martin pulled out two pair of rubber gloves as he headed for Thurston's terminal. "I'm just glad that they don't have motion detectors." He motioned for Julie as he put on one pair of the gloves. "We don't have much time. Let's do it."

She donned her pair as Martin typed in Thurston's private entry code and the screen in front of him came to life. "All yours." He vacated the seat in front of the terminal to make way for Julie.

She took the seat, adjusted it quickly as she inserted the floppy in the drive and typed the necessary commands to set the virus loose on the main frame and anyone else who was tied into it. She just hoped that the virus would be limited to this company and not spread to far. She paused with her finger above the enter button and then pulled it away. She looked up at Martin with a hopeful expression.

"Maybe I could hack into Struan's stuff from here. I really hate doing this."

Martin gently laid a hand on her shoulder, "You'll hate it even worse if Straun succeeds."

"I know, but all that data, all that time, lost." She held up her hand, "Yea, I know. They've got backups, but it'll take days or weeks to get it all back on line."

"That's all the time we'll have to get Straun."

Julie shook her head. "I can't believe Thurston would sacrifice his own work like this."

Martin turned away from the screen and looked about the room. "He's one of the few people that's not afflicted with vampirism that understands the consequences if Straun succeeds." Martin scuffed a spot on the floor with the toe of his boot. "That, and he's my friend," Martin said quietly, "one of the few I have left." He smiled as he looked up at Julie. "Also, he's an opportunist. Said it would actually help to push back a couple of dead lines he's facing." He nodded to the screen. "We need to be going."

"I know," she sighed, and hit the return key.

The virus did its job and started the system crashing. Julie stared at the screen, then pushed away from the console to join Martin where he stood by the door with his hand on the handle and his eye on the chronometer on his other wrist. He nodded at Julie then yanked open the door. The pair sprinted back the way they had come, easily making the stairwell before the camera completed its sweep. They glided down the stairwell, twin shadows blending with the brick wall next to them until they reached the door at the bottom of the stairs. Martin reached for the handle and then abruptly ducked, pulling Julie down with him and drew his sidearm as he went. A silenced bullet put a hole in the door where Martin's head had been a split second before. There was a deafening report from Martin's pistol as he squeezed off three quick rounds.

The vampire that had been hiding in the darkness at the back of the stairwell fell forward, the back of his head missing.

"Well, they know we're here." Martin picked up the other's gun, checked the clip and reholstered his own.

"I think I need some new underwear," Julie said as she pushed herself back to her feet.

"No need to be quiet anymore. Let's make a break for it before more show up."

"How did you know he was there," Julie asked as

they bolted out the door and headed for the exit where they had first come in.

"I smelled him," Martin called out as they raced down the hall. He was the first to reach the door and crashed face first into it when it failed to open. From the far end of the hall came the sound of running feet.

Martin and Julie both spun around to see two armed guards sprinting in their direction.

"Stop where you are," the first one shouted.

From their movements, they could tell the guards were human.

"We don't have time for this," Martin growled. He took a step back and lashed out with his foot, catching the door just below the locking mechanism. Brick, mortar and metal scrap flew from the outside of the frame. Martin and Julie wasted no time and leapt through the doorway.

The two guards stopped dead in their tracks, staring in disbelief.

Martin and Julie on the other hand were running flat out toward the truck. They raced across the lot and were to the first of the parked cars when Julie screamed a warning as one of Straun's watch-dogs leapt over the top of a sedan towards them. Martin caught him in mid flight and redirected him into the side of a mini-van. The vampire slid head first onto the pavement and was promptly shot twice by Julie.

"There's two more coming," Julie gushed out between breaths.

Martin judged the distance between them and their would be attackers.

"We can make the truck." He pitched her the keys. "You take the wheel."

The lead vampire was sixty yards away, sprinting hard when Martin suddenly stopped, turned and fired, catching him in the chest. The vampire's momentum carried him forward another half-dozen steps, to where he stumbled, plowing face first into the asphalt. Martin didn't know if it was a fatal wound and didn't wait around to find out.

Julie made it to the truck, jumped behind the wheel and twisted the ignition, causing the engine to spring to life. As Julie shot past him, Martin leapt onto the running board and grabbed a handhold. She didn't let off the accelerator as she bore down on the second vampire, intending to run him down.

The vampire sprang straight up into the air as the truck rocketed beneath him. As he came down, he rebounded off the roof executing a perfect flip to land behind them.

Julie glanced in the side mirror at the figure looking back at them. "Gee, do you think he used to be a gymnast?"

Martin opened the door and climbed inside. "I think that would be a safe guess."

Julie crashed the exit gate, sending the two guards there diving for cover. She handled the truck like an Indy driver as she steered it onto the street, straightened it out and tromped the accelerator. She smiled as the wind whipped through the cab stirring her hair. "I will say that Grant had one hell of a truck."

Martin grabbed the door handle as she slid around the corner at the end of the street. "I take it you like driving fast?"

Julie smiled again. "Comes with being a tom boy."

As the taillights of the pickup disappeared around the corner, the headlights of a black Jag could be seen speeding from the other direction. Straun braked hard and whipped the sports car into the drive of the lab and flashed a security card at one of the shaken guards.

"I'm sorry, sir," the guard sputtered out, between breaths. "We've had an—*incident* and we're not going to be able to let anyone in or out until the police arrive."

"I need to get in there," Straun began.

"As I said, I'm sorry. Even if it weren't against company policy, it appears that someone discharged a firearm, and for your own safety, I wouldn't be able to allow you inside. I'm afraid you'll have to come back tomorrow after everything has settled down and they're able to sort things out."

"I have some sensitive data that I must check upon and I will see it now." Straun stared at the man trying to impose his will upon him.

"Sir, you don't understand," the guard said finding something to focus his fear and frustration on. "You're not getting in there."

"No," Straun growled, "you're the one that doesn't understand." Straun slammed the Jag in reverse and stomped on the gas pedal, smoking the back tires until he cleared the guard shack. He wrenched the stick lever into drive and blasted through the exit that Julie had just demolished.

"Your supervisor is going to hear about this," the guard yelled at the retreating figure.

Straun was oblivious to the guard's threats, not that he would have cared if he could have heard them. Straun raced through the parking lot and screeched to a halt where one of his men was waving him down, forcing the man to backpedal to keep from getting hit.

"You were right, Mr. Straun," the vampire said as

Straun sprang from the car. His close-cropped, military style haircut mirrored his all business attitude. "There were only two of them. And, from the description Vic gave, it positively ID's them." The vampire fell into step with Straun as he headed for the building. "They also got Jeff, Craig and Nicky."

"And, you didn't get either one of them?"

"No, sir." The man faced Straun tight lipped.

"Damn." Straun made his way into the building and talked to the man following him as he went. "Check all the security tapes. Find out where and how they got in. Find out if anyone helped them and if so, bring them to me."

"We've already started checking out the tapes, sir and nothing yet."

"Keep looking." Straun strode on ahead and bounded up the stairs towards the lab he had been working in, not bothering to wait on the elevator. When he reached the second floor landing, he pulled the door loose from its hinges in his haste.

"This Daniels is really starting to bug me."

"Well? How'd it go?" Christine asked the weary looking pair as they came through the door that led in from the garage. "Did you get the bastard?"

"No, we didn't," Martin said with more apology than fatigue in his voice.

"Damn."

"My sentiments exactly," Julie said as she peeled off the body armor and let it fall to the floor. "That scumbag has more lives than a basket of cats." She stooped over, and then decided to sit as she undid her bootlaces. "God, I'm tired."

Martin, too, began divesting himself of his

equipment. As he did so, Christine noticed the holes in his shirt, pants and vest.

"Martin, you were shot?"

"That's an understatement," Julie said. "Straun's boys used him for target practice." She flopped back into the cushions letting them envelope her body and rolled her head to look at Martin. "Scared the hell out of me, I might add."

Martin placed both hands against his chest in mock surprise and mouthed the words "me?" to Julie.

"Are you all right?" Christine asked, genuine concern in her voice.

"I'm fine." Martin laid the vest beside the gun belt, duffel and shirt. He smiled at Christine. "Really. I'm fine, thanks."

Christine stared at him for a moment. At a glance, she counted more than a dozen holes in his shirt. Where there should have been gaping wounds and shredded flesh, there was only smooth skin over muscular arms. Not so much as a bruise to attest to the firefight they had just been involved in.

"You people really are impressive." Christine slowly shook her head. "I accidentally bump my arm and I'm bruised for weeks. You get shot up bad enough to kill an elephant and you don't have so much as a hang nail."

Julie and Martin both sat there, not knowing what to say.

"Grant used to impress me." Christine said slowly. She sat for a moment looking at Martin's hand and tears filled her eyes. "He was building a cabinet for me. That one over there in the corner," she motioned with a nod of her head. He was working on a table saw when I called out to him. He looked up to see what was wrong," she smiled to herself, "he was always so protective of me and he . . . cut off his finger. Blood went everywhere. I was horrified. It was his trigger finger. He tried to tell me it would be all right, but I couldn't stop crying. It was because of me that he had maimed himself. He's the one that was hurt and I couldn't stop crying. It grew back." She looked up from where she had been staring. "The whole thing just grew back. Not instantly of course, but he wrapped it and said he would be fine. The next morning I wanted to check it. Instead of a stump, there was a finger. Just like the old one. I found it difficult to believe. It was then that I actually realized he was truly different."

Christine drew in a shallow breath and looked at the pair who were hanging on her every word. "I think I've prattled on enough. You'll have to excuse me. I get started sometimes and just keep going." She folded her hands in her lap. "It's so hard to face that he's gone."

"I'm sorry." Martin crossed and laid a hand on her shoulder. "Would you like some help to your room?"

"No, thank you." She patted Martin's hand. "I think I'll sit here and dream awhile."

Chapter 21

The next day Thurston was at his console reloading some of his files when a shadow fell over the keyboard. He glanced up to the picture hanging on the wall in front of him and saw the reflection of a tall man in a long, dark coat standing behind him.

"I did not hear you knock," Thurston said as he continued typing.

"Maybe that's because I didn't."

"May I be of some service to you?" Thurston asked evenly, without turning around.

"I believe you can," Straun said in his baritone voice.

Thurston swiveled his chair around and looked up at Straun. "And, how is that?"

"I understand that you lost your I.D. badge yesterday."

Thurston crossed his arms. "Yes, I did lose it. Not that it is any of your business."

Straun's voice dropped further and he stepped closer to Thurston to look down at him. "You'd be surprised at what's my business." Then more lightly, "One thing though, Mr. . . . ?" Straun left the question hanging in the air. When it was apparent that no answer was forth coming he cast a glance around the room. "One thing Mr. Myers, did you lose it accidentally, or on purpose?"

Straun's shark eyes bored into Thurston's who placidly returned his gaze.

"One," Thurston held up a finger for emphasis, "if you knew what a hassle it is trying to get a new one, not to mention trying to operate around here with out it, you would realize that I would never lose it on purpose. Secondly, if you already knew what my name is, why did you ask?"

"I wanted to try and find out if you are who you said you were. Are you?"

"Am I what?"

"Who you say you are."

"Well, obviously." Thurston sounded annoyed at Straun's ignorant remark. "If I weren't, how could I function the way I do around the facility here?"

"Don't play stupid with me. I want to know if you're the mild mannered pencil pusher you say you are or if you had something to do with yesterday's break in."

"Oh, you're back to my losing my ID card. To what end would it serve?"

"That's what I would like to know?"

"Excellent," Thurston said as he stood up to face Straun a moment and then stepped around him. "When you find out, be sure to let me know."

"Actually, I have an idea or two." Straun followed him across the lab.

Thurston stopped in front of a cabinet littered with manuals and reams of paper. In the midst of the chaos was a pitcher of ice water and four glasses. Thurston started to reach for a glass and then looked at Straun. "I suspect you have some fascinating theories. Why not share them with me over lunch?"

Straun glared at Thurston for a moment, his temper barely contained. "That would not be . . . good for me."

"Oh, too, bad. Perhaps tomorrow then." Thurston took a long drink of the water and then returned the glass to its place on the tray and watched as sweat ran down the length of the glass. "I know this fabulous little outdoor cafe. It has the most wonderful fettucini." Thurston rummaged through the cabinet speaking to Straun as he shuffled papers. "The food is excellent and the atmosphere can't be beat, all that fresh air and sunshine. You really must join me sometime."

Straun growled low in his throat. "Let's dispense with the charades. I have some questions and you'd better have some answers."

"Well, that could be tough. In case you're not aware, our system is down."

"Don't dick with me, old man. You don't know who you're dealing with here."

"On the contrary, Mr. Straun, I know a good deal about you." Thurston paused his shuffling and raised his head, but looked straight in front of him. "You are a creature of the night. One of the undead. In short, a vampire. Although, in today's politically correct environment, I suppose you would be labeled hemoglobin dependent."

Straun started towards him, "Don't play games with me."

"I wouldn't presume to play games with you, Mr. Straun," Thurston said and spun around to face him with a gun in his hand.

Straun's eyes narrowed to twin slits and the tips

of his fangs could be seen protruding past the bottom of his lip. "Can you shoot me enough times to stop me before I kill you?"

"I only have to shoot you once," Thurston said and pulled the trigger.

Straun flinched expecting the bullet to rip into his chest. Instead there was a slight stick followed by a horrific burning in his neck that quickly started to spread to the rest of his body. Straun grabbed at his neck and yanked out the hypodermic dart that was sticking there, pulling bits of his neck away with it, as the acid started to eat his flesh. Straun tried to scream and fell to the floor, thrashing wildly.

Thurston didn't stay around to see the results. Instead, he sprinted from the room, out the exit, and headed for his car. He hoped that Straun hadn't perfected the sunscreen yet and that he wouldn't recuperate fast enough to catch him before he could effect an escape. Thurston gunned the engine on his Volvo and headed for the exit, never taking his foot from the accelerator.

The phone rang at Christine's several times before the recorder answered it.

"Hello, Martin. Pick up. Thurston here. I know you're not cavorting around on this lovely sunny day."

Martin rolled out of bed and vaulted the couch on his way across the living room to the phone. Martin answered just as Thurston was about to hang up.

"Ah, good of you to answer," Thurston began. "It seems your friend paid me a visit at the lab this morning."

"Straun?"

"That's the one."

"Out during the day?"

"It seems your escapades of late have, how should we say, infuriated the man."

Julie joined Martin at the phone, a worried expression on her face.

"Are you all right? Did he suspect you?"

"For the moment, I'm alive and well. Scared beyond measure, for certain." Thurston navigated the Volvo through the moderate traffic with one hand while holding the cellular with the other. He frequently checked his rearview to see if he was being followed. "To answer your other question, yes, I would definitely say he suspects me. I am still shaking from our encounter, and I will say that this type of activity is extremely harsh on a man of my advanced standing."

"In other words, he scared the shit out of you?" Martin couldn't resist teasing.

"Succinctly put, my friend, as usual."

"Where is he now," Martin asked as he started to pace. "Did he find a way to make the formula work?"

"I do not know about the sunscreen, my friend," he said seriously, "although, I doubt it because of his actions. I suspect that he was holed up in the building all day. As to where he is now, I do not know that either. I left him screaming on the floor."

"All right!" Julie blurted out.

"Good morning, Julie," Thurston said, "You two must save a fortune on extensions and conference calling."

"Wait a minute. You left him screaming? How?"

"I took your idea of the sulfuric acid one step further and employed a tranquilizer gun. It worked rather well, I might add."

"You mean you had him momentarily incapacitated and you didn't kill him," Martin said more harshly than he intended.

"Do forgive me for protecting my own life, but if he recuperates as fast as you do, I did not want to be around when the acid wore off."

"I'm sorry, Thurston. I didn't mean to sound ungrateful, really. You have literally put your life on the line for us. And, for that, I am eternally grateful. I told you to be careful and at least you listened to me this once."

"Well, I will admit that the whole thing has been rather invigorating."

"You can't go home," Julie spoke up.

"I know. I will purchase a few things and stay with a friend out of state. Although, I wonder how being chased by vampires is going to sound as a reason for a leave of absence."

"Come by the house here, if you would," Martin said. "There's a couple of things I would like you to double check. Just identify yourself at the door. And, Thurston, thanks again."

Thurston cut the connection and Martin replaced his handset. He turned to Julie and pursed his lips in thought.

"Well, it sounds like we rattled him."

Julie hugged him. "Yea, I just don't know if that's good or bad."

Shortly after noon Thurston rapped lightly on Christine's front door and called out, alerting those inside.

Martin yelled from the bedroom that the door was unlocked.

Thurston tentatively let himself inside, closing the door behind him. He stood for a moment as his eyes adjusted to the dim interior and finally saw Christine sitting in the living room.

"I would have let you in myself, but I'm afraid that would have been a major ordeal."

Thurston walked into the living room taking off his driving cap as he went. "No need to apologize, Mrs. Brewer. Martin has told me about your condition. Is there anything I can do for you?"

Martin and Julie came out of the bedroom and joined the other pair in the living room.

Christine turned her head slightly. "You were right, Martin. This guy is the epitome of a gentleman."

"Don't brag on him too much, he won't be able to fit his head through the doorway." Martin hugged Thurston and then patted him on the shoulder. "Thanks, again."

Thurston cocked an eyebrow, "Big head, indeed."

"Seriously, thanks for coming," Martin said. "There's something I want you to look at. You're not flying are you?" he added.

"No."

"Good. If you drive I don't think he can track you.

"I'll be staying with . . ."

Martin held up a hand. "I don't want to know. Write to us at this P.O. box in two weeks." Martin handed him a slip of paper. "If we don't call you, don't come back. It will mean we lost and you won't be safe."

Thurston looked at his friend. "I will see you within the month."

Martin just nodded.

"Now then," Thurston said clapping his hands together, "where is this material you wanted me to check?"

Chapter 22

Martin and Julie waited impatiently for the sun to finally dip below the horizon. They had checked the local listing for sunset and gave it another 20 minutes before deciding it was safe to venture forth.

"Will you be all right until we get back," Martin asked Christine.

She looked at him from under eyelids that drooped from exhaustion, but were denied rest due to the pain caused by the cancer that was eating her alive. Both Martin and Julie had noticed how gaunt she had become over the last couple of days. The pain pills she was eating did little to alleviate the constant agony she was suffering.

"What's to happen to me, dear boy?" she said weakly. "I'll either be here when you return or I'll die between now and then, which would be a blessing." She paused catching her breath. "I know I can't die until you've finished whatever it is you're doing, because when I go, you'll have to leave this place. But," she ground her teeth together against the torment she was experiencing, "I can't stand much more of this. I can't."

Martin looked down into pain filled eyes. "All right. How many pain relievers do you have?"

"Two."

"Not enough," Martin said matter-of-factly. He motioned for Julie to retrieve the pills and the glass of water on the end table. "You take these two," he said as he placed the tablets in her mouth and raised the glass to her lips, "and when I return, I'll bring something to finish the job." He gently stroked the top of her head, and his voice softened. "You won't feel a thing, I promise. You'll simply go to sleep."

She managed a barely audible, "Thank you."

They stayed with Christine until the medication had taken the edge off the worst of the pain and then left her there, the older woman's eyes shut tight against the agony that overwhelmed her.

Martin and Julie backed the truck out of the drive and headed it toward SUNCO, Inc., in silence.

"You're thinking of her, aren't you?"

"Among other things, yes," Martin said without looking at her.

Julie pursed her lips and propped her feet on the dash. "Why didn't you kill her?"

"I could have, obviously. But, I told her I would help *her* to do it, and that it would be painless. Without the medication, I couldn't guarantee that." Martin swallowed hard past the lump in his throat. "She has suffered enough because of me, and I don't want to add to that"

"You? You haven't made her or anyone else suffer."

"Yes, I have." Martin chewed the words as he spit them out, grimacing at the vile taste they left in his mouth. "It's because of me that her husband is dead. The one light in her life that would have made these last days bearable. It's because of me that she has hung on this long, dealing with pain no one should have to bear, so that we might accomplish a greater good." Martin closed his eyes and fought to maintain his composure. "I have made those I love suffer. For generations now. It's because of me that you suffered the transformation."

"Oh, that. I really don't remember much of it myself." Julie waved a hand absently.

A tiny smile crossed Martin's lips. "I appreciate your lying to make me feel better, but my transformation was well over a hundred years ago and I remember it all too clearly. Not to mention that I will never forget the way you looked or the sound of your screams. You were hurting so badly and there was nothing I could do to lessen your pain."

"Yea, but who injected themself?"

"Would you have if I weren't a vampire?"

Julie opened her mouth to speak and then closed it for a moment. "You can't argue with pure logic. However," she held up a finger for emphasis, "we are all responsible for our own actions. So, you are not responsible for all these people suffering."

"If not me, then people like me."

"Hence your obsession with Straun and his goons? Well, that helps. I was beginning to worry that you were starting to like boys, as much time as you spend chasing those guys."

Martin turned sharply to look at Julie who pantomimed a gun in her hand. "Got ya."

She had succeeded in breaking his melancholy as only she could.

Martin smiled, reached for her hand and brought it to his lips. He kissed it lightly and then bit the back of it.

Julie snatched her hand away. "That's more like it. You don't get serious too often, but when you do, you do."

Julie pursed her lips again and looked out the window at the passing city. "I have been wondering, are we going to be able to get in O.K.?"

"No problem. At least I think."

"That's what I love about you. You know how to install confidence in people."

"Getting in will be no problem," he said as he glanced at Julie who was leaning against the door staring at him, "getting out though . . . " he let his voice trail off.

Julie leaned her head against the glass. "Can I just wait in the car?"

"And miss all the fun?"

"You're idea of fun and mine are different. I personally don't like getting shot."

Martin smiled. "None of that tonight. Or, at least there shouldn't be; not for you. Like I was telling you earlier, the regular guard should be on duty when we arrive. Shift change isn't until 10:30. The guard Straun put in place should come on then. In fact," the tone in Martin's voice dropped, "I'm counting on it."

Julie looked at Martin, "Seeking revenge is not healthy."

"I know that. But, I also know that that scumbag killed Pete. The man didn't have a mean bone in his body and they slaughtered him. What is the law going to be able to do? Nothing. Even if they could prove it was him, they couldn't hold him. And, if they could hold him and convict him, with our judicial system, he'd be out in 3 1/2 years on good behavior."

They sat in silence for a moment.

Julie smirked, "Gee, couldn't you develop stronger opinions about things?"

Martin ignored her comment. "You did bring your badge like a good employee, didn't you?"

"Right here, Dr.," she said pulling her I.D. out of her shirt pocket and clipping it on her lapel.

Martin steered the Chevy into the parking lot. "Let's go pay our benefactors a visit."

They got out of the truck and looked around. The parking lot looked the same, yet different some how. All the lights were the same. Julie recognized some of the cars parked in their slots, yet, the place no longer had the familiarity that she had come to know.

"God, Martin. It seems like such a long time since I've been here." She took a step away from the truck and breathed deeply. All the floral scents she had been aware of before, now came to her a hundred fold. "Thinking back, it's like I'm viewing someone else's life."

Martin came up to stand beside her and put his arm around her shoulders; her own arm automatically sliding around his waist.

"I don't know if I ever thanked you for saving me from Straun. If I did, thanks again."

"For you, my Lady, I would walk through the fires of perdition itself."

Julie hugged him. "Where did you learn to be so romantic?"

"I've had 150 years to practice," Martin said as they walked toward the entrance.

The pair passed the guard at the front desk with a wave and an explanation that they were going up to talk to Chris Hankins. The guard knew that they were on an official leave of absence, but waved them on anyway.

"Down in a minute," Martin called to the guard.

"Take your time, Doc."

"Pretty sure of yourself, aren't you?" Julie asked as they got on the elevator.

"Sometimes." Martin punched the fourth floor button. "I just wish I could be more sure about this." Martin ran his hands through his hair.

"Thurston said it came out to your specs, didn't he? And, that Chris was holding the batch for us?"

The elevator stopped and the pair stepped out into the strangely familiar hallway.

"Yes, he did. Still, there's a lot riding on this."

"Oh, just our life," Julie said and knocked on the door they had stopped in front of.

"Come in," the voice said from behind the door. They walked in to find Chris Hankins, moppish dishwater blonde hair and wrinkled lab coat, kicked back, with his feet propped on Martin's desk. He had a diet Coke in one hand and a report in the other. He looked up from his reading as Martin crossed to his desk and almost fell backwards out of the chair as he tried to get up.

"Yo, Martin, Julie, how are you?" He shook Martin's hand and hugged Julie. "I heard the cops dropped the charges, so how come you're not back at the grind?"

"Just a little internal investigation. They want to make sure that the cops didn't miss something. They're pulling an inventory on everybody. Damage control wants to make sure the company's nose is clean and use this whole thing to put a positive spin on it and show the public a good wholesome image."

"So, that's why they've been up everybody's butt with a microscope. Thanks, Martin," Chris said.

Martin just shrugged.

Julie asked Chris, "Do you have that sample?"

"Oh, yeah, Thurston finished it up earlier," Chris said with enthusiasm, "He told me that you would be by to pick it up." He led them over to a file cabinet. "I had a hard time keeping some people's noses out of it."

"How many other people know about it," asked Martin.

"Just me."

Julie recognized the enthusiasm of the chemist. When presented with some new prospect or challenge, it's like giving a kid a new Christmas toy. She smiled as she followed Chris.

"I mean," Chris continued as he opened the second drawer. "It's one thing to have Thurston come in to synthesize something for you, when he has his own place and you guys on leave and all, but then to have Thurston tell me that if anyone read the results or analyzed the sample in any way, he would and I quote, 'Flay the skin from my body clean to my marrow.'" Chris produced a file folder laden with data sheets and a 12 oz. plastic cylinder containing Martin's sunscreen. "Here you go. If you don't mind my asking, how come you didn't wait and whip this up yourself?"

Martin thumbed through the data sheets. "Let's just say a certain competitor who stole my work is close to producing it. I needed to get there first. My lab's gone. I can't officially work here, so I needed help." Martin looked up from the sheets, "And, I trust you."

Chris blushed slightly under the praise. "Oh, hell man, you know I'd help you any way I can."

"We'll hopefully see you in a couple of days and you can bring us up to speed on what all has been happening around here since we left you." Martin shook the hand of the much younger man. "Thanks, Chris, you're a life saver."

"I hope so," Julie quipped as they turned to leave.

Julie started to press the elevator down button when Martin stopped her. "There's a side property of the sunscreen that I want to check out and now's a perfect time." He led her around the corner to the restroom and locked the door behind them.

"Take your clothes off, please," Martin said.

Julie arched her eyebrows. "Feel frisky, Martin? I didn't know you were into public sex."

"Believe me, you get me aroused in an instant, but that's not what it's about." Martin laid the file folder on the sink. "If I'm correct, this stuff will cover our scent just as effectively as the mask I made the other day. I incorporated it into the sunscreen."

Julie pulled her shirt over her head as she kicked off her shoes. "You serious?"

"Very," Martin said as he unbuttoned Julie's pants and tugged them down. Martin stood for a long moment taking in Julie's naked form when she had divested herself of bra, panties, and socks.

"Like what you see, big boy?" Julie asked in her best bedroom voice.

"Most definitely," Martin said moving closer to her as he opened the tube of sunscreen. This is going to be a labor of love." Martin applied the thick liquid to her whole body, covering every inch of her, lingering over her breasts, and the nape of her neck.

"If you keep that up," Julie breathed, "I'm going to throw you on the floor and rape you."

"You can't rape the willing," Martin smiled and then kissed her. "Now, my turn."

Julie finished coating Martin and both redressed.

"Let's go pay a guard a visit," Martin said and put the silenced 9 mm back in his shoulder holster. "He should be on duty by now."

They exited the elevator and made their way to the front desk. The vampire guard was on duty as expected. Martin and Julie stole up to the counter when he was facing the other direction.

"Hello, scumbag," Martin said.

The guard jumped out of his seat and spun around to face the pair. It took a second for him to realize that they had snuck up on him without his hearing or smelling them. "How in the hell did you get in here," he snarled.

"You'll never know," Martin said and pulled out the 9 mm.

"Now, Doc," the vampire said in his usual condescending tone, "you just pulled a gun on a law abiding citizen doing their job, and it's all on tape."

"Think again, asshole," Martin said and pulled an electromagnetic scrambler from his pocket. "Your picture has been toast since before we walked around the corner."

The guard cast a quick glance at his monitors and saw static on every screen. He looked back at Martin, sweat starting to bead on his brow.

"They're going to think that you had something to do with it, because they'll find the jammer and you'll be missing. Probably got spooked knowing that they're doing the extensive investigation. Any wrong doings around here will be contributed to you."

Martin's voice turned dark and menacing. "How does it feel to be in Pete's place, to know that you're about to die, and there's nothing you can do about it?"

The guard was visibly shaking and started to open his mouth when the bullet from the 9 mm ripped into his head. The guard staggered and started to fall, but was caught by Martin who had leapt over the counter. The vampire convulsed as Martin jumped back over the counter, carrying him in his arms and started for the front door with Julie on point. She opened both doors to the outside holding the last one open as Martin passed. He dumped the still twitching body behind some shrubs and put two more rounds into the vampire's head. Martin knew that the automatic sprinkler system would wash away all traces of the guard. Martin stood and watched with grim satisfaction as the other's body grew still and then burst into a brilliant flame. The flair was gone as quickly as it had appeared, leaving a pile of fine ash.

Martin turned and headed for the truck with Julie.

"Well," Julie said, "at least we know the stuff works so far."

"You want me to drive?" Julie asked.

"No. Thank you." Martin took a deep breath to relax. "Sorry for being so moody."

"Oh, just because you faced a supernatural killer, put one over on him and had to blow him away, I can't possibly understand why you would be upset. Want to talk about it?"

"It's just that Pete reminded me of someone I knew a long time ago. I loved that old man." Martin was silent for a moment and then continued, clinching his teeth in frustration. "I'm so sick of Straun and his goons hurting people and taking everyone I care about. With anyone outside of his group, I would have tried to communicate with the vampire. See if they had control of themselves. That dirt bag didn't deserve to live. None of them do."

"Well, you won't get an argument out of me there," Julie said. "What's next?"

Martin took another deep breath. "I've got to fulfill a promise."

Julie looked at him, but didn't say anything.

Chapter 23

"Listen, Martin," Julie said from the passenger side of the truck, "you can't be serious about Christine. You wouldn't do that, would you?"

"I am and I would," he said keeping his eyes on the traffic drifting around them as if he expected Straun to materialize out of the roadway itself. Martin glowered at the cars around him. For all of their intelligence, they had been playing catch-up to Straun from the start. Martin still couldn't put it all together as to why Straun would still be interested in them after he had gotten the formula. He was missing a key point and he knew it but was unable to come up with a logical answer. Maybe that was his problem; he was being too logical, the scientist in him wanting to fit everything in a nice, neat, little, orderly box. If anyone knew that not everything in life was neat and could be easily explained, it was him. After all the murders and deaths he had seen or heard about in his long life, he knew that most made no sense at all. He knew all too well just how fragile the human mind really was. Maybe that's what this was, he thought as he exited the freeway. Maybe Straun had taken that small step from genius to insanity.

"Hello. Earth to Martin. Come in Martin."

"What?" Martin gave her a puzzled look as he cruised the yellow light at the end of the exit ramp and turned right. "What? Did I miss something?"

"Oh, not much. I've just been sitting here talking to myself. I don't know where you've been," Julie said glancing out the window, "but, it certainly wasn't here. Any place interesting?"

"No, I'm afraid not. Just my brain working overtime. It's a good thing that I don't have to pay it time-and-a-half or I'd go broke."

"You mean you weren't having a sexual fantasy about me, "she asked, batting her lashes at him.

"Not this time. But, I'm sorry. What were you saying to me?"

Julie's voice turned serious again. "About Christine. You can't kill her. That would be murder."

Martin looked at her across the console, the green light from the dash reflecting off her sharp features. "I'm got going to kill her. I told you that. I'm going to assist her in committing suicide."

"It's basically the same thing."

"Not even close," he said checking the rearview again. "Murder is what the dope head does at the local convenience store, or when a jealous lover is incapable of coping with their emotions and stabs the object of their love to death. Murder is when some sick group thinks that to belong, you have to go kill someone. What I'm doing is helping someone preserve their dignity."

"How do you figure?"

"Think about it, Jules. Unless you oversleep with the shades open or step in front of a speeding train, you pretty much don't have to worry about it." Martin slowed to a stop for the red light at the intersection and checked the cross street for any potential traps and then faced Julie. "Christine doesn't have that option. She's used to being an active person. Someone who takes pride in doing for herself and her husband. They got her husband, and now, all that she cherishes, all that she is, is being taken away from her a little bit at a time. There's no stopping the disease, Julie. She's dead already; it's just that her body doesn't know it yet. This way, she gets to decide whether she wants to go now or later."

Julie was moved by the genuine emotion in his voice. "I'm sorry." She touched his arm, brushing up and down his biceps with the back of her hand, and added softly, "The light's green."

"Oh."

Martin pulled away from the line and headed off between the twin rows of mercury vapor lamps lining the street, their glow casting an on/off light to his face. They rode for several blocks in silence.

Then softly Julie said, "There is another way."

"No, there isn't," Martin said flatly. "Even if I could get her through the transformation, the loneliness would be worse than the disease."

Julie dropped the subject. At least outwardly. She turned to look out the window of the car not really seeing the occasional person walking the street or the teenage dropouts hanging out at the local convenience store. She entertained the thought of infecting Christine herself and cast aside the thought just as quickly. She knew how irresponsible that would be, not to mention she wasn't about to do anything stupid and risk losing Martin, now that they were finally together. Not only that, she still remembered the pain; the white-hot flames that seared her every nerve and totally reconstructed her body. Besides, she didn't have the foggiest idea what to do for a person going through the transformation.

Martin stared at the night as well. His mind circling thoughts of Grant Brewer. There was a man who had a near infinite number of years left to him, but had chosen a finite number instead to spend with the woman they were going to see for the last time and accepted the fact that his life would be that much shorter. As he turned into the housing addition where Christine lived, he wondered what he would do in the same circumstance and snuck a glance at Julie who was still lost in thought. The notion of going through the rest of his life without her smile to wake up to caused a lump to come to his throat. Martin turned the car into Christine's drive, killed the motor and then waited a moment before switching off the lights. Martin sat starring at the house, his eyes picking up things that would be invisible to most others.

Julie, who had been rummaging through the suitcase she called a purse, closed the bag and grabbed the door handle. "You waiting for an invitation or what?" She glanced sideways at Martin and then followed his gaze to the house. "What? Is she not home?"

"Something's wrong," he said switching off the lights and slowly opening the door.

Immediately she got that sinking feeling in her stomach. "Oh, shit, here we go again."

Following Martin's lead, she quietly opened the door and stepped out into the night.

Martin reached back into the cab and grabbed his walking stick. With a quiet click, the cane separated and the stick's concealed blade slid forth.

"No fair," Julie whispered. "I want one. You're

going to have to start sharing your toys with me or I won't play."

Martin ignored her and concentrated on the house. He knew Julie. Some people whistled when they got scared; Julie cracked jokes.

Julie watched in fascination as Martin tested the slight breeze that flowed through the neighborhood, like some lone wolf checking for possible prey—or peril. His whole demeanor changed. He was some feral animal, his whole body alert. She wondered if that was something that came naturally, was part of the change or if it was brought about by the necessity to stay alive.

Julie tentatively sniffed at the air and was amazed at the kaleidoscope of odors present there. She realized how much she had subconsciously tuned out. With a little effort she was able to discern different smells. She could smell the lilacs and honeysuckle heavy on the breeze, the lingering ashy aroma from someone charcoaling earlier in the evening. She turned her nose up when she caught a whiff of the animal, she didn't know what, that had died about four houses over. And, there was something else; there at the edge of her awareness. Something familiar, yet different. Vampire spoor. Julie growled low in her throat, her pulse rising while her breath quickened. She was shocked at the reaction she was having but she couldn't help herself. Her vision started to blur as she felt the urge come to life in her, the smell of the others, making a challenge she couldn't ignore.

Martin turned with a glare. He brought the tip of the sword around to point at her. "Control it Julie," he hissed barely audible to her, "don't let it control you. You have subconsciously suppressed the urge when you are around me. Do it now."

She looked at the blade and then into his face as if from a long distance away. With obvious effort, she shook her head and consciously slowed her breathing. Looking him in the eyes, she mouthed the words, "I'm O.K."

"Are you sure?" he asked without lowering the point.

Julie didn't trust herself to speak and simply shook her head.

"Good. Let's go." Martin turned and blended with the shadows that ran along the front of the house.

Julie's admiration of the man had just gone up several notches. She realized the amount of control Martin could summon forth, and the outward ease with which he did it. "How does he do it? He's had a hundred years of practice, that's how," she muttered to herself, her every fiber still vibrating as she started after Martin.

By the time she had made it to the front of the house, Martin had glided around the corner and was testing a bedroom window. Even with her hypersensitive hearing, she couldn't detect his passing. She rounded the corner of the modest frame house and stopped next to Martin who had the window screen off and the window jimmied.

Martin started to hoist himself into the window opening and then stopped. He leaned close to Julie, his mouth next to her ear, "Keep an eye on the front of the house and don't let them sneak up on me." Ever so lightly, he kissed her on the ear and turned back to the window.

"Wait a minute!" she hissed. "You're not going to leave me here are you?"

"That was the general idea."

"But, what if there's bad guys out here?"

"What if there's bad guys in here?"

"Sometimes I don't like you very much," she said with a slight pout in her voice.

She barely heard him say, "Liar" as he hoisted himself up and into the room.

Martin dropped head first into the room, broke the fall with his arms and rolled smoothly to one knee. Even in the near solid darkness he could make details in the room and recognized it as the one where Grant had kept his extra gear. He strained to hear any movement in the house. Silently, he skated across the carpet and stopped next to the doorframe. From there, he peered through a crack between the door and the stop and saw nothing. Softly, a moan drifted to his ears. It was so faint, he wasn't sure he had heard anything when there was no mistaking it the second time. Martin switched the grip on his sword, pulled open the door, and like a wraith, poured into the hallway. He hurried up the hallway, keeping alert for traps as he went, his heart beating quicker as he made his way toward the sound he had heard earlier. He could smell where they had been, but nothing was strong enough to make him think that any of them were still in the house. Martin glided past the opening to the living room towards the next doorway. Easing open the door, his fears were brought home with earnest. There, broken and bleeding, Christine lay sprawled across the bed. Martin hesitated before he entered the room, repressing the urge to rush to her. He scanned the room quickly and then crossed to were she lay like a discarded rag doll.

"Oh, Christine, I am so sorry." Martin stroked her arm gently so as not to disturb the break.

Christine moaned and turned her head in his direction, revealing more evidence of the beating she had taken.

"Lie still, and I'll call for help."

"Why," she coughed weakly. "I was going anyway. They just saved you the trouble, that's all."

"Why did they do this to you? Did they say what they wanted?" His mind searched desperately for some way to help alleviate her pain.

"They said that this was an attention-grabber. That you would understand." Her voice was a gurgle as her lungs started to fill with fluid.

"Shh. Be quiet and let go, it will be over in a little while," Martin said seeing another time from his past.

"Martin, I'm so hot."

Martin looked closer at some of her wounds and for the first time, what looked like several bite marks, became apparent. He knew in his heart what they had done. "They bit you didn't they?"

"Yes," she answered flatly. Then realization crashed through her pain shrouded mind and her eyes rolled wide, "Oh, God, Martin. Please don't let that happen to me!"

"I don't know if you're to far gone for the transformation to take place, but I'm not going to find out," he said pushing himself to his feet.

"I'm sorry." she choked out. "It looks like they didn't save you the trouble after all." Her eyes searched his face in the semi darkness of the master bedroom. "I just didn't think it would all end like this. Please hurry."

Martin brushed a stray clump of hair out of her face. "Just close your eyes and rest now."

Martin watched as Christine's eyes closed and ever so small a smile played across her lips.

"Say hi to Grant for me."

"I will." she whispered.

When his blade fell, it came down with such force that it cleaved the mattress set and came to rest against the floor.

Julie, who kept glancing back and forth between the front door and the side of the house she was on, was unaware of the happenings inside. Checking the front door one more time, she leaned her back against the side of the house giving her some sense of security knowing that at least nothing was going to sneak up on her from behind. She never thought to look up.

Martin stood looking at the shell that had once been a beautiful person when the phone ringing broke into his thoughts. The answering machine picked up on the second ring and dutifully gave the outgoing message. Martin's whole being snapped to attention when he heard the voice at the other end.

"How long have you been around, Martin, old boy? In all that time, they've come up with some rather nifty inventions don't you think. And, one of the niftiest is the cellular phone," Straun's rich baritone poured from the speaker. "Pick up, Martin, I know you're there."

Martin's mind raced. He ignored the voice on the speaker and started for the room that he had first come in through when Straun's voice continued.

"Really, Martin. Do pick up. I'm on peak time and these things can get dreadfully expensive. Besides, I have someone here that I think you will really want to talk to."

Martin was already through the door and almost to the window, the dry taste of fear in the back of his mouth.

"Martin. Pick up, please. It's me, Julie."

There was a receiver in the room and Martin nearly crushed the handset answering it. "Julie. Are you all right?"

"Oh, I wouldn't be too, concerned for her well being at the moment," Straun's voice cut back in, "I plan on taking very good care of her." The way he emphasized the words made Martin's skin crawl in repulsion.

"If you hurt her I . . ."

"Tut, tut, Martin. Please spare me the macho threats. I could snap her neck right now, torture her for hours, or," Straun's voice became darker with each word, "I could simply fuck her to death, literally, and there's nothing you could do about it, now or ever. So, lets get to brass tacks as it were. You have something we want. Again." Straun's voice had resumed that rolling quality that sounded as if he were talking to some college buddy about the upcoming weekend activity. "I will say that was a nasty bug you put into our system. My compliments. I didn't even know it was there until it was far too late to do anything about it. You really must show me the programming on it some time. But, I digress," and his voice turned serious once more. "You know what we want. And, I won't ask twice. You get one chance to play hero and save Miss Baxter's life. You mess this up old chum, and believe me, you won't see dear Julia again. At least, not in one piece."

Martin could hear Julie's cursing in the background and knew that at least for the moment, she was alive. His mind poured over the options in front of him as certain things started to drop into place, and he wasn't pleased with what he saw. "Where do you want me to bring it?"

"That's what I like about you, Martin. A man of action. An intelligent man. You didn't even pretend to not know what we were talking about. Fine. The old VanDel building. You know where it is. Fourth floor, southeast corner, there is a physical lab. You know, if I were a betting man, I'd wager that you have what we want on you. It wasn't in the old woman's house. Bring it, and be there in forty minutes, or we will practice vivisection on Miss Baxter. Oh," he paused for emphasis, "I won't even bother giving the standard speech about not involving the authorities. I know you won't call them because I know how you'd hate to see those innocent sheep get slaughtered."

Martin couldn't hear Julie anymore and wondered if she had simply run out of ammunition for her tirade, or something worse. He quickly abandoned that line of thought because he knew that either she was alive or she wasn't. If she were, no amount of worrying would help her, only his actions in the immediate future. If she weren't . . . Martin felt his soul grow dark at the thought.

"Listen to me, Straun," it wasn't a statement. It was a command. One that couldn't be ignored or turned aside, and Straun's voice fell silent on the other end of the connection. "If you do anything to her, I will see you dead. No matter the cost to me. If

I have to drag you screaming into the sun and burn with you, you will die."

The receiver went dead in Martin's hand.

Chapter 24

Martin gritted his teeth in frustration. Frustration with himself. Frustration at having let them get to Julie. He knew that what he and Julie had been doing would force Straun's hand, but he'd had no idea Straun would be able to pull this off. He'd known Straun's group would eventually trace Grant's address, just not this soon. Martin had figured that he and Julie would be able to get to Straun before he got to them.

Once more, Straun was one step ahead of him. And, Christine had suffered in the process.

Martin pushed the truck for all it was worth. As he drove, he slipped Grant's body armor over his head and strapped it in place. He knew with certainty that he and Julie were dead as soon as he turned over the data. Thankful that the traffic was reasonably sparse at this time of the morning, he turned the location of the VanDel building over in his mind trying to think of the best way of approaching the structure.

The building was only half leased now, falling victim to a building glut. There would be few, if any, workers present at this early hour. As a result, it would be obvious when he drove up. Martin cursed softly for not having more time to plan a counter attack.

"But," he chided himself, "they say necessity is the mother of invention."

He checked the clip in the 9mm he had taken off Grant and shoved it back in the holster he had strapped to his leg. He lifted the other one he had picked up during the fire fight at Straun's penthouse and checked the silencer to make sure it was secure, jacked a round into the chamber, and then nested it into the shoulder holster he was wearing.

Martin slid the truck into a deserted parking lot a little more than a mile from the VanDel building. He checked his watch as he got out of the truck and saw that he had just under eighteen minutes. Martin made sure his guns were secure and started off at a dead run through the back lots and open field between him and the VanDel building.

Martin covered the distance in just over a minute. He could have covered it faster but had been forced to jump fences and waited to let a paper delivery person go past. He had no idea if there were security cameras on the premises, or if Straun had posted guards at all four corners of the six-story building.

Martin sprinted the last 200 yards to the back of the building, a dark, silent blur in the deeper night. He paused at the rear entrance to catch his breath and scanned quickly for any video surveillance. Satisfied there was none, he cautiously made his way around the side of the structure. As he neared the front of the building, the concrete wall gave way to full glass panels that closed in the lobby area. He pulled up short as he looked through the glass to where two of Straun's men stood guard by the front door. One of the men was talking into a two-way radio.

Martin took a chance and put his ear to the glass, in what he hoped, was out of their line of sight. Straining to hear, he caught bits of the conversation. As he listened, he realized that they expected him to drive to the front door and be escorted upstairs.

"Not today, boys," Martin said to himself as he slunk back the direction he had come.

Near the corner of the building, Martin found what he was looking for; a drainpipe leading from the roof. He tested it and then started scaling the pipe like a monkey up a coconut tree. Once at the top, Martin heaved himself onto the roof and quickly scanned the area. He figured he could find a way downstairs since they expected him at the front door. He was just about to move, when the door leading to the roof swung open. Martin ducked behind a turbine and held his breath. From where he was, he could hear the person shuffling back and forth in the gravel that covered the roof, the crunching of the small rocks deafening in the cool morning air.

"Nothing here, sir," the vampire spoke into the receiver he was carrying.

Martin couldn't hear the person on the other end since the vampire was wearing an earphone, but assumed he was told to go back downstairs since he turned and headed back through the door.

"Maybe they're a little more cautious than I gave them credit for," Martin thought. His mind raced for possible solutions when something caught his attention. He spied a large spool of co-ax cable and an idea sprang to life. He glanced at his watch and then sprinted for the cable. As quickly as he could, he began to unwind the cable from the spool. Martin kept glancing at the door, certain that someone would hear the noise and come to investigate. Martin reeled off enough cable to reach the third floor and then doubled it twice. Satisfied that the cable would be long enough, he pulled on the cable, snapping it like twine. Martin gathered the cable together and made his way to the southeast corner of the building. Once there, he anchored the lines to an AC unit so that he had four strands of cable to work with. Holding onto the cable, Martin lowered himself over the edge of the roof, careful not to let the end of the cable dangle below the bottom of the fourth floor. He didn't know if they had anyone on the floors above, but he had to chance it. He eased himself down the wall until he was just above the third floor. Martin wrapped the cable twice around his arm and then inverted himself so that he could see into the room. When Martin peered through the glass, his heart skipped several beats.

Julie was seated in a heavy office chair with her hands tied in front of her and her legs strapped to the legs of the chair. Standing beside her was Straun. Martin couldn't hear what he was saying, but he knew he was talking directly to her, judging from her reaction and the look of pure loathing on her face. Suddenly, Straun's hand snaked out, grabbed her by the hair and snapped her head back. He leaned in, his face almost touching hers. He flicked out his tongue and lightly ran it down the side of her face, stopping just above her throat, his fangs protruding, preparing to bite her. Straun stopped just as his teeth touched her skin and laughed out loud as he slapped her head forward.

Martin had seen enough. He quickly noted the position of the other four men in the room and then scrambled back to the roof. Once there, he checked the placement and the length of his line again. Gripping the four strands with his left hand, he pulled the 9mm from his leg holster, took a running start and hurled himself as far as he could into empty space. Martin wanted to get as far away from the building as possible so that he wouldn't shock load the cable causing it to break, and so that he could achieve the greatest angular momentum. Martin's flight took him out and down in a rush of wind and gut churning exhilaration. The cable snapped taught and sent him careening faster toward the building.

One of the vampires chose that moment to walk to the window to look outside. He was the first to die. Martin put three quick rounds into him and targeted two of the others before impacting with the glass. When he hit, the window exploded inward sending shards flying to all corners of the room. The surprise tactic had its intended effect, causing chaos to erupt in the room. Pulling the other pistol, Martin rolled to one knee. He head shot the fourth vampire that had been standing a few feet away from Julie and who still had his eyes covered to protect them from the shrapnel. In the space of a heartbeat, Martin killed the other two and shot Straun twice as he was attempting to draw the pistol he had under his jacket. The force of the bullets staggered Straun, and Martin put another one into his left knee, collapsing him onto the floor. Straun grabbed at his knee and Martin shot him through the hand to keep him from drawing his gun.

"Those were because you're a scumbag and for all you've done to Julie and me. This is for Christine." Martin shot him in the other hand that Straun had been propping himself up with. "This is for Pete, you son-of-a-bitch." From point blank, Martin put two shots into Straun's groin causing the bigger man to cry out in pain. "How does it feel to have someone take you apart a piece at a time?" Martin bent over and seized Straun by the front of his jacket, hoisted him to his feet with one hand and carried him towards the gaping hole that he had made in the glass wall. "And, this is because you deserve to die." Martin put the gun to the front of Straun's head. "Say good night, Gracie."

"Good night, Gracie."

The gunshot reverberated around the inside of the room and the heavy slug tore into Martin's arm, hurling the pistol from his grip. Martin dove to his right on instinct and pulled the 9mm from the back of his waistband where he had put it moments earlier. He thought that he had missed one of the other vampires and got a bearing on the gunman as a second shot went wide. Martin rose to a firing position with his assailant in his sights, and froze. When he did, he paid the price. Another shot ripped into his shoulder, knocking him off his feet.

His attacker walked to were he lay and kicked Martin's pistol away from him.

"Hello, Martin. Get up, and take off the vest, but don't try anything stupid. I must say, though, nice entrance. I didn't expect that."

Total shock pinned Martin to the floor. He lay where he was, looking up, not believing his eyes. The exhilaration of seeing his friend alive was instantly dwarfed by the realization that he had been shot by him. Martin's emotions were out of control as they warred with each other. A thousand questions, accusations, and curses flashed through his mind as he stared in disbelief.

"Why?" was all that Martin could respond.

The pain in Martin's arms was nothing compared to the hurt inside his soul.

The whole thing had happened so fast that Julie hadn't had time to react and now, surprised as Martin by the sudden turn of events, she sat dumbfounded in the chair.

"Why, Bill," Martin pleaded again as he got to his feet.

"You weak, idealistic fool." Bill took a step further into the room and motioned for Martin to follow. "You always had a grand scheme of things, didn't you? To live your life quietly in peace while you wasted all the power you held at your fingertips. You, one of the most brilliant minds I know, have to ask me why?"

Martin, for the first time, noticed the half dozen or so armed men that had accompanied Bill into the room. Two of them had gone over to help Straun to his feet. He shrugged them off and stood on his own, flexing his hands where the bullet holes were no longer visible. With an animal growl, he drew the long slide .45 from its holster and crossed to Martin, placing the barrel against his head.

Bill looked at Straun and shook his head no.

"Fuck that. He dies now," Straun snarled and started to squeeze the trigger.

Bill, who still had his gun pointed at Martin, trained the muzzle on Straun instead. "I said no. I won't repeat myself."

Straun cut an icy glare at Bill.

"You're the boss." Straun's words dripped with venom as he slowly reholstered the .45 and turned away.

"That's right, I am. But, don't worry, you'll get your chance soon enough to watch him die."

"You still haven't answered my question." Martin winced as muscles put themselves back into place.

Bill took his gaze off of Straun and turned to Martin. "Look around you. The answer is standing all around you. They are the reason," he said pointing at the vampires standing guard around them. "I could have asked you to join me, to be a part of the greater good, but I knew you well enough that you would not. However, you had something vital to the plan, and we had to have it, no matter the cost."

Bill was talking faster now and Martin was becoming aware of just how unstable his former friend really was.

"Do you think I want to spend the rest of this generation slaving for others while my 'superiors' rake in the credit and the money for my accomplishments? Superiors, hah! I'm physically superior to everyone of them in every way except one, and you, Martin old friend, you remedied that." Bill gripped Martin on the shoulder in what at any other time would have seemed genuine appreciation. Now, the gesture was hollow and meaningless. "No longer will we have to hide from the light of day. No longer will we be subject to the whims of these puny . . . mortals. Yes! That's what they are after all." Bill was in his element and punctuated his statements with sweeping arm movements and spoke to the pair as if they were a throng of thousands. "Simply mortals, while we dear Martin . . . are the next step in human evolution. How long have you been around? And, no visible signs of aging. Think about it Martin. For all practical purposes, we are immortal. Ageless."

Bill was no longer talking to Martin. He was

preaching to no one in particular, swept up in his own rhetoric. It was clear to Martin that the man he had thought he had known for so long, was totally caught up in some sort of megalomaniacal fantasy.

"Listen to me, Bill. It won't work. You're kidding yourself."

Bill spun around with speed that belied the appearance of a man of his girth and stepped towards Martin. "No, it's you who are deluding yourself. When is the last time you had a cold, Martin? Had any trauma that didn't heal properly? You don't even have to worry about dying from cancer, or AIDS. You could go sell yourself on the street for the next fifty years and it just wouldn't matter, because YOU'RE NOT GOING TO DIE!"

Bill had stepped to within inches of Martin's face and the sound of his voice was something physical. "You don't have to worry about a stray bullet or some mugger ripping your chest open. Why should the rest of the people be denied the same opportunity?"

A part of Martin's mind actually saw the validity of Bill's idea. A world without disease. Man's ultimate goal. A world where children would not have to die from a killer that no one could see without the aid of a microscope, a world where the little ones would no longer feel the pains of hunger.

"My God, the children!" he whispered.

He realized in Bill's world there would be no more children. No more squeals of delight at the playground or a small pair of arms wrapped around a parent's neck. Martin's mind raced on, picturing the inevitable end. The human race would die off from attrition since vampires are sterile. Martin became aware that they were staring at him and clutched at the obvious.

"It won't work because most of them won't survive the mutation, Bill, you know that!"

Julie caught herself just in time before saying something about how it had been touch and go with her. She might turn out to be their ace in the hole, and she didn't know this man as well as Martin did. It was obvious to her that Martin thought this guy had lost his marbles. As much as she would like to tear into him for all he had done to Martin, she thought better of it and clamped down while Martin continued to try to persuade Bill to change his mind before it was too late.

"And, those that do," Martin continued, "most will be insane. What good is a world populated by gibbering, slobber happy, blood suckers?"

"You don't see the big picture, Martin," Bill said turning away. "If you haven't already guessed, I've developed a technique that enables me to bring the poor unfortunate souls through the transformation sane, safe and sound. Look around you, proof positive. Oh," he turned back to Martin and with a flip of the wrist said, "and, they all answer to me."

"So, that's it, "Martin said, his whole demeanor changing. Julie looked from Bill to Martin and she could feel the compassion draining out of him. "This has nothing to do with the betterment of Mankind. This is all for you. A means to an end. World conquest, Bill?" Sarcasm dripped from every word, "I didn't ever picture you as another Alexander the Great. What about free choice? What about people not being able to decide for themselves whether or not they want to spend the rest of their life, and now a very long life indeed, avoiding the sun and answering to one man?" Julie quietly took Martin's arm because she knew he was doing everything he could to keep his temper in check. "The populous as a whole doesn't get a say so, do they?"

"Of course they will." Bill looked at him as if he were talking to a not so bright student. "But, who would not embrace immortality. Your woman there, I would wager would jump at the opportunity. Why else would she hang around you?"

"I choose to spend my life with him, however long it is, because I want to. Not to try to embrace immortality, you fat ass, son-of-a-bitch." Julie snapped before she thought and now wondered if she was going to regret it.

Bill's eyes clouded over, and lightning flashed there, "You'd best learn to curb that tongue of yours, wench, before I pull it out." His hand shot out to grab her by the face.

Martin's hand intercepted Bill's at the wrist in a grip that would have turned a human's arm to pulp. As it was, it was sufficient to make Bill wince in pain. Martin simply said, "Don't," and then released his arm.

Bill massaged his wrist and stepped back to appraise the situation. "You really do love this—creature—don't you?"

"Yes, I do. And, that's why it's wrong to try what you're attempting to do. People need to be free to make their own choices, their own decisions, to choose who they want to love."

"Oh, they'll be able to," Bill said non-chalantly. "They can go where they want, do what they want, love who they want. As long as they do it my way." He was getting started again, warming to the idea of a utopian society created to his specs. Straun stood by with his arms folded over his chest, a picture of the killing machine that he was, with an uninterested look on his face while the others in his group were practically enraptured listening to Bill.

Martin saw this and wondered what he did in the process that would enlist such obedience.

"Think of it, Martin. Turn that great intellect of yours to the problem. Instead of wanting to stamp out what you are, embrace it. It's the next step in human evolution. Natural selection. The weak die off and the strong inherit. The mammals wrested it from the dinosaurs and now it's our turn!"

Bill was sparking with energy and Martin expected his group to erupt into applause at any moment, they looked so enthralled.

Bill's arms spread wide, "And, not just this world. Think of it. What's kept man from the stars? Not their equipment. Although not quite ready for interstellar travel yet, it won't be that far away. We already have the means for interplanetary travel. No, man himself has kept human kind planet bound. That frail body of his that would die from old age, if it didn't succumb to atrophy due to weightlessness. Not us, Martin!" He swept his arm indicating everyone present. "We could make the journey to Mars, or beyond and be ready to do cart wheels as soon as we stepped out of the space craft. The stars will finally be opened for mankind."

Julie could see why he had always been a leader. Although not a lot to look at, she realized neither was Hitler. She found herself wanting to get caught up in his ideals and enthusiasm, but Martin's voice broke the trance.

"It's a grand scheme, Bill. But, there's too many variables to take into account. As you said, 'We'll replace humankind.' What then? What happens when through accidents or time itself our numbers grow fewer and fewer? We don't multiply, remember?"

Julie blinked. She hadn't thought of what would happen if everyone were a vampire. Food supply was no problem with animals to choose from, but the thought of humankind winking out of existence was a sobering one. She associated with that thought very well, not yet thinking of herself as anything other than human.

Bill clapped his hands together congratulating that not so bright student for making an insight to a particular problem. "So, you have been thinking of the big picture after all. Very good, Martin, very good." Bill walked to a row of test tubes sitting in their holders on top of the lab table and lifted one clear of the rack. He turned it back and forth in his hand seeing the future in that small glass confine. He turned and tossed the tube to Martin who caught it without ever taking his eyes off Bill's face. "There's your answer, Martin. You hold the key in your hand."

"You bastard."

Julie leaned closer, "What's he talking about? I don't get it."

Still glaring at Bill, Martin raised the tube. "What he's talking about is test tube . . . "

" . . . babies." Julie finished. "You mean he plans to 'grow' humans to keep the vampire race alive?"

"You two really do catch on quick," Bill said in false admiration.

Martin's stomach twisted into a knot at the thought of the possible fate awaiting humanity.

"It will start out that they'd use the stock for propagation of the species. But, before long they'll keep the best of the genetic stock for vampires and then start to breed 'inferior' humans to do the grunt work that no self-respecting vampire would want to do. The human race will at long last achieve social equality because everyone will be subservient to this pack of jackals!"

A couple of the guards started forward, but where waved back by Bill. "Don't be ridiculous. We'll only breed what we need to replenish what we lose."

"And, don't you be stupid, Bill. You know it will happen. There will be those who will have enough free thought of their own to think that they shouldn't, not with their superior powers, be made to perform menial tasks and they will push for slaves! It's happened all the way down through history. You've got to have someone to due manual labor, to do the everyday work. And, what vampire, who's going to live for the next few thousand years, is going to want to haul garbage for a few millennia? The social order will break down and you'll have a world of chaos with NO ONE reaching the stars."

"No!" Bill took a step backwards physically agitated. "No, it won't happen like that. I won't let it!"

It was clear that he was shaken, and for a moment, Martin thought he had gotten through to him. Then more to himself then anyone else, Bill spoke again.

"No. I will have better control than that. They will all answer to me. Yes," he said gathering his resolve. "Yes, that's it. They will all answer to me and the plan will work." When he looked up, the gleam that had died in his eyes moments earlier was back brighter than ever and Martin knew that he had lost him. Still, he had to try one more time although he knew he would probably die in the process. But, he thought, they were going to kill him anyway and took a step forward.

"What about, Mary?"

Bill's eyes went wide with surprise like someone who is hit unexpectedly in the stomach.

"Would she have wanted this?"

Martin watched as the stone facade of Bill's demeanor crumbled.

"Would she have gone along with this?"

"Shut up," Bill whispered while the others looked on bewildered.

"Would she have held your hand and said you were doing the right thing?"

"Shut Up!"

"Would you have done this to Mary, Bill? Would You?!"

"SHUT UP!"

With a snarl, Bill sprang at Martin who easily avoided the lunge to send him crashing in a heap.

Two of the thugs went to aid Bill while another hit Martin in the kidneys as Straun clubbed him in the face with the barrel of the long slide 45. Martin went down under the onslaught. Before the one thug could hit Martin again, Julie burst the ropes as if they were silly string, and grabbed him in a wrist lock deflecting the kick that he aimed at Martin's head. Not letting the man regain his balance, she shifted her grip and drove the heel of her other hand against his elbow, breaking the joint with a satisfying snap. She turned to face Straun and instead looked down the barrel of the large automatic he held. Without any real conscious thought, she knew that at this range there would be enough massive tissue damage that her system wouldn't be able to handle it. She would erupt in a ball of fire a few moments later, even if she wasn't aware of it.

"Good bye, Miss Baxter," Straun said as he pulled the trigger on the 45.

Martin rose to one knee while simultaneously driving one hand against Straun's outstretched arm and the other into his groin. The gun jumped in his grip as the shot went wide, almost hitting Bill who was still on the floor. Straun gagged on his own bile and sagged to the tile. The others now produced guns of their own and started to bring them into play against Martin and Julie.

"Enough! Let them be," Bill ordered.

The others, obedient as ever, reholstered their hardware. Bill walked over to where Martin had gained his feet. "Close, Martin, but no cigar. So, Miss Baxter," he said turning to face her, "you're one of us. What a shame. Straun so did want to get to know you better."

Julie's skin crawled.

"Touché, Martin," Bill said clapping his hands in mock applause, "another first. You managed to mask her scent. Of course, you were always very ingenious. I had planned on converting her myself, but it appears I'm too late. Pity. I had planned on killing you quickly and painlessly for all that we've been through," as he spoke his voice took on a menacing tone. "I've changed my mind. If she wants to spend the rest of eternity with you, then she can have her wish. Although," he glanced at his watch and then tugged the sleeve back over his wrist, "eternity is going to be cut rather short."

The rest of the gang laughed at that as Martin stood staring at Bill, wanting desperately to choke the life out of him.

"You see, old friend, sunrise is in thirty minutes. Don't think of running. There's nowhere to run to.

That is, if you managed to get through the window, it would still be sunrise before you could get anywhere safe and—poof. But," he took a step toward them and turned a shark like gaze on them. "believe me, you won't make it to the window. That's where our friend Straun comes in. I would have had him kill you now, quick, painless. But, you blew that and so you get to be the main ingredient in Martin flambé. You see, he's wearing your invention. How does it feel to know that the one thing you invented to save your life is the one thing that is going to see you dead? A bit ironic, don't you think?" He turned once more and made for the exit. "I would really like to stay and see this through, but since we only have enough for one person from our original test batch, I will have to forgo the pleasure of your demise."

"That's all you've produced?" Martin asked not believing his ears.

Bill looked back over his shoulder, "Why?"

"Because it won't work," Martin said flatly.

"Oh, please," Bill said as he turned back to face the pair as he pulled on a light jacket. "Martin, Martin, Martin. I know it works. I saw you outside the house where you're staying. Outside in broad daylight. I've got it videotaped, plain as day. Don't try to deny it, Martin. I've known you were there for days now. How do think we got to the old woman?"

Martin cursed himself for being responsible for the old woman's death. He knew that she had wanted to die, but that didn't make him feel any better. He would have eased her out of this life, slow and peaceful. But, this pack of butcher's had raped and beaten her before she died. She didn't deserve it, and if there was anyway, he was going to make them all pay for it.

"Why does this surprise me?" Martin asked.

"Maybe because of your naive nature," Bill said. "I have contacts in places you'd never dream of. It was so easy to keep track of you."

Martin looked at Bill for a moment and shook his head. "You didn't have to stake out my house or any of the others. Hell, I told you everything you needed to know. I don't know why I didn't put two and two together before. You put the guard in place and he passed Straun right on through into the lab. You supplied him with the access code so he could get into my system. You masterminded it all, the virus and everything."

"I would love to take credit for that, but modesty prevents it. No, that was Straun's idea. He really is a computer whiz."

Straun took a mock bow, "It was nothing, really. Your much too gracious."

"He could have beaten your security system without my help. Your trusting nature just made it that much easier."

"I even accused Julie, you son-of-a-bitch." Martin shook his head slowly. "I have to admit, blowing up your own house was a nice touch to cover your tracks. But, why Jack, Paul and Mickey; why did you have to kill them, why did you have to kill all the others?" Martin said taking a menacing step towards Bill.

"Martin! Don't do it. They'll kill you." Julie said, grabbing him by the arm.

"Ah-ah-ah, Martin. Best listen to your lady friend. Don't make it any worse on yourself—or her."

The last part of his statement caught Martin's attention. Risking his own neck was one thing, but he had to stay alive to find some way to save Julie.

Bill glanced at his watch and then looked to the

horizon where predawn light was starting to make itself visible. "Listen, Martin, I'd love to stay and chat, but I've business elsewhere."

"I'm just glad Mary's not around to see this," Martin said quietly.

Bill glared at Martin. Their eyes locked, but Bill could not hold the gaze of his former, long time friend. He turned on his heel and strode to the door with the rest of his henchmen falling in behind him. As he reached the opening, Bill stopped and said over his shoulder, "You two—have a nice day."

Martin listened as their laughter flowed down the hallway. Straun closed the door with his foot; never taking his gaze off them, and then came back to where Julie and Martin stood.

"Well, Doc, there is no sense in you two being uncomfortable. Let it never be said that I was anything other than a gentleman. Have a seat." Straun motioned with the barrel of the gun for the two of them to sit in a pair of the plain back chairs sitting there.

"I'm not tired," Martin said.

"It wasn't an option. Sit down."

"Fuck you, asshole," Julie growled as she whipped the heavy chair around effortlessly, intent on smashing Straun's skull. The gun jumped once more in Straun's hand, the long silencer masking the concussion. The large caliber bullet ripped a jagged hole through her upper thigh, knocking her leg out from under her in the process. Julie screamed out releasing the chair in the wrong direction. She pressed her hand against the wound to try to stop the bleeding while she gritted her teeth against the pain.

Instinctively Straun turned the gun on Martin. "Don't even think about it."

The cold of space was nothing compared to the numbing stare of Martin as he slowly kneeled beside Julie.

"Let me see," he said gently as he pried her fingers out of the way. Already the blood flow had slowed to a trickle and the hole was in the process of closing itself. Martin glanced at some of the blood that had spilled to the floor and watched as the stuff, being deprived of nourishment, started to cannibalize itself. Martin looked at the minute puffs of smoke that rose there and then to the large window where the morning was beginning to make it's presence known.

"That's what's going to happen to you real soon, Doc," Straun told Martin.

As Julie listened to Straun, she thought that she should be more scared than she was, facing an imminent fiery death, but she couldn't help thinking of Martin and what Bill had said earlier. She couldn't stop her mind from dwelling on the injustice of the whole situation. Here was a man that had survived alone for the last 150 years, who had put all his energy toward one thing, and now it was that same thing that was going to get them both killed.

Martin ignored him and kissed Julie lightly on the forehead as he brushed a lock of hair out of her eyes. "You'll be all right."

"How touching. You two should get the Ozzie and Harriet award. Just remember Ms. Baxter, I could have popped you in the head, but I wanted you to experience the end." Straun sat the chairs back up facing the large glass windows. "Didn't your mother ever teach you chairs were made to be sat in, not played with? Now, this time, sit."

As Julie stood on her good leg and moved towards the chairs she whispered urgently to Martin,

"You didn't tell me that you had the formula working or that you went outside. Why?"

"Because I didn't."

"Do what?"

"He never taped anything. I told him all he needed to know about where we were or how to predict our movement. He was lying so as to mislead the troops. Particularly Straun." As they sat down, Martin said calmly under his breath, "He's a dead man."

Julie could barely contain herself, "So what. We're the walking dead too, remember. It's just that he has a few thousand years for his time to catch up to him!"

"Children," Straun said as he crossed to sit in front of them. "You know there's no whispering in class. It's as bad as passing notes. What were you talking about?"

"That you're a dead man," Martin said flatly.

Straun raised the barrel a little higher as his voice fell to a serious note, "Don't do anything stupid. I suggest you make this as easy as possible."

"No problem. All we have to do is wait."

"Martin," Julie said, "I don't really feel like dying today."

"You're not going to," he said ignoring Straun and turning in his chair to face her.

"You've lost me, Martin. Positive attitude is one thing, but I don't think optimism is going to keep the sun from rising," Julie said as she glanced toward the window where the sky was now a bright pink and warming toward a full blaze, cloudless sunrise. Bill had chosen this spot perfectly. By the time the sun cleared the hills to the East, it would be in full light.

"Julie," Martin's voice pulled her back from the view outside the window. "Last night when I put the sunscreen on you, I figured they would try something, but I didn't know what or when. I didn't tell you because I didn't want to worry you, and in my arrogance, I figured I could protect you. I could have walked in the front door like they wanted and we would be dead right now. Instead, I hoped to kill them all, or at least keep them engaged until morning light. On the way here, I ran figures back through my head. I was right about my earlier calculations. I'm sorry to worry you, Jules."

Julie's mouth fell open. "I don't get it, Doc."

"What I'm trying to tell you is, we're going to be fine."

Straun stood up and took a menacing step towards them. "What are you talking about?"

Martin continued to ignore Straun and rushed on as Julie absorbed everything he was saying. "When I found my handwritten notes and started loading them back into the computer, I discovered that I had indeed omitted a step in the process."

"What are you saying?" Straun was now towering over Martin.

Martin slowly looked up into the bottomless pools of Nelson Straun's eyes and for the first time saw a glimmer of fear hiding there. "Like I told you earlier, you're a dead man. The stuff you're wearing is useless."

"You're lying." Straun took a step backward.

"Am I? Why did Bill have you try out the formula and not himself? He's planning on killing you. Why look surprised? You don't fit into his grand scheme. You're a free thinker, a liability. He didn't bring you through the transformation, did he? I figure he found out about you and recruited you with large sums of money. Chances are, he knows the formula doesn't work and he planned to get rid of both of us together and perfect the formula at his leisure. If you noticed, he didn't ask for my data, because he knew I wouldn't bring it. He figures he can track it down later. What he didn't realize was that I'd had time to synthesize any for myself, and Julie was an incidental he hadn't planned on."

Straun pointed the .45 at Martin's head, "You-Are-Lying!"

Martin didn't blink as he looked down the black maw of the long slide just inches from his face and then cut his eyes to meet Straun's, "'Fraid not."

Just then the morning sun streamed into the room filling the space with a dazzling brilliance. Martin and Julie squinted their eyes against the glare as Straun whirled to meet the rising sun, throwing an arm in front of his face as if to ward off an attacker. Straun stood motionless for a moment and then slowly lowered his arm. He stood transfixed staring at the continually climbing orb.

"Ha! I knew you were lying." Straun spun to face Martin, his voice a mixture of accusation and relief. "I knew tha . . . " Straun didn't finish the sentence, the words catching in his now useless throat. He dropped the gun to the floor, his hands no longer able to hold onto it as great spasms ripped through him brought on by the fluids inside his body starting to boil. Straun fell alongside the .45, his body caught in throes of agony. Martin stared with a stone gaze and Julie watched in horror as Straun's clothing burst into flames caused by the extreme temperatures his body had risen to. The skin on his face blackened and peeled back to reveal the teeth and skull beneath. Then, as if all the potential life he had stored up were rushing to get out, what was left of Straun's corpse consumed itself in a brilliant flash.

Martin stood and slowly crossed to the pile of ash lying on the floor, "Like I said, 'fraid not.'"

He walked to the window and looked out where the sun was still on its way to zenith. Julie avoided the pile that had been Straun as she made her way to Martin's side. She stood staring out the window at the vista before them and took Martin's hand in hers. In such a short time, she had forgotten how beautiful a sunrise could be. She reflected on how the simple things in life were indeed the best, when suddenly Martin's hand closed vice like on hers.

"Oh God, Julie."

"What, Martin? What is it?"

There was no mistake to the look of horror on his face. "It's started, Julie." His voice was a rasp as his breathing accelerated. "I can feel it! My skin feels hot. I am so sorry, Julie."

Martin was near panic for the first time since she had known him and her mind raced over the situation. She couldn't understand. Why him and not her? Why not both of them? They had both put the block on at the same time. She should be feeling something. . . .

"Doc! Listen to me. Martin." She worked to make herself heard. "You're not going to die, Martin. At least not yet." She took him by the face forcing him to look at her, "Martin. It's the warmth of the sun. It's been over a century for you and you've forgotten how it feels. See. I can still talk. I'm not going up in flames and neither are you."

Martin stared at her like he knew her, but couldn't place her face. He reached up and touched her hands as his breathing started to slow. He looked out the window and back to Julie. He stepped forward and tentatively placed his palms against the panes.

She waited patiently as he stood with his hands still pressed to the glass. After a few moments he dropped his head with an audible sigh and turned to look at her, his cheeks wet.

"You O.K.?"

"It's beautiful."

Julie looked at him sideways. "You thought you were going to be Martin flambé, didn't you?"

"And then some," he said as he hugged her looking out at the beginning of a new day.

FIN

BVG